Train to Freedom

Train to Freedom

Debbie —
I hope you
enjoy the book.
Jonathan A. Pohl

12/24/13

Jonathan A. Pohl

To order additional copies of this book, contact:
Xlibris Corporation
1-888-795-4274
www.Xlibris.com
Orders@Xlibris.com
41739

CONTENTS

ACKNOWLEDGEMENTS

I would like to recognize those who helped me along my own journey. My wife, Alison, and my children, Richard and Andrew, who waited patiently while I said, "One more minute, I just have to write this last line." Mike Gilles, thank you, for travelling to Kingston, capturing images on your camera, and getting us in to the real estate office to see where slaves were kept in the old house. Many thanks to Dave Horne for doing the copyedit work. This novel never would have reached you without his stupendous performance. I want to thank those that read earlier versions of this work and instead of telling me it really wasn't that good, helped me to persevere: Rudolph Pohl, Jean Pohl, Jeff Broadnax, Linda Donnelly, Carol Jite-Ogbuehi, James Howard, Robert Dores, and Judy Grenier. In so many ways, we are all on a journey to freedom.

CHAPTER I

Transfer to Points North

Wind blew in a distant gentle hush that crescendoed in a cooling breeze. James Penn welcomed the cool air, as it eased the temple-pulse of his beating heart. In the humid summer night, his sticky tongue failed to moisten his dry lips. Lanky arms pressed close to his body, he leaned against an ancient oak to help bear his weight, his trembling right hand clenching the iron handle of a kerosene lantern. He gazed up at the cloudy night sky and noticed that the tip of the oak was lost amid the dark. He forced himself to slow his breath, vainly trying to clear the thoughts in his head, fleeting intrusive images of imminent capture. The handle of his lantern slid roughly onto the stubby branch of the tree. Penn glanced to the left and to the right, searching the shadowy woods. He listened, but heard only the chirp of crickets amid the rustling of leaves; each breath that he drew. His imagination turned the shifting branches of a willow tree into all sorts of irate creatures, but there was no sight of another human.

Penn's shaking hands knotted a blue ribbon onto the metal handle of the lantern; he slipped back into the safety of the shadows, to wait impatiently for the signal. Each passing moment brought an ever-increasing intensity to his fears. He worried whether this meeting might have been an elaborate ruse by clever slave catchers. His mind could do all but focus on the fear, as his body responded. He could barely keep himself from retreating further into the dark woods, to escape. Sweat trickled down his temples and into his woolen shirt collar; he ignored the itch. Penn was unaware that his muscles were tensed and prepared to act. He focused on escape, as his temples throbbed and his throat dried. He thought of the chores on his farm, more than willing to return to the plow. Simms's comments echoed in his mind: "patrollers with slave dogs in Virginia." Slave dogs were bred to literally tear apart slaves when they attempted to run free. Sweat dripped into Penn's left eye, causing a sting, but he stared with his good eye at the lantern on the tree. Flame flickered, as the lantern swayed slightly with another gust of wind. Penn drew in a long deep breath and wiped the sweat from his brow with an old handkerchief.

He silently cursed himself, asking for God's forgiveness, then made an easily broken promise never to return to the fields, never to conduct again. He wiped his upper lip and leaned harder into the tree. He reminded himself of the stories from Quaker Jowett, about the beatings, canings; the cruelty the passengers endured at the Master's hand in the South. He knew in his heart he'd be back to conducting on the Underground Railroad—if he survived this journey, his fear added. He rolled his tongue from side to side in his mouth, trying to find any moisture. He stuffed his handkerchief into his coat pocket and looked up to see the second lantern. He watched as the lantern was hung.

Penn's stomach twisted, knotting up into a ball. He stepped from the shadows into the light of the moon, as clouds parted for a brief respite from the darkness. He placed his right foot down on the path; twigs crackled beneath it. On the edge of his vision another figure moved from the shadows, across the clearing. Penn froze and gazed in the direction of the movement. The other man was dressed in a dark cloak and broad-brimmed hat. Penn took a deep breath to draw in the courage to lift his lantern, as the other figure came into the light.

Penn whispered, "Mr. Keagle? Is that you?"

Mr. Keagle, a slender, lanky, thin-faced man, whispered, "Mr. Penn, if I was not Keagle, you'd be facing a firearm."

Penn's voice cracked as he uttered, "That I pray never happens. Unfortunately, I am a rather impatient man under these circumstances." Penn noticed the cooling breeze.

The two men removed the kerosene lanterns from the oak tree, shifting every shadow in the clearing. Penn briefly searched for his handkerchief, retrieved it from the pocket of his coat, and coughed into the thin cloth. He returned the handkerchief to his jacket pocket.

Keagle said reassuringly, "I was not followed, but did have difficulty with men in search of bounty."

Penn asked in a worried tone, "Trouble—you weren't followed, were you?"

"No, we spent yesterday in the swamps to avoid the bounty hunters and their dogs," Keagle softly responded. "Just seems to be more of them around since the price of a runaway slave has gone up. And then the Slave Act forcing innocent bystanders to take action or be imprisoned." He placed a comforting hand on Penn's shoulder for a moment.

Penn stated bitterly, "I wish this whole damn business could be over. Slave Act has only made matters worse." His gaze was attracted to the woods opposite him as a breeze shifted the branches of willow trees. A few vague figures cautiously moved into the edge of the clearing.

Keagle defeatedly remarked, "Not going to happen; always be slavery, Mr. Penn. We think differently than those who would own another human being."

Keagle turned, gesturing for the figures to come closer as Penn's demeanor softened. Penn tried to count the number of passengers.

"How many made it with you?" he asked.

Keagle replied, "I lost one and another conductor was captured, so I have a total of six passengers. An older man and woman, two girls, and two boys have made it this far. One of the boys, Trent, has a wound on his leg from chains. Miss Alice has a raspy cough. Miss Hattie, the older woman, knows about medicinals and has helped Smitty care for the boy's leg. All of them know about the dangers; they listen to every word I say as if it's the gospel." Keagle's expression was one of worry.

The figures moved closer; Penn saw the apprehension in their faces. He stepped forward to greet them, tipping his hat to Miss Hattie. The long-faced, dark woman didn't make a motion. Penn stood still. A large, dark-skinned man in coveralls reached out with a leathered hand to shake Penn's hand. Penn gently took the scarred hand in his, and felt the man's strength.

"My name is Penn, I'll be taking you through New York, the Catskills," he offered.

"I's called Smitty by mos' folks," said the man. "Thank you kindly."

Keagle added, "Smitty is the only one who talks to me. He's the leader."

Penn nodded to the others to recognize them. They stared blankly back at him. Penn directed his speech to Smitty.

"My buckboard here has space beneath the planks—" He cleared his throat and continued, "Space fits four, but I don't know about six."

Keagle rested his hand on Penn's elbow and gently drew him back.

Keagle urged, "Mister Penn, the six of them came together in New Jersey. You have to take all six of them, or those left behind will surely be captured."

"I don't know if six will fit. Night riding won't be so bad, but I'll have to travel during daylight some to get them through the Catskills. I'll have to have them hiding beneath the planks. Better one or two be captured than all six."

Keagle replied in mild defiance, "Then make your choice and tell Smitty. I'm certain the slaves you do not choose will stay."

Penn looked into the eyes of the passengers, one pair to the next. Without noticing, he had crossed his arms across his chest; after a long moment they dropped to his sides. Penn surrendered to his own sympathy for the travelers, but remained confused about how to proceed.

"When there is a will, God finds a way," he muttered.

Keagle offered, "Miss Alice, the one with the cold, is lighter skinned and can pass as your niece from the South. You take chances, but they all go."

Penn pondered while examining Miss Alice, a slender, fair-skinned young woman.

"Miss Alice will not speak unless you tells her to," Smitty added.

Miss Alice nodded in agreement.

"Then we all go together, with God's grace."

Miss Hattie, in her patchwork dress, let a smile slip from her lips. She turned to face Keagle and gave him a hearty hug, a hug that wished their paths could cross again, but knew they wouldn't. Keagle couldn't help but wrap his lanky arms awkwardly around the portly woman. Keagle nodded a farewell to the others and shook Smitty's rough hand.

"God Bless, Mr. Keagle," Smitty drawled.

"He has, Smitty. Go with God."

The rag-tag passengers turned toward Penn as conductor of the next "railcar" toward freedom, points north. Penn led the band of six along the dirt path to his buckboard off the edge of the dusty road. He flipped open the edge of a tarp that flapped in the wind. Several burlap bags of cornmeal rested on the edges of the tarp in the buckboard. Miss Hattie pulled up the edge of her dress to avoid tripping on the cloth, as Penn helped her into the buckboard. Calvin shifted the weight of his brother Trent so that he leaned against the wagon instead of Calvin's firm shoulders. Calvin held Miss Dorothy's arm to steady her slender frame as she stepped up into the wagon. Smitty's sweaty arms glistened in the moonlight as he boosted a coughing Miss Alice onto the wooden seat of the wagon. Trent hopped twice to steady his body against the wooden wagon. Miss Alice let out a few barking coughs.

Calvin and Smitty moved in close to Trent's sides and lifted him up from beneath his armpits, grabbing hold of his sweat-soaked shirt. Perspiration dripped from their foreheads as they lifted the slender boy into the buckboard. Trent let out muffled groans, winced, as his wounded leg bumped into the side of the buckboard. Miss Hattie steadied the leg as best she could, while Penn quickly glanced about to make sure again that there was no one else to hear the cries.

Smitty reassured Penn, "Boy will be good, once we get moving."

"Certainly hope so," Penn replied.

Smitty climbed in back and buried the other four as well as himself beneath the heavy cloth tarp. Penn moved three sacks of cornmeal one at a time to secure the tarp. The movement of each sack brought a glimpse to the woods. Penn's uneasiness hadn't changed—neither better nor worse, just a persistent nagging. He climbed aboard the buckboard and took the reins in hand. Miss Alice let out another bout of muffled coughing. Penn tugged at the reins, made a clicking sound in his cheek, and eased his horses onto the road. The horses appreciated the slow pace at the beginning of the journey.

CHAPTER II

A Bitter Taste of Life

A glowing fire in the stone fireplace and hanging lanterns from the Heifer Hill tavern brought light through the windows to the dark road that Simms had traveled not but a few moments before. The tavern lay nestled along a busy road on the western side of Kingston, New York. Simms heard thunder in the distance, as he hung his soaked, woolen cloak beside the fireplace. Nate, the short, burly bartender with a mild limp had already poured him a frothy tankard of golden ale. Nate's thick hands wrapped easily around the handle of a tankard. Simms appreciated Nate's hospitality, almost as much as Nate appreciated Simms's hand-rolled cigars. Simms saw beyond the scarred cheek and furrowed brow of the quiet barkeep. Nate could appreciate a cigar, unlike most of the farmers in the region, who preferred the sturdier Dutch clay pipes.

Scent of a wood fire had long ago penetrated the plaster walls of the appealing tavern. Nate's heavy Dutch accent could be heard in any corner of the place, even during the winter months when twenty or more farmers came in for a pint and a chat. The summer rain kept a few of the regulars away; there were only four others in the place, one too many, thought Simms. Simms preferred the loud banter, when the place was crowded with forty or more at the seven tables.

Simms and Nate nodded toward each other with the swap of the pint for a fine cigar, each with a warm smile. Barnaby Bathers, a tall, brash fellow, slapped Simms on the back, causing the younger man to drip ale on his shirt. Simms recognized Bathers's scarred knuckles, which belied a tendency to use force to make his point. Simms would almost rather befriend him than find him a foe. He turned to face Bathers's tight, leathery face; drink and smoke added further years to Barnaby's face, strangely making him all the more menacing.

Bathers chided, "Can't keep out of the rain?" He shifted slightly on his feet to maintain his balance, his breath holding the blended scent of ale and stale tobacco.

Simms replied, "If it means spending an evening with you, I'd rather be in the rain." Simms allowed the words to trip from his lips before judging Bathers's state.

Bathers stepped away from the short bar in the back corner of the tavern, while Nate and Simms chuckled. Simms spotted Hubbartt and Dillancy at a wooden table closer to the tavern's back door than to the crackling fire. The two gentlemen made a pleasant pair, one a stocky, short fellow, Hubbartt and the other tall and lanky, Dillancy. Hubbartt's skin was pale though he spent many hours in the sun. Dillancy was tan; his ready smile often brought one in return. They could never be confused for brothers. Mud had dried on their boots, as well as the sweat on their cotton shirts.

Bathers continued, not to anyone in particular, "Coldest spring I've ever known. Too much rain, means we'll have a dry summer." He paused to catch a "breath" of ale, Hubbartt thought that Bathers himself had never seen a dry day in Kingston for all the ale he consumed, more fish than man. Bathers then remarked loudly, "My sheep won't last through a dry summer." His tongue raked across his upper lip, licking off the foam.

The oak floorboards creaked softly as Simms joined Hubbartt and Dillancy at the table. The legs of Simms's chair made a grunting sound as he pulled it back from the table. He set down his pewter tankard and sat back in the chair, remarking to the other two, "That man is exhausting."

Hubbartt nodded in agreement, finished his ale.

Dillancy interjected, "He's been like that for the past hour, all through supper; talking as if any of us cared to listen."

Hubbartt stood up and took his tankard to Nate to be refilled. Nate looked wearily at Bathers as he poured the ale.

He said softly to Hubbartt, "Wish that man would head on home. The devil gets hold of him when he drinks like this."

Hubbartt replied, "Devil's always got a hold of him; the ale just loosens his tongue."

Nate's attention was on Bathers as he absently passed Hubbartt the tankard. Foam from the pewter tankard sloshed over the lip and onto Hubbartt's hand. Nate passed Hubbartt a towel and an apology, watching as Bathers moved closer to him.

Bathers rested a muscular arm on the bar and jiggled the tankard in his hand. Nate eyed the tankard, but ignored him.

Bathers said insistently, "Need another ale, Nate."

Nate looked at Bathers and then down at the bar. Bathers impatiently thumped his pewter tankard on the wooden bar.

Nate replied, with what courage he could muster, "You want another ale? I need coin."

Bathers shifted himself from an alcohol-induced slouch and stared down at Nate, who stood a full foot beneath him. Nate's whiskers fluttered, as he breathed quickly through his nose. Bathers leaned over the bar; Nate got a whiff of Bathers' beer-bated breath. Bathers continued his intimidating stare as he pulled three coins from his pocket. He placed the money on the bar.

Nate slowly reached out and picked up the silver piece. He took the tankard and filled it to the brim, foam sliding down the side of the tankard. Bathers reached for the other two coins, and as he did, noticed a brass coin on the floor next to the bar. He picked up his two coins, and tucked them away, then knelt and grabbed at the brass penny on the floor. He examined it closely to discover it actually was a button, an ornate button. He held it against the buttons on his vest, but found no match. He thought for a moment and recalled Penn purchasing a fancy vest not too long ago.

"Must be Penn's, from his vest," he thought to himself. He tucked the ornate button into his pants pocket, as Nate brought the ale. Nate made certain to wipe down the outside of the tankard before returning it to Bathers.

"What was that?" he asked.

Bathers absently said, "Nothing, wasn't much of nothing."

Nate placed a penny on the bar and Bathers quickly put it in his pocket, lest Nate think he was deserving of a tip.

He rudely snarled to Nate, "Been here most every night for the past six years, and you worry about a little coin."

Laughter erupted from the three farmers. Bathers turned his attention to the three men. He staggered a little, moving closer to them as they quieted.

Bathers demanded, "There a joke, here? Tell me the joke." He was unaware his upper body swayed as he spoke.

Simms retorted, "No joke, just something funny that happened with a plow horse." Behind Bathers, Nate tended to the fireplace. He kept a poker close at hand if needed, as he threw a fair-sized log on with a thud.

Bathers wobbled a little, distracted by the thud while comprehending the words. He glared at the men, then snidely remarked to Simms, "Probably has to do with a relative of yours then." He snorted a lone laugh. The tavern fell silent as the men looked uneasily at one another.

Bathers commented to the tavern, "Sheep won't last a dry summer, need water."

Simms responded matter-of-factly, "I heard you Barnaby—"

Bathers leaned down to Simms's face. "That's Mr. Bathers to you, Jeffrey."

Simms conceded, "Fair enough, Mr. Bathers. I know you want water rights to the land I purchased from you, but I just can't give you the water. Sheep would destroy many of my crops just getting to the water."

Bathers snorted, "I'll pay you for the damn crops." He took a long draw off the tankard of ale and continued, "When I sold you the property, I thought you'd be gentleman enough to give me a little water." Bathers tipped the tankard a bit too far forward, spilling ale on the table.

Simms glanced at his friends to determine if he should be more frightened of the inebriated Bathers. He replied, "I wish I could, but that just will not do. I cannot rely on keeping my accounts when I cannot supply them with vegetables."

The farmers jumped inadvertently as Bathers thumped his tankard on the wooden table with a loud thud. Bathers roared with laughter, drops of saliva spraying from his mouth. He motioned for Nate. Nate saw the empty tankard on the tabletop, but was leery of refilling it.

Bathers growled, "Run me a tab!"

Nate replied, "Neither a lender nor borrower be." An awkward silence added to the tension. Simms's hands clenched to fists and relaxed beneath the table, as his nostrils flared.

Nate sheepishly commented, "People forget what they owe." He wiped a bar towel across his brow.

Bathers sternly replied, "That ain't like me." He looked straight through Simms. "I remember everything about what I owe and what is owed to me." He reluctantly placed a coin on the table. Nate took the coin and tankard back to the bar.

Bathers commented loudly, "Didn't expect no drought, neither." Nate returned with the ale and placed it in front of Bathers. Bathers blew the froth toward Nate; he took a long drink. He wiped his face on his sleeve, letting loose a voluminous belch nearly as loud as when the tankard hit the table.

"If I knew a drought was coming," he added, "I never would have let you have the land for such a good price."

Hubbartt broke off a piece of brown bread from the loaf at the center of the table and began to slowly chew on it. Dillancy sipped from his tankard, gazing at Bathers over the rim.

Simms responded evenly to Bathers, "I paid a fair price for the land. You had no other offers."

Bathers ignored Simms's reply and continued to ramble. "Can't stand a man who takes advantage of others when they are in trouble."

"Think what you will, I can't change that," said Simms.

Bathers face was a cigar's length away from Simms's ear as he openly expressed his agitation. "Course I'm going to think that way; it's the truth. A man like you should get whipped for what he's done. Should be against the law to let a man's sheep die of thirst cause you got the water and won't let them drink."

Hubbartt slipped the bread knife into his sleeve and slowly moved his arm beneath the edge of the table. His fingers pulled along the dull edge of the knife to get it over to Simms' lap.

Simms' fists tightened beneath the table as he shifted his body away from Hubbartt to confront Bathers. His heart raced, his nostrils flared, and sweat trickled down his cheek. Bathers was breathing directly into his face. Hubbartt raised his hands to urge calm, while Dillancy shook his head slowly from side to side. Simms took a long breath and held onto the arms of his captain's chair as Bathers stood up tall before him.

Simms was a full half-head shorter and forty pounds lighter than Bathers, but was hoping the alcohol had slowed the other man down a bit. He briefly considered grabbing the bread knife from the table, but calmed himself with a quick prayer. Simms noticed out of the corner of his eye that the bread knife was gone.

Simms stared off to a point on the wall. Bathers was little aware of the shift in Simms's demeanor and chided him, "I'm talking to you, Jeffrey." A drop of his sweat flicked onto Simms's cheek, but Simms dared not move to wipe it away for fear he would strike at Bathers. A long slow silence filled the room. Bathers began to back away from Simms. Simms's hand came above the table as he wiped away the sweat. The bread knife Hubbartt thought he had slipped Simms under the table tumbled to the floor with a dull thump. The four men looked at one another again.

Simms stood up, apparently to head toward the bar. Bathers reeled behind him, having moved only a pace from the table. Bathers stepped between Simms and the bar. Dillancy and Hubbartt instinctively stood, tugging at Simms's sleeves. Nate squeezed between Simms and Bathers, facing Bathers.

"I don't need any trouble in here," he said decisively.

"No need for trouble," Bathers angrily replied. "I just need Jeffrey to understand the truth."

He shifted unsteadily on his feet, then stumbled toward Simms; Nate caught him. In the moment, Bathers reached past Nate, grabbing Simms's money pouch. Bathers stared at Simms while his fingers clenched the leather pouch; he realized he had the money pouch and tried to bring it in close to his shirt. As Nate got him to his feet, Bathers's arm slipped, the pouch falling lightly onto a nearby chair.

"Mister Bathers, you ought to get a breath of fresh air," Nate suggested. "You look a bit tired."

Bathers slurred, "I feel a little off. Must have been that kidney pie you fed me." His eyes half-closed as the ale caught up with him.

Nate escorted the staggering Bathers toward the door of the tavern, past the crackling fireplace. Dillancy's slender arms pulled his chair closer to the table as the two passed by. Simms's breathing slowed slightly, vigilant of Bathers's every move.

Nate repeated, "Let's get you some fresh air." Bathers turned quickly, considering his drunken state, and stared at Simms. With rage in his eyes, he said, "This ain't over, Jeffrey!" He pointed in the direction of the table.

Nate coaxed Bathers by the arm to get him out the door of the tavern and into the cool night air. Dillancy slowly closed the heavy wooden door behind them. Hubbartt retrieved the knife from the floor and sighed in relief.

"That Bathers is nothing but trouble," he said. "Penn knows how to handle him, but he's home with a sour stomach He was in a bit of a scuffle with Bathers himself just yesterday at the bar." His chair creaked as he sat back down, grabbed a piece of bread, moved to take a bite of it, but hesitated. He lowered the bread, spat in Bather's tankard, and then took a bite. Simms laughed, as did Dillancy as he returned to the table.

Simms said, "Penn twists Bathers's own words, so Bathers thinks what Penn wants him to think." He sipped his ale, then added, "Bathers is always looking to cheat someone." Simms brushed his curly brown hair back, wiping sweat from his temples.

"You're telling me," replied Dillancy. "He once sold a plow to farmer Johannsen, and stole it back from him three weeks later. When Johannsen got the law on him, Bathers was able to convince the sheriff that *he* was wronged, not Johannsen."

"That's because he's friends with the sheriff. There's not a man, woman, or child within three counties who would cry at that man's funeral." Simms pulled his tankard toward his mouth, hesitated, and placed it back on the oak table.

Dillancy swallowed a bite of bread, sipped his ale, and said, "The man will have a big funeral." The others looked at him quizzically. "Everybody will be present to make sure he's dead."

Hubbartt laughed, adding, "I will assuredly earn some coin that day. I will be selling sharp sticks with which to poke his body, just to make sure he is truly dead."

The men laughed, and tankards clanked as they toasted Hubbartt.

Dillancy excitedly added, "I can sell fistfuls of earth to throw down on his coffin." His eyes twinkled a bit at the thought.

"You don't think people will bring their own dirt to toss at that man's funeral?" questioned Simms. "Hell, a few of us will have wheelbarrows full."

The men broke into laughter once again, toasting one another. Simms had to catch his breath, causing the other men to laugh harder.

"You can be the auctioneer at his farm the day after the funeral," he said to Dillancy. "We can all buy back our belongings." Simms laughed while the others chuckled. During a pause in the conversation, Simms drank the last of his ale. He stood up and placed his tankard at the bar.

"I have an early day tomorrow," he commented.

Dillancy warned, "Watch out for Bathers. He's a man to hold a grudge."

Simms said defiantly, "He's all talk, but I'll be cautious."

Hubbartt rose from his seat, grabbed another chunk of brown bread, and reached for his cloak. Dillancy took his cloak from the iron hook beside the fireplace. Simms came back to the table, throwing his still-damp cloak over himself. The heavy wooden door's latch clacked, and the men turned to watch as Nate stepped through.

"He's sleeping it off near the shed," he said, smiling.

The men left the tavern and passed by a snoring Bathers. Bathers's head rested on a clump of moss at the base of an old oak tree. The three men passed by slowly, but then Hubbartt stopped short and returned to Bather's side.

Dillancy asked, "Hubbartt, what are you doing?"

Hubbartt laughed through an inebriated shushing by the other men. He whispered loudly, "Quiet," but broke into laughter before he could finish his sentence.

Simms and Dillancy looked at each other in a confused fashion, until they heard trickling water.

Simms asked Dillancy to confirm, "Is he . . . ?"

Dillancy said, "I believe he is." They both broke into hearty laughter, while Hubbartt vainly tried to hush them. The men went to retrieve their horses.

CHAPTER III

Respite on the Run

A fire just large enough to warm the hands of seven people crackled at the center of a circle of fatigued travelers. Lightning flashed off in the distance, followed by a long gust of wind, a brief pause, and a low rumbling of thunder that lasted a full breath. Miss Dorothy covered Trent with an old horse blanket and used the frayed hem of her dress to wipe away the sweat from his brow. She cradled him in her arms to keep the poison in his leg from reaching his heart, like Miss Hattie told her. Years of keeping her tongue still kept her from doing more than singing softly to the young man. She closed her eyes and gently rocked him.

Miss Alice's slender arms stretched out to grasp the water jug by Trent's side. Calvin was quick to assist her, helping lift the white ceramic jug. She sipped water to ease her coughing fit, while Calvin finished chewing on a piece of dried beef.

Penn stood up, walked over to the buckboard, and drew out a small cloth bag. His horses turned, snorted, and sniffed the humid air for the scent of a carrot or Jonathan apple. Sure enough, Penn pulled two apples from his coat pocket and provided each of the horses with a treat. His right hand held the fruit while his left brushed his open palm along their muscular necks. He noticed the dust left on his hand. Penn set himself down against a log beside Smitty and just beyond Miss Hattie.

Penn said, "My name is James Penn." He looked over at the slaves and then back to the darkness of the night.

Smitty held a thick tree branch in his left hand and a small pocketknife in his right. He whittled on the branch, cleaning the wood of bark. Penn almost repeated his words, but held his tongue when Smitty looked up at him.

"Dey calls me Smitty. I's a blacksmith, and dis here is Miss Hattie." Smitty pointed toward the older woman sitting next to him.

She smiled at Penn, looked away, and nervously added, "Used ta like wearin' da nice hats. Pleasure to makes yer 'quaintance Massah Penn."

The darkness hid Penn's embarrassment. He said, "Please, call me James."

Miss Hattie promptly corrected herself. She innocently said, "Yessah, Massah James." She returned her gaze to the ground.

Penn, fearing an insult to Miss Hattie, hesitantly said, "Please call me James, you don't have a master here." They smiled at each other awkwardly. Hattie nodded in agreement, and gazed at the campfire. Miss Alice continued to cough between sips of water, while Trent let out a low groan. The imprint from the shackle remained on his leg just below the wound he had suffered when the leg irons were removed. Smitty looked over at the boy and thought to himself that he could have removed that shackle without the wound.

"I thought it best to rest for a bit and then press on to my farm near Kingston," said Penn. "This place seemed far enough off the road." As if he didn't believe his own words, he glanced about the wooded area.

Smitty and Miss Hattie responded in kind, looking warily about. Penn caught them out of the corner of his eye. He said, "Just the wind. We can rest in Kingston for a day and then move on through the Catskills."

Smitty looked at the four young travelers. He pointed to the young man with the leg wound. Trent rested against a log with his feet closest to the fire, his breathing labored from the obvious pain. His britches were frayed at mid-calf, and he wore tattered shoes held together with twine.

Smitty said, "Dat boy is Trent." The boy raised a hand and pulled the brim of his hat toward Penn; he was a bit apprehensive for failing to stand up, but was unable to do so.

Penn put his hand up as if to prevent Trent from standing. He said a little too loudly, "Nice to make your acquaintance."

Trent replied, "Yessah, I's happy to meet you."

"Over dere is Trent's brother, Calvin," continued Smitty. Calvin nodded to Penn, and Penn returned the nod. Calvin eyed his brother's leg wound, and scratched at the mosquito bite bumps on the left side of his head. He was concerned about his brother's leg wound and the promise he had made to their mother. His firm features gave a reassurance about him, even while he took a "less than" position. Penn thought some might take this quality as a sign of arrogance. A shucking sound emanated from Smitty's knife as it raised another layer of bark from the branch.

Smitty took another stroke of his stubby knife to the shaven piece of wood in his hand. Penn opened his mouth to ask about the young women, but again Smitty looked to him before a word was uttered.

"Miss Alice, she don't have the consumption, Miss Hattie seen to that. She's the coughin' one wid de lightah skin." Smitty worried that Penn might leave Miss Alice behind; this wasn't the first time he had been North.

Penn smiled slightly at Miss Alice, and she returned a slight smile. She coughed softly, in the way a young lady did so at a dance. Penn was taken aback by the thought that leaped into his head. Her skin was lighter than the others; she could pass as white.

Thunder rolled through the woods following a flash that lit up the sky. Smitty glanced up, saying "Den dere's Miss Dorothy. She has a pretty voice when gived a chance ta sang." Smitty enjoyed a woman singing; his mother's singing brought comfort to his childhood. He focused on the whittling to fight the thought of her sale.

Penn smiled at Miss Dorothy. She rose up and curtsied, and it occurred to Penn that she wanted to act older even if she couldn't be older. He scrambled to his feet to bow. Her slender physique and slight voice gave away her age She sat back down on the hard earth coated with pine needles.

Penn said to the cluster of slaves, "Nice to meet you all. God willing, I'll get you to Oneonta. From there, you can head north, cross over into Canada and freedom We can't use the Albany route anymore, too many slave catchers about."

Smitty returned to his whittling. While shaving the edges of the stick smooth, he said, "We sure does 'preciate yor kindliness." Smitty kept his eyes on the smooth wooden stick in his hand.

"You can say a prayer for the Quaker Jowett. He was the one to get me involved in conducting," confessed Penn. He looked into the cloth sack he had pulled from the buckboard, searching for something.

Smitty said, "I's'll be thankin' him when I's sees him, Massah, er, Misser James." Smitty knew he would never lose the "Massah" when talking to a white man.

Penn noticed the "massah" and hoped to spend this journey with the slaves calling a white man "Mister." Miss Alice broke the quiet with a coughing fit; Miss Hattie patted her on the back to relieve her suffering. Another flash of light from the sky accented the beleaguered state of the passengers.

Penn listened to the rumble of the thunder rolling in from the distance. His hands grabbed the wooden crate from the buckboard, as the covercloth fell aside. He placed the crate between Miss Hattie and Smitty.

"I have a bit of hardtack, a few Jonathan apples, brown bread, and ale for you. There is water as well. Not much, but it will fill your stomachs while we travel."

Smitty smiled and replied, "Hungry makes dem beans taste a whole lot sweetah. Anything you has ta eat will stills da rumblin' o' my belly."

Silence ensued as Smitty waited for Penn to hand him the food. Penn stood waiting for the passengers to help themselves. A flash of light startled Miss Dorothy; she gasped. The others looked in her direction. The thunder brought a sense of relief in the clearing. Penn reached into the crate and distributed the hardtack, water, and ale. Smitty thanked him with each gift bestowed upon the slaves.

*   *   *

Smitty's gracious attitude reminded Penn of slaves traveling with Southerners through Kingston. He had thought of them as paid servants, entitled to all of the dignities of that station in life. One day, as he piled supplies from the general store into his buckboard, he saw a child of one of the wealthy Southerners tease a slave with a piece of candy. The child held the candy out toward the young man dressed in cotton shirt and pants that clung to his sweating body. As the dark-skinned man reached for the candy, the child pulled it away with a fit of laughter. The lad eventually gave the peppermint stick to the young male slave who waited patiently for the return of his owner. The slave thanked the young boy as if he was the child and the boy was a man. The boy's face lit up with the excessive gratitude. Penn had fought a sudden urge to strike the lad down with the back of his hand. Rage filled his mind as he fantasized slapping the child to the ground and kicking him. He had never felt such an urge in his life. The slave smiled graciously at the boy and ate the candy.

When the boy returned to the cool of the general store, Penn discreetly walked over to the young black man and gave him three pennies. The young slave didn't understand the gift and put the coins back into Penn's hand. His master saw the last of the exchange and growled at the young slave. The slave jumped toward the entrance of the store. He was ordered to the back of the store to put the supplies in their wagon.

The Southerner's fine linens of deep blue, his gentile ways, and his snow-white hair and goatee portrayed a gentleness betrayed by the glare from his slate blue eyes. Penn glared back, knowing that if he did anything else, he would be allowing this man an opportunity to feel justified in striking out in anger. Penn swallowed hard and watched the man and his child walk along the wooden porch around the corner of the store. He prayed to himself, "God still that Southerner's hand should he feel his slave deserves a beating for my actions."

*   *   *

Penn sat down next to Smitty as the gathering ate supper. He relaxed his body.

He said, "I would have brought fresh meat, but the fire has to remain small." He placed a small log on the flames. Tiny sparks flew into the air and quickly faded to ash.

Smitty used his whittling knife to cut a piece of apple for Miss Hattie and then himself. He chewed the apple chunk. "We un'erstan's, Misser James, we surely does." He ate another chunk of apple, juice trickled down his hand.

Penn eyed the group as he chewed on a piece of hardtack and sipped ale from the same jug as the others. The slaves stared at him, and he felt a growing unease. Penn felt an air of insult, but wasn't able to determine in what manner. Smitty's smile at Penn grew into laughter the others shared with him. Penn sat stunned, searching his shirt for a stain from the ale, but none was there. This led to further laughter among the passengers.

Smitty eased Penn's worried look with an explanation. "No white man ever done drank from a jug I's drank from. Dey always treats it like it was downstream from a pissing mule. The cluster of rag-tag travelers broke into laughter again, as Penn took another swig from the jug. This time he joined in the laughter. Another strike of lightning hushed them.

Smitty declared in a somber tone, "We gets caught an' da bests dat'll happen to us is returns to da plantation an' you goes ta jail, Misser James."

"We'll pray they don't catch us. Leave ourselves in the hands of the Lord," assured Penn.

"Amen, Amen Misser James," said Miss Hattie. "Den we has you up ta Canada and I's makes us chitlins, collared greens, grits an' gravy, an' mouf waterin' corn on the cob." Penn reached back into the wooden crate.

Smitty began to carve holes in the piece of wood. He added, "What dem Massahs throws away, Miss Hattie makes in' a feast." He turns to Miss Hattie. "Can we'se have peach cobblah for dessert?"

Miss Hattie gave a broad-faced grin and said, "Jes for you, Smitty." She smiled to herself.

Penn pulled out a small, off-white sack with a string tie at the top. He untied the cloth sack and offered up tobacco to Smitty.

"I don't smoke, so I don't know if this is good tobacco," he declared.

Smitty accepted the small cloth bag and sniffed the tobacco. He said, "Dis here's mightah nice, Misser . . . James. I enjoys a good pipe."

Smitty pulled a hand-made corncob pipe from his coveralls and packed in two pinches of tobacco. His thumb tamped down the tobacco as he searched for a twig near the fire. He took the twig, lit it in the fire, and then lit his pipe. Smoke curled around his eyes as he puffed the tobacco to flame. He let out a cough as he continued to puff on the pipe. Lightning flashed again, followed more closely by the thunder. He took a puff and passed the pipe to Miss Hattie. She took a draw on the pipe and slowly exhaled the warm smoke.

Smitty observed in his plain-speaking style, "One nice thang 'bout gettin' oldah, dis here pipe fits easy in dah hole dat toof done lef'." He chuckled. Miss Hattie smiled and passed Smitty the pipe. He took a few puffs and blew out a smoke ring. The passengers and Penn watched the cloudlike ring dissipate in a gust of wind.

Penn, searching for small talk, asked, "Miss Hattie why don't you wear hats, anymore?"

Miss Hattie looked to the ground as if embarrassed, and Smitty responded, "Massah's young wife thought she was bein' sumpshus."

Penn didn't quite understand, and clarified, "Presumptuous?"

Smitty stopped whittling and looked Misser James in the eye. He said, "Yes sah, dat's it. Massah said if'n she wears anudder hat, she'da been whopped. Ain't worn one since." Smitty paused on the verge of saying something, but the words never breached his lips. Penn just sat stunned as he took in the thought of being whipped for wearing a hat.

Smitty asked, "Misser James, any poltices in dat box o' yers?"

Penn replied, "I have whiskey and an old cut-up shirt for bandages." He knew if he had asked for medicines from the pharmacist it might draw suspicion.

Smitty and Penn took the stout jug of whiskey and cloth strips over to Trent. Smitty unwrapped the filthy cloth that covered the wounded leg. He used his stubby knife to cut the cotton shirt into smaller strips, while Penn examined the wound. A raised red mound encircled a crusted area that oozed a yellow puss. The thick yellow ooze ran in stark contrast to

Trent's dark skin, as a trickle dripped to the ground. Miss Alice coughed while watching over the healing arts of the blacksmith. Smitty took a quick look and complained, "Cain't see a dang thing ova here. Trent, we gots ta git you by dat fire."

Trent gazed at the small flame, but felt the sweat in his clothes. He said, "I'se too hot, cain't stands da heat."

Miss Hattie added, "He's burnin' wif de fevah. Smitty, we's got ta git him ta de fire's light so's you cain sees ta de wound." Calvin stood up and stepped closer to the fire.

Smitty and Penn helped Trent hobble toward the campfire, while Calvin cleared a spot on the ground. Trent moaned every time his wounded leg touched the ground, but he kept hopping along with them. He slipped on a stone; Penn caught him under the armpit. Sweat seeped through to Penn's hand.

Penn remarked to Smitty, "He's soaked to the bone."

"We cools him down latah. I's got ta git de devil's spit out o' him."

Miss Hattie added, "Devil's fevah gots a hold o' him good, Smitty." She put her arm around Miss Dorothy.

Smitty leaned over Trent's leg as the others looked on. He placed a firm hand above and below the raised red mound on the leg. Trent winced at each touch. Smitty gave him his neckerchief, and motioned for him to put it in his mouth.

"Bite on dis here when you feels like yellin'," he said. "Dis here is gonna hurts a bit." Several tears rolled down Trent's cheeks in anticipation of the pain.

Trent placed the cloth in his mouth and turned away from Smitty. Smitty took the clay jug of whiskey and poured a trail onto the wound. Trent shrieked into the bandana while he struggled to keep his leg still. Penn placed his hands on Trent's thigh, while Calvin grabbed Trent's leg just below the knee to hold him steady. Trent let out a long, low guttural scream as Smitty pressed on his skin. He pushed down on either side of the puffy reddened area. Trent let out a shrill scream even louder than before, as thick, yellow-green puss oozed from the wound. Trent's head rapidly moved from side to side stirring the dirt beneath him.

Smitty said to Trent, "Hurts like hell, son." He looked up to Miss Hattie. "Beg pardon, ma'am."

Miss Hattie nodded.

Smitty spoke back to Trent in an even tone, "But dis here whiskey's gonna save dat leg o' yers."

Smitty pushed again on the sides of the raised reddened welt to move more puss to the surface. Trent cried out for God to save him, but the others only heard a muffled scream. Calvin's worry spread across his face and settled in his eyes—tears came from the corners, as he held his brother to the ground. Trent clenched his teeth on the neckerchief. Penn understood the boy had to suffer to relieve the infection, but found it was all he was worth to strain against the boy's leg muscles. Smitty coolly administered to the boy's wound. When a third pinch brought forth yet another guttural scream with a mix of puss and blood, Smitty doused the leg with whiskey and bandaged him quickly.

Trent moaned, and puffs of dust rose near his mouth, as he breathed deeply. He remained on his belly, immobilized by the pain. Smitty walked to the edge of the clearing and returned to his whittling. Penn left Trent to the care of his brother Calvin as he joined Smitty.

Penn asked, "He going to lose the leg?"

"Don't knows, dat's up to da Almightah. I don' what I cains for him." Smitty carved two more holes into the stick.

Miss Hattie doused Smitty's neckerchief with water. She instructed Miss Dorothy, "You takes dis here cloth an' wipes down Trent's forehead. Keeps him as cool as you cain. When he starts ta sweatin', puts a blanket on him, as da devil's fevah will be weakenin'. Stays wid him, chil'."

Miss Dorothy took in the instructions and said, "Yessum, Miss Hattie."

Calvin held his brother in his arms, as the throbbing pain in Trent's leg began to ebb. Tears streamed down Trent's face, but his moaning subsided. He caught his breath, as Miss Dorothy came over to minister to his fever. She placed the cool cloth on his forehead; he smiled at her. Calvin stepped aside, as Miss Dorothy was giving Trent what he couldn't. Miss Hattie picked up the corncob pipe and stuffed it with the tobacco from the cloth pouch. She took a twig and in the midst of a flash of lightning lit the pipe. A trail of smoke left her lips as she passed the pipe to Smitty during the roll of thunder. Smitty puffed on the pipe, while Penn sat silent, wishing he could do more for Trent. Miss Alice fought another bout of coughing; she swigged water. Thunder rolled off into the distance.

Penn asked, "You think that fever's going to break?"

"I doesn't know," Smitty replied. "Dat boy, he's a strong spirit, but da devil's got a hold o' his leg an' is tryin' ta pulls him ta dah grave."

"Can he travel?"

"Cain't stays here. Dis ain't no place to starts a new life."

CHAPTER IV

Catching a Train

Harper Jones took comfort in the cool winds. He ran his fingers through his matted brown hair to loosen it from his scalp. His damp clothing clung to him, making him appear even thinner than his slight build. Jones scanned the clouds for rain, a distant misting up the trail. The hunger pains in his stomach went ignored, as always during the chase.

When Jones was coming up, his mother told anyone within earshot that "Harper must'a been part bloodhound in another life, 'cause that boy can catch anything." She'd say he could come back from a hunt with a deer, a rabbit, a wild pig—whatever was in the woods, Harper could catch it. He sniffed the air again; another reason why he liked the breeze. His tan, flat-brim Stetson returned to his head as he brushed his heals into the haunches of his horse, heading the hard-breathing animal toward the dirt road.

A flash of lightning lit Jones's face; Harold Kingman saw the intensity and smiled. Harold was done in, plain tired and hungry. So far the venture through the swamp had done more for his smoldering rage than his spirit. He couldn't wait to get hold of the slaves and whip the crap out of them for running so hard. He'd wait. Kingman was a patient man; that was his strength. He'd get them slaves in an iron-caged cart and wheel them back down South. He'd parade through every damn town in the North to show those sympathetic bastards who help slaves run that the South wouldn't tolerate interference. Stealing a man's property, and acting righteous. Kingman's chaw slid across his tongue and stuck between his lip and gum. A stream of brown ooze flew from his mouth to the damp ground. He thought to himself, they'll get whipped all right; they'll feel the sting of leather.

Thunder rolled through the valley, as Jones pointed up the dirt road. Kingman smiled, not looking so old now; Jones must have picked up their tracks. The bloodhounds had had trouble in the swamp; two of the five had died, and the others had been left behind. Kingman let loose another long stream of brown spit, as he jogged the clump of chewing tobacco in his mouth. The six men pulled taut the reins on their horses and took the fork in the road that led to eastern New York. Slaves didn't head straight north, knowing they'd get caught. This conductor was smart, but not smart enough to let it be.

The horses needed an extra spur to get moving. They had been run hard in the heat of the day and protested a need for rest. Jones figured they had another couple of hours of daylight, possibly enough to catch up with the slaves. Problem was, there were too many paths off the road to hide along by daylight. Jones and Kingman had decided that traveling by night gave them the best chance of sneaking up on the slaves, but it was the toughest time to see them. The wind picked up, and a light rain began to fall on the men.

Kingman grabbed a clump of leaves from the branch of an oak tree that stretched across the trail. The horses slowed a bit as the gentle rain brought a deepening darkness. Jones wanted to continue at the quicker pace, but had to give in to the weather. He pulled up, and the six men clustered together on the trail.

Jones said, "Too dark, can't afford to have a horse come up lame."

"We'll get them in the morning," Kingman agreed. "Can't get too far with that lame boy."

The men dismounted and took the horses to a nearby clearing next to a stream. The horses tried to wander to the water but were pulled back, as the men removed their gear. An impatient horse stepped on Willis's right foot. Willis shouted, and quickly drew his pistol. He lowered the barrel just behind the horse's right ear; the hammer clicked open, causing the horse's ear to rise up. Jones stepped up to Willis and spoke softly.

"We'll have fresh meat for tonight, but you plan on walking home." Willis slowly slid the hammer back down, holstered his pistol, and slapped the horse's shoulder.

"Dumb animal nearly broke my foot," he moaned.

Jones got a fire started, and Kingman pulled out jugs of whiskey. Jones eyed Kingman, but Kingman ignored the glare, as drink at campsites eased the tension. Jones lit up a pipe and drew deeply on the warm smoke. Smoke curled past his left eye as he thought about distances, directions the runaways could travel.

Willis wondered, "How far ahead of us you think they got?" Willis grabbed dried beef and a loaf of rye bread. He slumped down on an oak stump.

"Near as I can figure, them slaves are 'bout a day ahead," replied Jones, still staring down the road. He tipped his hat up to cool his forehead.

"How the hell you know that?" challenged Davis, a man whose mouth led him into trouble on many an occasion. Kingman turned quickly to see Jones's reaction to Davis. "We don't even know if we're on the right trail." Davis wanted nothing more than a night with a warm woman.

Kingman said, "Jones is the best in tracking slaves. Nobody he's tracked has escaped, alive anyway."

Davis acknowledged Kingman, took a swig from the jug of whiskey, and wiped at his lips with his shirt sleeve. Jones sat smoking his pipe, looking off into the distance, and ignoring the jug Davis was attempting to pass to him. Flashes of lightning highlighted the droplets of falling soft rain. Willis chewed a bit of dried beef, took the jug from Davis, and slumped down on a nearby rock. He was the oldest in this cluster of men and thought this might be his last hunt; his body ached from the day's ride. The flaming wood in the fire sizzled with the rain, as Kingman placed a small makeshift lean-to of sticks over it.

Davis broke the silence; he said, "I'm spendin' my share on a piece of land. What you spendin' yours on, Willis?"

Willis replied, "I don't count my chickens before they hatch." He scraped mud from his five-dollar boots; undertaker was always good for a pair.

Kingman replied, "The six of them are probably worth near four hundred dollars, depending on the owners. I know they aren't worth much dead." Kingman shot Jones a look that Jones didn't turn to see, but the words sank in.

Jones said, "I had no choice, he was going after Green with a chain." He puffed hard on the pipe clenched between his teeth. "If I didn't shoot him, Green would be dead."

"Two hundred dollars," Kingman chided, "we lost two hundred dollars. Couldn't just wound him?"

Jones never looked at Kingman, just stared off down the road. "I hope the rest of you understand that if one of them slaves comes after you, I'll be shooting to wound him, making him a might angrier."

Kingman let loose a long stream of brown spit just in front of Jones's boots. Then he saw the pistol Jones was pointing in his direction. Kingman backed away and wandered over to the stream to check on his horse.

Jones sat smoking his pipe in the soft rain, wishing he could go ahead on the trail to spot for the slaves. He knew they had to be close, and if it wasn't for the others he'd be on the trail. Like a barking hound at the base of a tree, Jones yearned for his quarry. He thought to himself that the man aiding them must know these woods well. He wondered how he knew to head east; how did he contact the next person on the trail, or was that planned? Six slaves would be hard to hide. He liked knowing the numbers. The Slave Act would let him jail any person helping the slaves.

Jones thought to himself, "Doesn't matter how long I wait, I come back with my quarry." His eyes focused more intently on the trail before him.

Willis and Davis scared up more firewood and tended to a putting up a lean-to for shelter during the night. The twins shoved handfuls of oats into feedbags and strapped them on the horses. Kingman came back over to the fire and saw that Jones was still staring at the road. He knew Jones was disappointed at the delay, but the men needed rest. Kingman swallowed hard and reminded himself he was lucky that Jones never attempted to challenge his leadership, because he wouldn't be able to stop him.

Kingman lit a pipe and stood near the fire for a moment smoking. He finally lay down on his bedroll to sleep; Jones stared at the trail.

CHAPTER V

From Points South

Dawn's light was several hours away from the horizon as the woods held on to the chill of night air. Miss Alice watched Trent sleep restlessly with his head in Miss Dorothy's lap. Trent appeared much younger than his brother, who looked more of a man. Miss Dorothy slept propped up against an old willow tree. Miss Alice closed her eyes and rested her head on Calvin's shoulder, but another coughing fit kept her awake.

Miss Hattie's left eye opened and stared at the young, light-skinned girl. She rolled over, handed Miss Alice the jug of ale, and motioned for her to take a drink.

Miss Hattie said, "Go on, chil', takes a drink, good for the coughin'." Miss Alice took a long draw on the jug, suddenly pulling it down when she felt the burn of the alcohol. She winced at the taste more than the sensation. Calvin felt Miss Alice's body bumping up against him. He turned toward the two women, yawned, and let out a moan as he stretched.

Calvin collected some fresh water from a nearby stream while the others slept. Miss Hattie put a twig to the last embers of the fire and lit her pipe for a quick smoke. Calvin came back to the camp to find her beside the fire.

"How comes you smokes dat tabacca?" he asked Miss Hattie.

"Keeps 'way da consumption."

Penn waved a hand in front of his face, then slapped his cheek and picked off a bug.

Smitty added, "An 'dose squitoes. Deys biggah in da South, but still's pesky." He puffed on the pipe that was passed to him, sending smoke trails past his nose.

Miss Hattie said, "Squitoes da devil's helpah. Dey ain't no bit o' good and a worl' o' troubles. Bring on da sleepin' sickness." She stopped Miss

Alice from placing a small piece of wood into the fire. Penn stood up and stretched his arms and legs. He let out a long yawn.

"I hears 'bout dat," said Smitty. "Makes people sleeps more'ns healthy."

Calvin yawned, followed by a yawn from Miss Hattie.

Calvin said off-handedly, "I won't be sleepin' 'til I sees my Mother agin."

Miss Hattie asked, "She in Canada, Calvin?" A flash of lightning threatened to betray Calvin's tears, but the others failed to see them. Miss Alice coughed more softly and appeared to fall asleep.

"Don't knows exactly," said Calvin. "We's separated somewheres in Mary'sland. I cain only prays she done made it 'fore us. I knows me and my brother needs ta git ta Canada, only place she cud be."

Miss Hattie responded reassuringly, "Den we's got ta git you all ta Canada." She packed up another pipe full of tobacco.

Penn stepped away from the smoldering fire and stared off into the cloudy night sky. A few stars poked through here and there. Smitty placed the stick and blunt knife in his coveralls and walked over to Penn. In the moment of silence that passed between them, Smitty felt the breeze and no longer heard the crickets; it would rain soon.

Penn stared at the sky and said, "Must be hard when families separate."

"Mos' hard fer folks dat don't wants ta seprate. We's been parted all da time. Families can scarce stay togethah, bein' auctioned off regular like."

Penn's confusion came out in his words, "I don't understand how they can do that?" Smitty now felt a might confused.

"Auctionin' off propertay?" he asked.

"I don't believe a person can be property, not like a horse."

Smitty drew in a deep breath and slowly exhaled. Penn just stared off at the sky as if God himself was going to come down and give him the answer.

Smitty said, "Figured as much, you willin' ta risk yer own freedom fer our'n."

"It's just not right, that's all, just not right." Smitty wanted to place a hand on Penn's shoulder, tell him he knew of his sympathies, but a lifetime of seeing black men whipped for placing a hand on a white man kept his hands still.

"My great grandmothah was brung by slave ship," he said. "Round de kitchen fires she tol' us 'bout what she remembers. De clankin' o' de chains in de belly o' dat ship. When dey sets sail, de clankin' was loud, but de longah deys sail, de more tired an' starvin' dey be. One day, de clankin' done stops. Some ain't sahvived de voyage . . . ."

Penn shivered, as Smitty breathed in deeply and blew out the air from his lungs as if blowing out a match.

Smitty continued, "Rights or wrong, dat is what dat is. I wants my freedom more dan my life." A light rain started to fall, and Penn watched droplets of water trickle from Smitty's face. Smitty looked back at him and asked, "Is you sad, Misser James?" Penn looked into Smitty's eyes.

"No sir," he replied plainly, "smoke from the ember's stung my eyes."

"Tis fine Missah James. We's gonna be fine. De Lord watches out fer folks like us."

Smitty had a pensive smile on his face. The cool air reinforced the chill in Penn's bones. He pulled his light coat closer.

Penn asked, "Why don't more slaves revolt? I've read about a few revolts, and the harm that comes to those who revolt, but if everyone revolted . . ." Smitty had a look of utter defeat.

"How many o' you peoples in de North believes in slavery?" he asked.

"I don't believe there are many who actually own slaves."

Smitty politely asked, "Den why doesn't dey makes e'eryone gives up deir slaves? Why doesn't dey marches on down ta Georgia or Souf Carolinas and takes dem Southern slave owners by dey's necks an' wring 'em likes deys chickens fer dinnah? Just picks 'em up an' twirls dem round 'til yous hears da snap . . ." Smitty's eyes glowed with inner rage, but he forced his breathing to slow, his muscles to relax.

Penn answered apologetically, "I don't know. Many of us are anti-slavery. I don't know why we don't make a change." Smitty turned away.

"Sorry Misser James," he said, his face downcast. "I knows you's tryin' ta he'p. Sometimes, I gets 'way from myself."

"No need to apologize. We all have to do what is right."

Alice coughed again, over by the coals. Another roll of thunder came through the clearing. Miss Hattie continued to puff on her pipe as the mist formed into beads of water on her weathered face. Droplets fell through the wrinkles and onto her calico dress. She made no effort to wipe away the droplets, but rather puffed harder on the pipe. Calvin stared off into the night. When Trent let out a particularly loud snore, Miss Dorothy brushed his hair for a stroke or two, and then fell back asleep.

Calvin spoke, not to anyone in particular, as he said, "Rains reminds me o' when I runs 'way."

Miss Hattie said, "Mhhmm, chil'."

Calvin continued in an even, faraway tone, "Dat night was darks wid de storm clouds, an' de rains was a startin'. We doesn't hears de pattyrollers. Dey was right on top o' us, so's we lights inta de woods. We was runnin' fer our lives wid de tree branches a whippin' us in de face. I thought I cud feels de hand o' de pattyrollers reachin' out ta my shouldahs, but I doesn't look back."

A flash of lightning followed closely by a clap of thunder stopped Calvin momentarily. Miss Hattie made curls of smoke rise up from the corncob pipe. Miss Alice swigged on the jug of water to calm the burning in her throat. A moment of silence ensued.

Miss Hattie said, "Mhhmm."

Calvin sighed, and then continued, "My heart was a poundin' an' de tree branches whippin' on my face. Dey was from de devil's hand tryin' ta push me back inta de hands o' de white-faced demons. I was a fightin' de very devil fer my freedom. I foughts an' foughts an' foughts, 'til I got free . . ."

Another flash of lightning and burst of thunder filled the sky. Penn and Smitty stood by the tree, looking back at the camp. Penn's curiosity was overcoming his concerns about prying. He asked, "I still don't understand something, though. You hate the slave owners, but you work so hard for them. That I don't understand, don't understand at all."

Smitty cleared his throat. He said, "Well, we has pride dat no massah can takes away. We works hard 'cause we believes dat de massah owns de body, but God owns de soul. We works hard an' makes de plantation prosprus, den de massah has no reason ta sell off propertay. Families git ta stays togethah. We cain git a little times togethah on Sunday fer prayahs an' times a picnic."

Penn's eyebrows raised as he said with surprise in his voice, "They let you have religious services on the plantation?"

"Not sahvices 'xactly, as we gits togethah an' prays. The massah don't come down ta de shanties. We's like da horses, he don't thinks 'bout us when we's not in de fields. As fer de field boss, he don't care what we's doin' if'n de crops is good an' de works on de buildin's is done. I use ta slip 'way ta sees my wife." A slight smile curled up on the edges of Smitty's mouth, as if he wanted to be happy but had to hold himself back.

Penn's confusion was expressed in two words, "Slip away?" Light rain continued to fall, but he didn't want to end the conversation with Smitty. A flash of lightning lit up the clearing for a moment and the two men instinctively scanned the woods.

"We cain't lives togethah," he explained. "Only de ol'er married folks cud lives togethah."

A muted boom of thunder sounded. Behind the men, Miss Hattie poured a bit of whiskey from a small brown jug into a tin cup and gave it to Miss Alice. Miss Alice's face cringed at the taste, but appeared soothed by the drink.

Penn said, "We should go back to the camp. I don't know what kind of storm is brewing, but we'd best take cover. I have a tarp we can tie up to the buckboard to stay dry."

Smitty and Penn took to tying the tarp.

Smitty said, "Ain't much rain comin'; my corns is feelin' fine. My knees ain't hurtin' de ways dey does when de rains is a comin'."

A last tie was pulled taught and secured, and the shelter was finished. Penn tossed several blankets under the tarp on a pile of leaves. Miss Alice woke up with a coughing fit. She saw the shelter; felt the mist in the air. She yawned and rose to Miss Dorothy's side, then gently shook her.

Miss Dorothy woke a bit disoriented and looked around. She saw the lean-to and gently rubbed Trent's arm, but he didn't wake. Calvin and Smitty moved over to the sleeping Trent. They carried Trent's limp body under the lean-to, cautious of his leg.

Miss Hattie got everyone settled in for the night. Penn fixed himself a spot just under the edge of the lean-to, just enough to be able to see the stars if they returned to the sky. Smitty checked the horses one last time and sat down next to Penn.

Penn asked, "You taking first watch?"

"Yep."

"Wake me in two hours." Smitty just sat there looking up at the night sky.

"Nope," he said. Penn raised himself up on one elbow.

"You planning on staying awake all night?" he asked. Smitty just kept looking to the sky.

"Nope," he smiled. Penn's confused look shifted to relief when Smitty said, "Calvin's gonna take us to mornin'. We wants you rested."

Penn thought for a moment about protesting the division of labor, but realized their survival depended on his ability to think quickly if they were stopped. At that moment, he said a prayer for safe passage to Kingston. He felt he would never calm his nerves enough to sleep, but physical fatigue outweighed mental anguish, and he dropped off to the sounds of the falling rain.

CHAPTER VI
Devil in the Night

Bathers woke up on the treeside, moss clinging to his scraggy beard, and he wiped spittle from the corner of his mouth onto his white sleeve. Sweat kept the cotton shirt close to his body. He pulled the fabric away from his skin; a breeze filled the cloth, cooling him. The sky was dark and cloudless. Bathers cleared his head and watched the kerosene lanterns in the tavern dim. He gathered himself and stumbled toward his horse, but stopped short.

He heard a rider coming from the west. He leaned back behind an old oak tree, covered in shadows. Simms rode up to the tavern and dismounted. He tied his horse to the post, and the horse eased over to the watering trough. Simms tried to enter the tavern, but without luck. He pulled the cord to ring the bell inside.

Nate came to the door with a dishcloth in his hand. He opened the top half of the Dutch doors and saw Simms standing before him.

"I thought you had an early morn?' he said.

"I do, but I lost my coin purse," Simms replied.

"None here that I know of, but you're welcome to search."

Simms went in and searched the table and chairs where he had sat earlier that evening, then expanded his search to the surrounding area, as Nate finished placing tankards behind the bar and stacked the plates to wash. Nate cranked the handle of the pump with a loud clatter of metal striking metal. Water gushed forth and he stoppered the basin, beginning the wash.

"Found it," Simms suddenly declared.

Nate said, "Very good my friend, hate to lose money myself." Nate began scrubbing the plates.

Simms left the tavern and got back on his horse. As he rode off, Bathers stepped out of the shadows to be sure Simms was heading toward his farm.

Bathers waited for Nate to leave and then followed the path Simms had taken.

Simms rode swiftly, but his horse had tired from the night's previous rides. Bathers soon caught up to his quarry, but held the reins back on his stallion. He needed to surprise Simms to add to his intimidation. Simms rode to his barn, dismounted and took the saddle from his horse. He ushered the horse in his stall and was on his way through the wooden door. He needed to pee before brushing down his horse. Bathers stepped from the side of the barn to block his path.

Startled, Simms said gruffly, "Bathers, what the hell are you doing here?" His body tingled with the sensation to flee.

Bathers responded evenly, "Came to get you to sign off on water rights." He pulled a rolled-up piece of paper from his pocket.

"I will not sign off on water rights! What do I have to do to get that through your thick skull?" Simms's eyelids narrowed and his hands began to shake with his rage. Bathers sensed the rage and realized he could use it to his advantage, to get Simms off guard.

"We are adults and can rationally work this out," Bathers said calmly. "If I could find a way to keep the sheep in a narrow path to and from the water, put up a temporary fence that came down before harvest?"

Simms replied, "That's preposterous, no sensible man would put up a fence that big for such a short time."

"If it meant keeping peace with my neighbors, I would. I know I'm not well liked in this town, but I am trying to better myself. What do you say, if I build the fence?"

Simms rubbed his mouth, trying to keep himself from an agreement that would harm more than help him. Groping for reassurances, he said, "You build the fence and then take it down?"

Bathers sensed the ambivalence and reassured, "I build the fence and I . . ." A blunt metal object slammed into Simms's face. He reeled backward, confused, dazed. Bathers swung the shovel again and knocked Simms to his knees. Simms struggled to remain conscious, to stay upright on his knees, unaware that if he fell forward it most likely would have saved him another blow. Bathers snarled; spit flew from his mouth as he raised the shovel's scoop above his head and brought it down with andrenal-enhanced force. The metal banged into the right side of Simms's head, crashing it against the wooden stall. Simms's horse made excited grunts as its front legs rose up and over the edge of the stall in alarm.

Bathers angrily struck the limp body of Jeffrey Simms three, four times more. Blood trickled from Simms's mouth and ear on the right side. His left leg involuntarily spasmed, and Bathers struck it with the shovel.

Spit flew from Bathers's mouth as he barked, "You made me do this, you made me do this, Simms." His rage forced him to pace in the barn as he considered his actions. "All I wanted was water, water for my sheep this summer, and you couldn't do that!" Bathers kicked a clump of hay onto the body. He pointed his left index finger in Simms's face, as he knelt next to the body. He blurted out, "Why didn't you give me the water, you dumb bastard? You had to know I would get it. You made me!" Blood continued to drain from Simms's body, a pool forming near his head.

Bathers left the barn. Lightning flashed across the sky and lit up the stark emptiness of Simms's farm. Bathers breathed in deeply, as if trying to catch his breath. He slumped down next to a willow tree for a moment, his chest tightening and his thoughts confused.

He said to himself, "Got to think, got to think."

He stood up and returned to the barn, to stare at the lifeless body before him. His rage returned.

"I told you, you shouldn't steal from me. Now look where you are, you poor bastard. You're dead. You are dead and ain't nobody gonna bring you back. Not even that friend of yours, Penn."

Bathers rested for a moment, leaning against a post. He noticed a knife beneath the straw near the stall. The clover insignia on the handle, the knife Penn used. This was Penn's knife. He looked about the barn. Bathers reached into his pocket and pulled out the copper button. He smiled while placing it in Simms's left hand. Bathers took the knife and set it in the pool of blood collecting beneath Simms's mouth. Blood trickled onto the shiny blade.

Bathers said calmly, "You know what I'm gonna do. I'm gonna make it look like your friend did this to you. I'll make everyone think Penn killed you." He took a few breaths and rubbed the sweat from his face. "Need to rest; need to rest, but not here. Go to my place. Wait, have to make sure Penn is alone. Then make it look like he done you in for your land."

Bathers rode off Simms's property toward the main road to Penn's place. He was on his way along the road when he ran into Jacob Knufield. Jacob always hurried as if he was to be there yesterday. He spent many hours listening to and believing the tall tales of the old men in the tavern. Bathers quickly raised his arms up, frantically shouting for him to stop along the roadside. He'd have to trust that Penn's absence from the tavern meant he was alone on his farm.

Bathers reported, "Jacob, thank God I found you. Simms is hurt. He was bleeding." Bathers noticed the blood on his hands and shirt. He added in a panicked voice, "I tried to help him, stop the bleeding, but I couldn't. He died right there in my arms."

Jacob stuttered, "W-w-what happened?" His neck seemed to stretch an extra inch. Bathers knew he had a witness to work his alibi.

Bathers said, "Over at Simms's place. He's hurt, maybe dead. He told me Penn did it. He must mean James Penn."

Jacob quickly said, "Get to the sheriff, I will get Doc Hamilton."

Bathers acted confused, "Yes, the sheriff. I'll go now."

"God speed."

"God speed," Bathers replied.

He rode down the dirt road east toward the sheriff's office in Kingston. Jacob rode north over to Doc Hamilton's place. Bathers smiled cruelly as he rode along creating the lie that would turn Penn's fate. He recalled the ways Penn had been a thorn in his side. The most recent event was when Bathers had tried to purchase land the town would need for docks along the Hudson. With the completion of the canals, Kingston's port was booming, and the town needed a last stretch of land. The loss of that land cost Bathers a small fortune, hundreds of dollars. Penn had stepped in before Bathers could buy up the property. He had to pay.

A gust of wind removed Bathers's hat, and it had to be retrieved. He thought to himself, "What is the waiting period before I can get the deed back from Simms's estate?" He rode on to the sheriff's office wondering if he could get some of Penn's land as well. The high from the alcohol was replaced with the high from getting his land back, cheap.

CHAPTER VII

A Wolf in Sheep's Clothing

Penn and Smitty rode side by side on the buckboard, but that was the only equality they could share. The wooden wagon creaked along the dirt road with five of the passengers lying tucked in one against the other, with just room enough to move one's head back and forth. In the cool, sunny morning, Penn saw a more hopeful future for the passengers. The two men had placed the five passengers in the two-foot-deep false bottom of the buckboard, lined with a woolen Army blanket tacked to the top boards. Penn had been unaware of Miss Alice's tears when she was first placed in the back; it reminded her of a coffin. Miss Hattie had joked about moving their bones when they got to Canada. Smitty looked pensive, causing Penn to feel ill at ease.

Smitty said in a low tone, "I'm worrie't 'bout runnin' inta folks."

"We have our story," Penn said reassuringly. "I'm returning to Kingston with a slave I purchased in South Carolina."

"What cha gonna calls me?" asked Smitty.

"I'll call you Smitty." Penn shifted the reins to his left hand, moving back on the wooden bench.

'You think dat's de bes' thing to do? Seein' as dey may be lookin' for a colored Smitty?"

"What do you want to be called?" asked Penn.

Smitty said, "Calls me Slim, ain't nobodah calls me Slim." They both chuckled, but a silence quickly separated them.

Simms asked, "What's bothering you? You worried about our story?" He wished Smitty would stop waiting to be asked.

'Dat don't bothah me none." Smitty said. "You gonna treat me too good."

"How's that, Smitty?" wondered Penn.

"Well, you should treats me more like that horse o' your'n, and less like a man. Nevah waits for me, no matter what, you just keeps walkin' and let me catch you."

Penn said defensively, "But I naturally treat you this way."

"An' it cud gets me killt," said Smitty plainly.

"I understand; I'll remember," promised Penn His backache returned; he tried to shift to a more comfortable position.

"If'n you don't, I reckon' I won't has to worries 'bout it for long," said Smitty with a big grin. Penn smiled back at him, the horses took them northeast.

As the sun rose above the treeline, the dirt road became wider, enough for the passage of three carriages and at times four. The buckboard rambled over every bump in the road. The only sound from the cargo was a low moan from Trent or a random cough from Miss Alice. If anything could give them away, it was the coughing.

An Amish family rode toward Penn and Smitty. Their black surrey was decorated with a circular splash of color. Dressed entirely in black and white, the family of an older man, his slightly younger wife, and their adult child looked rather dour as they came close. Penn tipped his hat and bid them good morning while Smitty looked down at the ground, but there was no reply. The family ignored Penn. Penn kept moving; he didn't look back.

"Reckon folks ain't kindly 'round dese parts," said Smitty.

"Wasn't that, it was us, me owning you."

"I kinda like dem folks."

"Me too."

*   *   *

Jones was awake and may have been so throughout the night. He sat in the same position Kingman had left him in the evening before. Kingman wasn't pleased when Jones didn't sleep. Jones's attitude would go from irritable to impossible. Kingman knew well enough not to ask. Willis and Davis had drunk too much whiskey before sleeping and were the slowest to rise. Kingman kicked their boots for a second time to wake them. If they didn't wake, water was the next approach. The Clemmons twins were up and ready to get into the saddle That's what Kingman liked about the Clemmons twins, two burly brainless men who could hogtie a bear if need be. If it hadn't been for the size of their horses, they would have looked like a pair of over-aged kids on a pony ride at the carnival. They had no initiative of their own, but took to a leader like a beaver to water.

Willis rubbed the sleep from his eyes and began gathering wood for a fire and most likely coffee. He placed a pile of dry twigs in the firepit and gathered up kindling. Jones scrambled to his feet and kicked the kindling out of the firepit. Willis lunged for Jones, but was caught up in Kingman's arms.

Kingman quietly said to Willis, "Step away before Jones gets angry." Willis took a step back from Kingman. Jones returned to staring down the road.

Willis replied, "He ain't got no right to treat me that way." Willis's thoughts flashed forward to the end of the hunt; he'd settle up with Jones.

Kingman said gruffly, "Right or not, we have slaves to catch, and we best get to it." Kingman raised his voice for everyone to hear, "Saddle up, men. The sooner we catch 'em, the sooner we go home." Kingman knew his patience was being tested by the Almighty.

They gathered their belongings, strapped bedrolls to the horses, and crammed everything else into saddlebags. Jones put on fresh socks, a lesson from his days in the cavalry, rose up, and glared at Willis, as if to blame him for the late start. Kingman stepped in front of Jones's glare.

"You sure about going east?" he asked.

Jones replied snidely, "If you ain't, go north." Kingman hated the challenges, but that was Jones. He reminded himself that Jones was the best he'd ever known at this.

Davis thought about taking off, leery of the tension, but he had too much invested in catching these slaves. Jones was the only one who knew Davis, a private man. One evening in the swamps, Davis had let Jones know he had joined this hunt to buy a small farm for his family. Davis touched the brim of his hat to Jones.

Jones returned the gesture. He knew that he could count on Davis for most anything, except killing a man; always vital information to know, just in case.

The men rode east, into the bright sunshine. Rested horses obligingly began to gallop toward the fork in the road that would lead them due east or northeast.

*   *   *

The quiet steady movement of the buckboard and idle conversation between Smitty and Penn were interrupted when a man and his young son rode by with supplies in a wagon. The man tipped his hat to Penn, who responded in kind. The boy eyed Smitty just a little too long for Smitty not to feel leery of the boy. Smitty smiled at the boy, as he had done so many times in the South, but without the same recognition of dominance.

Smitty recalled that Southern boys liked the slaves to smile at them—it made them seem more kindly, less frightening. Smitty hated smiling at the young men who might one day inherit him, but he smiled none the less.

He remembered one young child who was sitting on the long shaded porch of the Master's house. Smitty was working close to the house, clearing brush away. The boy smiled at Smitty, so Smitty smiled back at him. When Smitty bent over to clear a bit more of the brush, that boy took a stick and whacked Smitty right on the ear. Smitty's ear stung as he rose up enraged; blood trickled down his neck.

The young boy, no more than nine, said delightedly, "Whip that niggah."

Smitty's chest rose and fell quickly as he stared at the child. He had considered it might be worth losing his life to crack that boy's smile off his face. A prayer to the Lord eased his muscles and suppressed the rage.

Smitty felt a tightening in his body. He took his breath slow, steady like the rocking of the wagon. "Such a chil'; such a worlt," thought Smitty to himself.

*   *   *

Penn saw the pile of supplies in the back of the wagon and assumed the farmer saw his "supplies" as well and thought nothing of it. Penn wanted to stop and wipe the sweat from his brow, but didn't dare for fear of being noticed. The five passengers hidden in the false bottom of the buckboard lay still, sweating. Alice coughed from time to time, and Trent moaned, but when they heard another carriage or horse, everyone became still as the night.

Miss Hattie wanted to say prayers aloud, to comfort the others, but dared not speak. She knew in her heart that her silent prayers would be heard.

*   *   *

Jones and the others arrived at the fork in the road. An Amish family was riding through. Kingman rode over to their surrey, as the older man drew to a stop.

Kingman asked, "You seen any slaves?"

The older Amish man politely shook his head back and forth, struck his reins, and started to ride along.

Kingman held the tack of the surrey's horses, causing them to stir uncomfortably, rear their heads. He repeated himself in a threatening tone.

"I said, you seen any slaves?"

The older Amish gentleman gazed at the taller Kingman, then at Willis and Davis flashing their holstered guns. Kingman said, "One last time, any slaves?"

The older Amish man said plainly, "No, no slaves."

Kingman told the others; they started down the road that led due east. The Amish man hesitated for a moment, then drove his surrey west. He smiled to himself.

Jones halted the group a mile down the road. He looked Kingman in the eye.

Jones said, "They travel northeast."

"Are you sure?" Kingman asked. Kingman wanted Jones to be damn sure.

Jones hesitated a moment, then begrudgingly repeated himself, "They travel northeast." He was ready to travel on alone.

The men raced back up the road and headed down the other fork, northeast. Kingman didn't like the pace Jones was setting, but the man was on a mission. In a brief while, Willis and Davis were lagging behind, Jones was a good half mile ahead, and the rest were in between. Kingman wanted the others to catch up, rather than he slow down. He knew if he slowed, Jones would travel ahead on his own.

*   *   *

A lone rider trotted up from behind the buckboard and surprised Penn and Smitty. The morose rider, dressed in dark clothing, asked, "Where you from?"

Penn briefly looked at Smitty then recalled his words, "cud get me killt." "From Kingston, and you friend?" he answered.

The lone rider replied, "I'm a sheriff from Albany, been chasing runaway slaves." He nodded in Smitty's direction, "You own him?" Smitty just looked at the ground.

Penn looked over, "Yep, I calls him Slim."

"Where you buy him?" asked the stranger.

"South Carolina, got the bill of sale in my pocket," said Penn.

"Must have a bit of money to own a slave," challenged the stranger.

Penn quickly responded, "Not to own a broken down old mule like this one. He can't do much of nothing, but he holds a plow and can fetch well water."

The stranger tipped his hat to Penn and appeared to ride off up the road. Penn and Smitty sighed and smiled at one another.

Smitty said jokingly, "Broke down mule?"

"You told me to treat you like a horse," Penn reminded him.

"Yessah, I said horse, not no broke-down mule."

Penn joked, "Well you are, Slim; haven't looked in a mirror lately."

They both smiled, until they heard the click of the rifle. Smitty and Penn raised their hands as the returning stranger approached.

The stranger said, "Keep 'em up." He paused for a moment. "What you worth, slave?"

Smitty replied, "Don't reckon I know'd. Ask the Massah how much he done paid for mah."

The stranger said angrily, "How much you pay for this nigger?"

Penn didn't know how much a man cost and hadn't discussed it with Smitty. He looked at Smitty to look for any clues, but none were found. Penn replied, "I spent fifty dollars."

"Get down off the buckboard," demanded the stranger. Smitty just kept looking to the ground. Penn had to give him a bit of a shove to get him off the buckboard.

"Bring me the reins," demanded the stranger. Penn sat stunned, unsure what to do. Smitty reached over with his left hand, hidden from the stranger, and pushed on Penn's leg. Penn noticed the gentle shoves, and he pushed Smitty with his boot. Smitty bowed slightly and ran to get the reins, as if Penn had reminded him of his place in the world.

Penn slowly stepped down from the buckboard with the gun barrel following him, as Smitty reached up to hand the reins to the stranger. As the stranger reached for the reins, Smitty wrapped them around the stranger's hand with his left hand, while grabbing onto the back of his vest with his right hand. As the stranger tumbled to the ground, Penn pulled the horses away from him, causing his hands to be pulled away from his body. Smitty grabbed the rifle and struck the stranger with the butt. The stranger grappled at Smitty's right leg. Another strike of the rifle butt left the stranger limp.

Smitty had never hit a white man in his entire life. Every colored man who ever struck a white man was hanged. Smitty started shivering and couldn't stop. Sweat dripped from his forehead and the world took to spinning. He wasn't sure if Penn grabbed him before or just after he hit the ground. Penn said something to him, but Smitty couldn't recognize the words. Penn was yelling something about getting into the buckboard.

Smitty recognized the rifle when it was aloft. Penn threw the rifle into the woods. He helped Smitty into the buckboard, and they rushed off. Penn didn't want to slow the horses, but had to let them rest some. Late in the afternoon, they stopped by a stream to let the horses drink. The other five remained in the buckboard. Smitty slipped his hands beneath the tarp and poured water onto the wooden slats, so some of the water trickled down to them.

Penn was quick to return to the road, and had done so just before a sheriff came along. Actually, the badge was that of a deputy, but Francis Calhoun didn't mind being called sheriff. He'd outgrown his baby-faced features and kept his curly, sandy-colored hair short cropped to make him look older.

Deputy Calhoun asked Penn, "You see a man dressed in black? He's fairly tall with dark hair; two days growth of beard. I've been chasing after the thief."

Penn said, "I haven't seen the man you described, but if I do, I'll steer clear." Penn's fingers clenched the reins.

The deputy said, "Remember, this man is dangerous, so if you see him get to the nearest town to report him."

"Absolutely, Sheriff."

Calhoun took back to the road, heading southwest. He thought he should have caught up to the thief by now.

*   *   *

Jones was in the lead by a fair stretch with the others following behind. Willis and Davis had fallen back, as their horses were older. A huge groan came from a tall oak tree shading the road. Willis and Davis looked up just in time to see the branches of an uprooted ancient oak tree crashing down on them. Horses fled as the men fell to the ground with the force of the tree. Willis shrieked and Davis moaned loudly. Kingman quickly turned and raced back toward them. The Clemmons twins arrived first and took to pulling branches off the groaning men. Kingman fired two rounds into the air, not that it would do much good; Jones was well down the road and wouldn't return without the slaves.

Willis couldn't feel the fingers of his left hand; his arm was in an awkward, unnatural position. Davis had branches pushing against his chest, causing him to breathe deep, barely catching enough air. While the brothers lifted the huge tree branch that pinned Davis, Kingman pulled him out by his legs.

Attaining Willis's release from the timber was more difficult, as he screamed every time the branch on his left arm was moved. Kingman tried to immobilize the arm, to no avail. Finally he just lifted Willis's left arm with a jolt. Willis screamed, louder than the two gunshots, his arm flopped over, and he passed out. He was removed from under the tree. Kingman sent Davis with Willis to the nearest town, and thought again with aggravation about Jones not returning. Kingman didn't like a split party—something always went wrong. He thought to himself, "Like a damn tree falling on the trail." The Clemmons twins, as predicted, stood beside their horses watching Davis ride off with Willis slung over the back of his horse. Willis's twisted arm made it appear as if he was saluting; the Clemmons brothers stood returning the salute. If Kingman wasn't ready to spit nails, he would have enjoyed the moment.

Jones came across an area on the road where it appeared a scuffle had taken place. He dismounted and checked the trampled tall grasses. The scuffle had been recent. He wasn't able to determine what happened. Along came a rider heading south, a lone man with a deputy sheriff badge pinned to his cotton shirt.

The clean-shaven man said, "I'm a deputy sheriff in search of a thief, a man in black clothing, dark hair, two day's growth of beard."

Jones said, "I didn't see anyone traveling south on this route. I'm part of a hunting party. I told the others I'd go on up ahead to scout for a location to rest for the evening. There are five others behind me."

The deputy warned, "You may want to rejoin your party while the thief is on the loose. He knows he's being chased."

Jones replied, "I'll keep that in mind."

The deputy asked, "You see what happened here?"

"Some kind of scuffle took place here, but I wasn't here when it happened. Could have been the thief, but who knows?"

"I don't want to lose him; I'll stick to the road." The deputy peered down the dirt road.

Jones waited for the deputy to ride off down around a bend in the road. When he was certain the deputy was out of sight, he followed footprints into the wooded area adjacent to the road. He found nothing in the woods, unaware that the thief's head lay only inches from his boot, hidden beneath brush carefully placed there by Smitty and Penn. Another step and he would have been certain he was on the right track to find the slaves.

Jones mounted his horse and continued northeast. The warmth of the sun on his right side had him remove his coat. He preferred the cool comfort of the shade on the narrower roads. He hoped the deputy would run into Kingman first, as he would readily remember the story of a hunting party. Jones wasn't about to clue in a deputy about slaves, so that he could take away their bounty. He had wanted to ask the deputy about other travelers on the road, but knew better than to tip off a lawman. Couldn't say the hunted party included as many as six slaves.

Jones wanted desperately to find the slaves before nightfall. When the bounty hunters came up on a camp at night, it was too easy for the quarry to slip away into the darkness. Jones thought about the money he would be getting and hoped of finding himself a new life. Nothing left for him back in Georgia, nothing but pain.

CHAPTER VIII

With Age Comes Loss

Penn spied the western side road off the main road and pulled the buckboard onto the narrower track. Smitty sat quietly next to Penn. Shade from the elms lining the road brought relief from the humid heat. The two glanced at each other, and then back at the road.

"You don't want to ask me about taking this road?" Penn wondered aloud.

Smitty replied, "You knows better'n I 'bout where you goin'."

"You do trust me," Penn said. He was mildly surprised that these runaway slaves would follow him anywhere; trust him with their lives.

"Figuret we done beat up a thief an' outwitted a deputy. Cain't be much mor'n dat in a day."

Penn said with a deep sigh, "Thought we should get off the road for the night; travel again at first light. Thought about traveling at night, but there's too much of a risk of running into the wrong person on this road."

"I's sure dose in de back'd prefers ta stretch dey legs an' relieves dey bodies."

Another five hundred yards up the side road, Penn stopped the buckboard in a clearing beyond the trees. Penn and Smitty scanned the woods, then released the horses to graze on the fresh grasses. The two men removed the burlap bags and tarp from the buckboard. Wooden "two by tens" lifted easily off the back of the buckboard, exposing the five passengers to sunshine and fresh air.

All five blinked their eyes rapidly as they adjusted to the sunlight. Trent let out a moan louder than that of Miss Hattie as they climbed out of the buckboard. Miss Alice's coughing fit grew louder as she stood upright. Smitty handed her a jug of water.

Miss Hattie said, "A might cramped in dat wagon. I hopes we cain rides in back durin' the dark o' night."

Penn replied, "Absolutely."

Miss Alice lifted the jug to take a long sip of water. She quickly lowered the jug and spat out the liquid. She started coughing and choking. Calvin patted her on the back as Smitty took a swig from the jug.

Smitty said, "My apologies Miss Alice, I done gived you de whiskay. Here's de watah." He passed a jug to Calvin to hold for Miss Alice.

Miss Hattie said, "Whiskay may clear dat coughin'."

Penn started gathering firewood while Smitty helped the travelers get settled in. He noticed his white skin was tanning an even darker brown on this trip. His friend Simms always remained pale for a farmer. He gathered up branches and twigs for the fire. A roaring fire would surely be pleasing to his passengers, but only attract attention.

In the camp, Trent shivered uncontrollably, and Miss Dorothy ran over and got him a blanket from the buckboard. She tucked the blanket around his boney frame.

Calvin glanced over toward Trent while he gathered supplies from the buckboard. He silently petitioned God to see his brother through this, get them to Canada. Supplies placed at Miss Hattie's feet, Calvin sat down on the other side of Trent.

Calvin said, "We're gettin' a fire started. We gets you warm." Trent turned his head toward Calvin, his eyes struggling to focus on the familiar face.

"I's so cold," Trent said. "I cain't believes how cold I's feelin'."

Calvin placed an arm around his brother and said, "Trent, we's gonna git through dis trial, an' when we gits ta Canada, we's gonna find Momma. You lookin' bettah, brothah," he lied.

Miss Hattie added, "'Tis dat fevah breakin'. Miss Dorothy, gets him un'er dat blanket an' sits next ta him. Don't you's worry chil', de devil cain't jumps from him ta you's."

Miss Dorothy huddled with Trent under the blanket. Trent continued to shiver; his teeth began to chatter. Calvin swept away the fresh pine needles and placed a cluster of rocks in a circle. Miss Hattie stacked up smaller sticks in the center of the circle and struck a match to them. Smitty returned with a bundle of sticks and placed them next to Miss Hattie. He fed the wood to the smoldering fire as he blew on the fresh flames. Penn dropped an armload of dried branches and headed off to collect more.

Miss Hattie's nerves got the better of her, and she puffed on the corncob pipe; smoke curled toward Miss Alice, who sat downwind from her. Miss Alice broke out in a coughing fit and sipped the jug of water.

Miss Hattie, with concern in her soulful eyes, said, "Miss Alice, you bes' sits upwin' from me. I doesn't wants ta makes de coughin' worse."

Miss Alice took a swig of water and replied, "But de smoke's good fer consumption."

Miss Hattie smiled knowingly. "De smoke's only good fer de consumption 'fore you gits it, not aftah." She blew a mouthful of smoke away from Miss Alice, then leaned in close and said, "You doesn't have de consumption young lady. You has a plain ol' chill."

Miss Alice picked herself up, brushed off the backside of her dress and walked over to Calvin. She sat down next to him. Smitty had a small fire crackling in the firepit. He turned his attention to Trent's leg, examining the wound. He gently pushed the leg back under the blanket.

Miss Hattie puffed on the pipe, understanding the look in Smitty's eyes. Smitty groaned aloud the stiffness in his old bones as he found a place to sit down near her.

"You groanin' like an ol' man," she teased.

Smitty replied matter-of-factly, "I's an ol' man."

Miss Hattie passed Smitty the corncob pipe. He took a sizable pinch of tobacco between his large fingers and stuffed the pipe. Miss Hattie gazed at the young ones, while Smitty lit the pipe with a burning twig. Miss Alice and Calvin shared a blanket.

Miss Hattie said, "Even in de midst o' de storm dey cain fin' comforts wid each othah."

"Tis only when we gits oldah dat we's wantin' ta cling ta life," Smitty replied. "Young 'uns knows bettah dan dat."

"No needs ta change it, just de way it is. Dey're mos' likely talkin' 'bout tomorrah an' de farms dey'll lives on in Canada."

Smitty placed a larger piece of wood on the fire, causing a shower of sparks to fly a foot into the air and disappear. "I wud likes a small stretch o' land an' a nice blacksmithin' shop," he said. "Doesn't you wants a farm, Miss Hattie?"

"I cain't run a farm, but I cans do well in a househol'," she replied. "I doesn't know what all happens ta me in Canada. Dats in de han's o' de Almighty, but I knows I'll be free dere. Dat's what makes me dream o' crossin' de river Jordan."

She softly began to sing a gospel song. She sang in a soothing whisper that rose into a speaking voice. Everyone silently listened to her voice as she sang of leaving the fields behind and entering the lands of Heaven. Smitty smoked his pipe, listening to her sweet voice. She finished the song and was most surprised to see the others had been listening to her sing. She smiled shyly at them.

"Dat was nice, Miss Hattie," Smitty said. "You mights finds you a husban' in Canada."

Miss Hattie replied, "Nevah has much of a needs fer a husban'. No offenses ta you all, but mos' men wants one thang, an' I's had my fills o' dat."

"Miss Hattie?"

"Well maybe not quites my fills, but I doesn't know if'n I wants anuddah husban'," she said plainly.

"What happens ta yer husban'?" Smitty asked.

Miss Hattie looked down at the ground for a long moment. Penn returned with an armload of wood and a pail of water. He knew he had walked into the middle of something, but wasn't sure what. Smitty regretted asking the question, but knew he couldn't really take it back, not now.

Miss Hattie spoke slowly, "He died o' de influenza ten year ago. He were a good man, always lookin' aftah me."

Penn lowered his load of wood onto the pile. He said, "Sounds like my wife."

Smitty and Miss Hattie noticed Penn and looked at him. Miss Hattie sat quietly; Smitty passed her the pipe.

Smitty asked Penn, "How long has you been married?"

"My wife died three years ago. We had been married for six years . . ." Penn grew quiet and stoked the fire. He sat down next to Smitty.

Smitty asked in Penn's direction, "You has any child'en?"

Penn paused for a moment and cleared his throat. He said, "No, she died in childbirth with our only child." He looked away from them. "She had a lot of bleeding and the child didn't . . ." Penn's voice trailed off.

Thunder rattled in the distance, followed by a cooling breeze.

"Hard ta lose a wife," Smitty said. "Dat I knows."

Penn asked, "You were married—that's right, sneaking away to see her."

"Dat I was, married, when I doesn't has dese gray hairs or dis here belly. She was de pretties' woman in de' whole worlt, wif de soul o' an angel. I nevah knows what she done saw in me, but I wasn't gonna questions it."

Smitty had a smile on his face; a twinkle in his eyes, as he spoke of his wife. Penn and Miss Hattie understood the smile of his heart.

Miss Hattie said, "She sounds beautiful."

"Yes Ma'am, but dat was her undoin'. A Georgia plantations ownah took a shinin' ta her. She was sol' ta him. I tries ta slips out ta sees her, havin' ta stay clear o' da pattyrollahs . . ."

Penn interrupted, confused, "I'm sorry, pattyrollers?"

Miss Hattie passed Smitty the pipe.

"De men whos watchin' de roads lookin' fer runsaway slaves," Smitty explained. He repacked the corncob pipe and lit it with a burning twig.

"Oh, the patrollers."

"Yessir, Misser James. I wud takes ta de woods. We has trails 'tween mos' o' de plantations." He puffed on the pipe. "Well, I goes ta sees her one Sunday, an' she weren't no wheres ta be foun'. De massah has taken her ta de slaves market dat Satahday. If'n de othah slaves hasn't been hol'in' me down, I'd a choked dat man 'til his eyes done popped outta his head. His face would'a been blue six days aftah he were done buried in de groun'. I hated her massah more'n my own."

The passengers watched the fire for a moment, as there wasn't anything that could be said to ease Smitty's pain.

Penn said, "I don't know if I could have restrained myself. I'm a peaceable man, but that could bring any man to rage." He took a swig from the jug of ale and asked solemnly, "You ever see her again?"

Smitty exhaled a long sigh. "No, I nevah sees her agin." He wished he could spit the anger from his soul.

"Never got the chance to say goodbye," Penn remarked softly. "At least I was able to hold Rebecca's hand and say goodbye before I lost her." Shadows filled the clearing as the sun began to set.

Smitty said, "E'ery night, I looks ta de stars an' prays ta God dat she cain hears me. Dat she cain hears me tellin' her I loves her. An' I asks God dat one day we's'll be togethah, doesn't mattah how long it takes as long as we's togethah."

"I pray God answers your prayer. You're a good man, Smitty." He felt the urge to pat him on the back, but knew it wasn't his place.

"Thank you kindly, Misser James," said Smitty. "Dat's why's I cud nevah marries agin, 'cause she cud be out dere."

Another silence blanketed the gathering. Miss Alice let out a few coughs. Trent moaned a little, restless in his sleep. Smitty picked up a stick and began to whittle.

Penn said to Smitty, "At least you have that hope. For me, I won't marry again, can't go through that kind of pain."

"But what 'bout de joy of bein' in love?" Miss Hattie asked. "Havin' someone ta be dere wif you in de sorrow an' de happiness?"

"I lost her and I couldn't stop it," Penn replied. "She lay there growing weaker and weaker, and I couldn't change that. She just slipped away while I sat there. Her hand fell from my own and I . . ." Penn's voice trailed off.

Miss Hattie said, "You got ta say yer good-byes."

Smitty said, "We's all done los' somebody; dat comes wif age, too. Los' too many peoples in my life. Dat's jus' de way it is in life."

Penn looked over at the others. He said, "That's why those young people over there are so important. They are searching to be with others while we want to be alone."

Miss Hattie nodded. "Young'uns always brings us back ta wha's importan' in life."

Penn said, "We best get some rest. We'll be traveling again early in the morning."

Smitty asked, "How much longer to Kingston?"

Penn said, "About another day."

The travel-weary group settled in under the tarp as thunder continued to boom off in the distance.

Miss Hattie said, "Praise de Lord, He held de rain from drownin' us.

Smitty added, "Amen ta dat, Miss Hattie.

CHAPTER IX

Derailing a Train

Jones's horse panted hard as he pushed on along the dirt road to cover more territory than a bunch of slaves on foot. He pulled up tight on the reins to the relief of the horse. They slowed to a stop at the edge of the road next to a puddle left by the rains.

Jones looked about, wiped a neckerchief across his forehead, and glanced at the streak of sweat and dirt left on the cloth. He made a few more swipes and sipped from his canteen. He thought for a moment, a long moment, as the sun was just starting to set. He'd hoped the others would have found him by now, but that was less of a worry. The slaves had gone into hiding. He gazed about the woods on the edge of the road.

Jones had to think this through, not his strength. He often found himself talking things out with Kingman, not so much to get the man's opinion as to hear his own words and find the errors in his reasoning. He needed to forget everything, everything except this hunt. He needed the hunt. He took another swig of warm water from the canteen. A trickle dribbled down his neck, leaving a clean trail along its path. His horse found the puddle and lapped loudly.

Jones spoke softly to himself. "I rode hard, and slaves on foot couldn't get this far. Must be on foot, because everyone I come across tells me they haven't seen any slaves. There is a thief in these parts, and he may have taken them in, if he knew they were runaways. Could be behind me, hidden somewhere in the woods. Hiding in the woods, I won't find them. Need to find them on the road. Is there another trail, a foot trail through the hills? Slow them down, but safer than the road." Fatigue hampered his concentration. Jones didn't want to admit to himself that thoughts of his wife were distracting him.

He smacked a mosquito while wondering if he was thinking in circles. He would know if he was walking in circles, but without rest, he might not know if he was thinking in circles. Jones pulled on the reins, and his horse was slow to respond, licking at the puddle water. Jones wasn't of a temperament to wait on a horse, and his spurs let the animal know that. Jones tried to clear his head and think it through, but he needed Kingman. He felt something was wrong in his reasoning, but couldn't tell what. If he was right, the party should head north and wait for the slaves to come passing through.

*   *   *

Dusk arrived with a gentle breeze and distant thunder, as Kingman and the Clemmons twins rode past a man dressed in black tending to a gash on his forehead. The man looked to be in a sorry state, but that was of no mind to the Clemmons brothers, as Kingman paid it no attention. Kingman had lost two good men and worried that those remaining might not be able to subdue the slaves even if they were able to catch up to them. His anger toward Jones for being away from the hunting party intensified with each passing moment. Kingman was beginning to blame Jones for Willis and Davis getting hurt. If Jones hadn't run off, then the others would have had to keep up or at least try. This hunt was going from bad to worse. Kingman wondered if Madame Lebuque's voodoo curse was to blame for their misfortune; he never had a hunt go as badly as this one.

Kingman wasn't one to believe in voodoo and the like, but a dark cloud was hanging over them. Jones getting lost in the swamp had never happened before, and then this huge tree falling on his men. Kingman kept trying to sort out what was going wrong; he wondered how he could change his luck. He smiled to himself when he came up with catching the runaways. He said to himself, "Yeah, that would change my luck."

Kingman worried that Jones was injured up the road, or had just plain taken off. Jones was moody this time, moodier than in most other hunts. Jones was a private man. Kingman respected his privacy, but it made him feel uneasy; the kind of uneasy that had a man keep one eye open as he slept.

*   *   *

Kingman and the Clemmons brothers were a bit surprised when Jones appeared around a bend in the road. Light was barely holding on as crickets chirped and frogs croaked. Stars began to peek through the evening sky. The men broke for camp at a clearing near where Jones had found the scene of the scuffle.

The Clemmons twins searched the wooded area for kindling and firewood, while Jones and Kingman set up camp.

Jones asked, "Where's Willis and Davis?"

Kingman declared, "Freak accident got them. Tree fell right on them, almost killed Davis and broke Willis's arm. Could have used your help back there." Kingman's tone reflected his suppressed anger.

Jones replied, "Didn't know anybody was gonna get hurt." He eyed Kingman, but let it go. He turned his back, taking down his bedroll from his saddle.

"Best if we stay together," Kingman added.

Jones said curtly, "I'm here to find six runaway slaves and bring them back to their rightful owners. I'm going to get the job done."

Kingman understood he had pushed a bit, but it needed to be said. Kingman asked, "How are we going to catch them?"

Jones said, "We have two choices, we can ride along the road until somebody spots them, or we can pick a spot and wait for them to get there. Slaves on foot can't travel more than twenty miles a day. If we wait north of Kingston, where the road narrows by the Hudson, we can see anybody coming through."

Kingman pointed out, "If we wait along the road, other travelers may tip off the slaves." Jones hadn't thought about that; sympathies ran with slaves in the North. Jones didn't understand how so many people whose folks owned slaves, and who had servants themselves, could deny the South their property. It didn't make any sense in Jones's mind.

"We can pick up a few more men in New Paltz and have two parties covering the trail," said Kingman.

"More men can lead to trouble. We don't know if these men can be trusted. Either they'll let the slaves go, or they'll take them in for the reward."

"You have a point there. At least we know they're headed to Canada through Albany."

"Looks like that's the trail they're following; wouldn't make any sense to go any other way."

"We have to catch them in the States," said Kingman.

Jeremy and Jesse Clemmons were almost identical, the only difference between them was a crooked pinky finger Jeremy had broken while chasing

Jesse with an axe handle. The men came out of the woods with a couple of armloads of wood. Jeremy had a piece of cloth hanging from his side pocket. The twins emptied their arms and awaited orders from Kingman.

Kingman looked up at the men and said, "You can sit and rest boys. I'll get the coffee on. Any water around?"

Jesse replied, "Just the canteens, sir."

Kingman bit his tongue and said, "I mean any streams within walking distance?"

Jeremy said, "No, we didn't cross any."

Kingman conceded, "Then I'll use the canteen water."

Jones was busy getting bread and dried beef together. He hadn't the need for coffee; the food would keep his muscles from twitching. Jones laid his head down and fell fast asleep. He'd wake in three hours for his watch. He never slept more than three hours at a time, not since his days in the war.

Kingman heard the slight snoring and knew he had three hours before Jones would pop up and take a shift. Kingman spent the time studying his map. New Paltz was the next nearest city on the route north.

Jesse asked, "Where we going?"

Kingman pointed to their approximate location and the road north. He poured water into the coffeepot and waited to put in the coffee. He watched Jeremy unwrap a slab of dried beef and place it under his armpit. Kingman wondered why, but refused to waste his time asking. Kingman noticed the cloth hanging from Jeremy's pocket. The calico cloth was familiar.

Kingman asked Jeremy, "Where'd you come across that piece of cloth?" He pointed at Jeremy's pocket.

Jeremy replied, "It was in the woods over yonder." Jeremy handed the swatch of cloth to Kingman. Kingman studied the cloth and put it into his own pocket. Kingman knew the cloth was of a design used by the slaves. He took out his neckerchief and handed it to Jeremy.

Jeremy said, "Trade for a trade."

Kingman said, "Jesse you stay here and watch the road; Jeremy, show me where you picked up the cloth."

The two men went into the woods a short distance. In a clear area spotted with crushed brush, Jeremy pointed to the ground. Three types of footprints could be seen in patterns around the area, one of which was a bare foot. Kingman thought slaves had been through these woods, with a couple of whites, or in an altercation with whites.

Jesse was in the camp drinking whiskey upon their return. Jeremy rushed over, grabbed the jug out of Jesse's hands, and took a long swig. The brothers begrudgingly shared the jug until it was finished. Kingman searched the clearing, but found nothing further. If there *was* an altercation, someone else was hunting the slaves.

A rustling on the road shifted everyone's attention. The stranger in black was there. He pulled up and dismounted. The stranger walked up to the fire and warmed himself. The blood on his brow was dried into a forming scab.

He said, "Name is Parker, and I've gotten a bit lost. I hope you don't mind me sharing your fire."

"No, help yourself. We'll have coffee in a moment." Kingman didn't want company; he wanted information.

Parker sat near the fire and warmed himself. He pulled out a packet of tobacco and pulled off a chaw. He offered the packet to Kingman, who followed suit.

Kingman took notice of Parker's reconnaissance of the camp, the cut on his forehead. Parker eyed the sleeping Jones a few moments too long. Kingman placed his hand on his pistol and nodded to the Clemmons brothers. After four years, the boys understood the signal: watch everything carefully and be ready to jump the intruder.

Parker caught on to Kingman's hand on his pistol; he tried to warm him with conversation. "Been having some strange storms lately. You get caught in the rain last night?"

Kingman said, "Yeah, a little, but we are pushing on to Albany to buy a farm."

Parker nodded. "Farm isn't a bad business, but I got to tell you, the ferries are making the money in Kingston. Some of the ferrymen have nice stone homes in town." Parker knew that land cost money, and these men must have money. He wanted to appear local. He didn't know anything about the ferry business, but neither did these Southern folk. He knew he couldn't overpower the big guys, but even with a foot on him, he thought he could take Kingman.

Kingman said, "Have to think about the ferry business. Had my mind set on a farm."

"Lots of good farmland by the river, but you got to be on your toes. A lot of land is used up and won't be good farming for several years, after the next flood. Best check with the county clerk's office about the land."

"That's a good suggestion," Kingman agreed. "You come from upstate?"

"Yeah, I've been up there for a few years."

Kingman used a stick to move the coffeepot off the fire. He poured himself a steaming cup and offered one to Parker. Parker leaned in closer to the fire to accept the coffee. Kingman saw the abrasions on his face; the man had been beaten recently. Parker noticed Kingman looking at his face.

Parker joked, "Had a bad run-in with a bear."

Kingman said sternly, "As long as it wasn't the law. We don't want no trouble with the law." The Clemmons twins relaxed a bit, feeling the buzz from the whiskey.

"No, it wasn't the law, just a jealous husband." Parker knew that most men were willing to readily accept that as an excuse for almost any injury. Parker spit a long draw of brown ooze and sipped his coffee.

"See many people in your travels?" Kingman felt it was time to get his answers.

Parker replied, "Seen an Amish couple, and this guy with his slave."

"I thought you Northerners didn't take to having slaves."

"Most don't," Parker replied, "but you still find one or two that take on a slave."

Kingman wondered aloud, "Must look pretty odd seeing a slave. Bet he was dressed in coveralls and a plain white shirt."

Parker put his cup down, an amazed look on his face. Inside, he told himself not to overdo it.

"Yeah, how did you know?" he asked.

Kingman had overplayed his hand. He backtracked as he said, "Most of the slaves wear coveralls and white shirts, best for working the fields. We plan on doing all the work ourselves."

Parker decided to fall back and let them think better of him. He said, "Yeah, the one man I saw had this old slave sitting next to him on a buckboard. The two of them was heading north, but I don't know to where. Looked like farmers with the supplies they had stored in the back."

Kingman joked, "Best not be after my farm. I want that land."

Parker and Kingman laughed while Jeremy took the dried beef from under his armpit and split it with Jesse. The others watched as the men pulled apart the beef and began chewing.

Jeremy smiled and said, "Warm and soft, just the ways I like it." Kingman just stared at him, while Parker used the distraction to grab some rations.

CHAPTER X

A Rat in the Switchyard

Bathers arrived at the sheriff's home. He pounded on the thick oak door and shouted, "Sheriff, I think a man's been killed." He paced to the end of the porch and back. His thick fist pounded on the door again. He yelled, "Sheriff, Simms has been killed."

A kerosene lantern appeared, followed by the slightly pudgy figure of Sheriff Tom Calderon. His graying, auburn hair was pointing in every direction at once, as he yawned. Sheriff Calderon despised the minor emergencies most townfolk woke him to care for, but murder wasn't one of them. Murders in a town like Kingston were rare.

"You say murder?" Calderon asked. His eyes were thin slits as he looked up at Bathers. Calderon refused spectacles; squinting worked just fine.

"Yeah, Tom, I was there," Bathers said excitedly. "I was with Simms when he died. His last words to me were 'James Penn'." Calderon and Bathers had been friends at one point, but a few too many favors in Bathers's direction had left the sheriff feeling a little less than friendly. Bathers liked to get drunk and then forget about it in the morning. Some of the townsfolk didn't take too kindly to forgetting the intimidation. Calderon pulled up on his suspenders to keep his pant legs from getting stuck on the heels of his boots.

Calderon was still half asleep as he asked Bathers, "Who was murdered and how?" His head was clearing, but not fast enough, he realized.

Bathers was all too quick to respond. "Simms was murdered," he explained. "I went to his farm to get a deed signed and he was murdered. He said Penn did it."

Calderon yawned and invited Bathers to come inside.

In the living room, Bathers sat in Grandmother Calderon's rocker as he recounted the events of the evening. Bathers said, "I was going over to see Simms about signing off on water rights, so my sheep could have water during the summer. Well, when I got there, Simms was laying on the ground and bleeding. I thought he was dead, until I saw he was breathing. I told him I was going to get Doc Hamilton. Then he grabbed me and said 'James Penn.' Then he stopped breathing. There was a lot of blood around him and a knife."

Bathers sipped the whiskey he was given by the sheriff as he continued to think up his story. He added, "I raced out of there and ran into Jacob Knufield. He went for Doc Hamilton; I came to get you. I don't know if Simms is dead, but damned if he weren't breathing." Bathers finished his whiskey and had to fight the urge to smile. He put the empty glass to his lips to prevent the sight of his smile. Inside he was telling himself that Penn was about to get what he deserved and that Simms already had.

Calderon brushed his index finger along his mustache, thought for a moment, then decided to have Bathers write out what he had witnessed. He said, "Bathers, I'm going to Simms's farm; you head on home, and I'll be by in the morning." Bathers stared into the sheriff's eyes, as if to burn the image into his memory.

He said, with a tinge of sadness, "There was nothing I could do, nothing, blood all over and the words, I won't ever forget the name James Penn." He glanced at the sheriff again, then looked down and turned. Tom Calderon had never seen Bathers so distraught, but then he figured Bathers had never seen a man murdered. The sheriff put his hand on Bathers's shoulder. Barnaby Bathers smiled on the inside, despite his downcast appearance as he walked out of the sheriff's house.

Bathers walked slowly off the porch, to his horse. He mounted the horse, waited for a moment, and then took to the road. He wanted to hoot and holler, having just put the figurative nail in Penn's coffin. He felt a surge of energy and a need in his loins.

*   *   *

Penn woke with a start and sat up in the middle of the clearing. He was breathing hard, in a panic, waking Smitty and the others. Smitty grabbed a large stick and stared out into the night searching for intruders. Calvin started to drag Miss Alice toward a cluster of trees. Miss Hattie grabbed hold of Miss Dorothy and began muttering a prayer. Penn could scarcely catch a breath to tell the others what happened.

As he regained his composure, Penn said, "I had . . . I had a nightmare. A nightmare is all . . ." He continued to shake his head clear as the others calmed down.

Smitty asked, "You okay Misser James?"

"Yes, I will be fine," he muttered. "Please, forgive me for waking you up."

Smitty laughed a little. "We doesn't mind you scarin' us as long as it's in the mornin'." Miss Alice and Calvin returned to the lean-to.

Penn replied, "I don't think I can sleep." He looked about the camp, then up at the night sky, where a bright moon lit up the night.

Smitty asked, "Cain we travel by da stars?"

"Absolutely, we'll head north and make my farm around midday." The others collected up their bedding.

Miss Hattie wanted a pipe before traveling, but she was used to doing for others. Miss Alice coughed a bit, but only needed a few swigs of water to get relief. Calvin helped Miss Hattie and Miss Dorothy into the buckboard. He turned to gather up his brother, but Trent was already hobbling toward him.

Calvin smiled and said, "You's gettin' 'round pretty good now."

Trent said, "Won't beats you in no foot races, at least not for a while."

"Then we's'll have ta race e'ery day, 'til you cain beats me." They both laughed while Calvin helped his brother into the buckboard. Calvin climbed in and sat down next to his brother. They shifted their bodies about, getting comfortable. Miss Dorothy passed around the blankets, each huddling within one.

Penn had a worried look on his face as the last of the supplies was placed in the back of the buckboard. Smitty wondered about the look, but didn't feel comfortable in asking. Penn and Smitty climbed onto the seat and with a tug of the reins, the buckboard pulled out of the camp. Penn still looked worried.

*   *   *

Smitty was reminded of a time when he was a child. He was with his father at a Sunday gathering. There must have been forty people all gathered together, women gossiping about the massah's households and the men watching the young ones perform for them. Some of the little children sang and others danced, as the old men pointed, laughed, and cheered. That day was one of the most peaceful Smitty had ever had. He was standing by his father's side.

A man with a funny looking eye came walking over. Smitty noticed that eye right quick. He just sat staring at the eye that looked nowhere, while this man spoke to his father. The eye just seemed to float on the man's face. Finally curiosity got the best of him; Smitty tugged on the man's pantleg and asked him, "Why is yer eye like dat?"

Smitty's father shot him a look that would have scared a grizzly bear; Smitty was confused and terrified of him. The man placed an arm on the forearm of Smitty's father. The stranger knelt down and said, "Dis here eye's fake, comes rights out. Massah takes my real eye one day; done plucks it out." Smitty trembled with fear at the thought of an eye being plucked out. He imagined it rolling around the floor, seeing the world spin. The man started to take the eye out, but Smitty ran off. He heard the men laughing behind him, but he was scared to death. He remembered peeking around the edge of the shanty when his father found him.

His father said, "I hopes dat taught you ta leaves well enough 'lone."

Smitty recalled saying, "Yes sah, I learnt mah lesson."

*   *   *

The wagon creaked along the side road, jostling those in the buckboard. Miss Hattie was thankful she had taken the time to prepare for the long journey, although she was suffering powerfully from the mosquito bites. The jostling actually helped to scratch the itch. She thought to herself, "De Lord does works in myster'us ways." The wagon reached the turn back onto the main road. Calvin felt the changes—fewer bumps, a more even rut for the wheels. He and the others were silent, as they had been the day before. No words were exchanged between them, though they could send messages through facial expression in the dim moonlight.

Words weren't being passed between Penn and Smitty either. The two men sat silently following the road back to Kingston, just as riders did in the South. Smitty glanced over at Penn and saw that he still looked worried.

Smitty said, "Now you gots it."

Penn, as if awakened again, wondered, "Got what, Smitty?"

Smitty smiled and said, 'Now you's treatin' me likes a slave."

"I didn't mean to treat you poorly," Penn said apologetically.

Smitty chuckled and declared, "You got somethin' powerful on you's mind."

"I—I had a nightmare, a terrible nightmare."

"Don't tells me anymore o' dat. Dreams cain be tellin' de futures."

Penn wanted to purge himself of the nightmare, as he had done so many times as a child. He remembered crawling up into his parents' bed and talking to his mother, trying not to wake his father. She listened to his whispered fears of lions in the house. Then she'd tell him a fable that included lions. He'd snuggle close to her breasts, comforted in hearing her heartbeat, and would fall fast asleep. Penn wished he could return to that sense of security.

He wanted to tell Smitty that he had seen them all, all the slaves in the back of the buckboard, dead, as if in a giant coffin. He was standing there as the mortician looked at all of their bodies in the back, put up the planks, and banged nails into them. Penn caught his breath short remembering the horror. He appreciated that the passengers were able to ride out in the open at night. He breathed in the cool night air and forced the image from his mind.

"Smitty, tell me a story, anything about the plantation." Smitty heard the urgency in the man's voice. Whatever was haunting him was sitting on his shoulder.

"Well, on de plantation we's got a place ta stays out in back o' de big house. Our places wasn't really our'n but we stays dere. I has a small gardens in back o' my place. I growed de bes' corn and I has a tree dat jus' rained peaches. Dey was de juiciest peaches ya ever has de pleasure o' eatin'. I's trade dem peaches ta de women folk, and dey brings back cobblahs." Penn was comfortably distracted.

"I like to get my hands into the earth, into the soil," he said. "On my farm, I grow corn, beans, peas, tomatoes, and squash. I have an apple orchard; some of the best cider gets pressed on my farm in the fall. Growing crops, a man can see what he's done with his life."

"Seems likes my life is jus' gittin' started," Smitty pondered. "I chooses what ta grow."

Penn smiled and said, "That's right, you choose what you grow. If you want, you can grow peaches, or pears."

"If'n I wants, I kin grow apples, potatoes, corn, beans, wheat, peas, and melons."

"You're going to need a bigger farm," Penn joked. Smitty smiled at the thought, revealing a few missing teeth from his smile.

Smitty said, "I's gonna has me de bigges' farm in all o' Canada." Penn felt his stomach begin to settle down.

"Won't be hard for me to find when I come up there to visit."

"No sah," Smitty replied, "but if'n you comes, comes ta work cause a farm dat big needs lots o' work." The men smiled as the wagon creaked down the dirt road.

*   *   *

Jones awoke to the snores of Kingman and the Clemmons brothers. If he hadn't been used to the loud sounds, he'd have sworn a ferocious bear was in their camp, "gonna rip yer head off" mean bear. Stars filled the night sky, as a gentle breeze hushed the world. Jones cleared the sleep from his head. He thought about packing up his gear and heading north, but a moment passed and he thought better of it. Kingman would somehow still get his money from the plantation owners, and Jones would have done all the work.

The camp reeked of cheap whiskey and farts. Jones was unaware of the stranger called Parker visiting the camp twice earlier that night, or he'd have checked his saddlebags more carefully. He grabbed a chunk of dried beef and set about starting a campfire. He didn't want a fire, but knew the others would need one at the first light of day. Jones thought a cup of coffee might do him good. He smiled to himself as he thought about the others sharing the pot in the morning, eyes wide open from the strong brew. Jones preferred the solitude, except when the thoughts of her intruded.

His small pile of twigs and kindling lit quickly. Fanned by the slight breeze, the flames took to the wood. Jones sat staring at the flickering flames, watching the fire shifting with the wind. He wished he were able to move that freely.

He thought about his wife, her auburn hair and hazel eyes. He wanted to see the image of her smiling in his memory, but all he could remember were the tears. Standing by the door, she held her cloth satchel in hand, and she said . . .

Jones turned away from the warmth of the fire. He wanted to grab the jug of whiskey and wash away the memory, but whiskey only stopped his mind for a moment, and he needed to think as clearly as possible. He sat staring into the darkness of the night, just staring at the empty road. Scarred hands clenching the stick in his hand.

The Clemmons brothers snored in unison, as Jones struggled to empty his head. He focused on the hunt. He had runaway slaves to retrieve, possibly as many as six. Jones had been on chases before, but not with so many this far north. He wasn't about to lose his quarry to the rabbit hole of Canada.

Jones thought about the slaves and how they might be traveling. He felt that if they were on foot, he would have found them on his day's ride yesterday. Could they have hidden for the day and be traveling at night? Could they be on horseback or wagon?

If they traveled by horse or wagon, surely others must have seen them. The Amish fellow had said he had not seen any slaves enroute. That many slaves would have to be in a covered wagon not to be seen. Jones thought long about a covered wagon, possibly a wagon with a tarp. Slaves knew how to hide, get in the smallest place possible. He recalled finding one young slave girl in a cabinet drawer. She had lain under a thin layer of linen.

The young girl struggled when he grabbed her ankle and pulled her from the drawer. It was like landing a fish when he was a kid, squirming all around. She hit her head on the cabinet and yelped loudly. Much like the trout he caught, one good hit on the head and they didn't squirm so much. He carried her limp body back to the iron cage. Jones tried to recall how much he had gotten for her, but somehow that eluded him.

Coffee was ready, or at least he had lost the patience to wait for it any longer. He poured a cup and watched the steam rise up into the night. He sat before the warmth of the fire, with his back cooling off, and sipped the brew. Jones reflexively jerked his head back quickly from the cup, feeling the sting of his burnt tongue. He set the cup down on a rock, then stepped over to Kingman's saddlebags and retrieved the map. He tried to see the route, having to take the map closer to the fire for a better view.

Jones squinted as he traced the route with his finger. Sure enough, the road narrowed beyond Kingston, a good place to watch and wait. It would be a hard day's ride, but certainly one worth the effort if they got beyond the slaves. Then it wouldn't matter how they were traveling.

Jones studied the trail, tracing his finger all along straight up through Albany and into Canada. He didn't want the slaves to get beyond Albany, it would be too easy for them to take to lesser roads and even foot trails at that point. They couldn't really scatter until after Albany, needed a guide until then. Jones returned the map to Kingman's saddlebags and rested next to the fire. He was thankful the thunder was off to the west of them, probably meant no rain until morning. He hoped the storm would move north. Jones sat quietly with his thoughts. He wondered how Willis and Davis were getting along. Figured the men were nestled into feather beds with clean sheets, maybe a warm body next to them. Kingman would figure their share, not as much as the others, but he would be fair, well almost fair. Jones thought, "If you ain't there for the capture, you ain't entitled to a share."

He turned to stare into the starry sky. A shooting star raced across the horizon as the moon shone brightly amid scattered clouds. He thought about childhood wishes made on shooting stars; wishes that often didn't come true. He watched as a few moments later another star streaked past, and another.

CHAPTER XI

Next Stop Kingston

Jacob Knufield and Doc Hamilton raced to the Simms farm in the darkness of night. Doc Hamilton was comfortable in a surrey, not on a horse, but speed was of the essence and Jacob knew the trails between the farms. Doc Hamilton crouched low behind Jacob, but from time to time gave in to the urge to raise his head. When he didn't feel Doc Hamilton's head pressed against his back, Jacob hollered, "git down." Inevitably a tree branch brushed against the doctor's head.

Doc Hamilton was relieved when he saw Simms's barn. The men slid off the horse and ran for the barn. Jacob pulled a kerosene lantern off the side of the barn, lit the wick, and stepped through the barn door first, bringing light to the dark space. Farm animals grunted, or let out a low guttural sound as the men stirred them from sleep. As Doc Hamilton entered, he saw Jacob staring at the lifeless body at his feet.

Doc Hamilton gently pushed Jacob to the side to get to the body of Jeffrey Simms. He knelt down and reached for Simms's wrist, checking for a pulse—nothing. He laid the wrist down. He took his stethoscope out of his black bag; he listened for any sounds of a heartbeat—nothing. Doc Hamilton checked for a breath, his ear close to the mouth of Jeffrey Simms—nothing. Jacob stood staring, watching Doc Hamilton shift from place to place, and sensed that Simms was already in God's hands. Jacob realized he was saying a prayer aloud as Doc Hamilton closed the lifeless eyes of the man known as Jeffrey Simms.

Doc Hamilton rose to his feet and joined Jacob in praying over the body. At the close of the prayer, Doc Hamilton placed his hands on Jacob's wrist and elbow, guiding him out of the barn. They took a few steps toward the house. Jacob noticed the gray hair creeping up the doctor's temples. The glow of dawn was climbing over the treeline. Doc Hamilton looked older now in the early light.

He said in a fatherly tone, "You did everything you could, son." He could see the question in Jacob's eyes. "Simms was dead for quite a while before we got here." Doc Hamilton wanted to examine the body, but knew Jacob needed him more.

Jacob asked absently, "Nothing we could do?"

"No, nothing more could have been done. I'll wait for the sheriff to come. You should go home and get some rest." Jacob shivered—he was cold, so cold. Doc Hamilton breathed into his hands to escape the morning chill.

Jacob asked, "How will you get home?" Doc Hamilton patted Jacob on the back.

"Tom Calderon will see I get home. You need your rest." Doc Hamilton saw Jacob shivering. "Now, go on home son. I'll stop by later." Jacob nodded his head in agreement.

Doc Hamilton returned to the barn. He proceeded to feed the horse, three cows, and a couple dozen chickens. He could have used Jacob's help, but knew Jacob would be staring at the body the entire time. Doc Hamilton had learned from experience that if he didn't care for the animals, they'd get in his way. Once the chores were complete, he took to examining the body.

He started with the head. He took a bucket of water and a neckerchief and washed the blood away from the head. To Doc Hamilton, this wasn't Jeffrey Simms, a young man whom he had brought into the world, whom he had stitched up on more than one occasion, whom he had watched closely as the measles passed through him, and who stood fast as his parents passed away from the influenza. This was just a body, so he could concentrate on his examination.

He noticed portions of the skull soft to his touch. They were on the right side of the skull, indicating a blow to the head. He looked around and thought Simms may have hit his head on one of the posts for the stall. Doc Hamilton spied the knife with blood on it. He gently picked up the knife, examined the blade, and placed it in a cloth for the sheriff. The body was stiffening from rigor mortis. He searched the remainder of the body, and found bruising, but no other potentially fatal wounds.

The body's left hand was clenched shut. Doc Hamilton had to force the fingers, and they cracked as they opened. In the palm of the hand was a copper button. Doc Hamilton placed the copper button in the cloth and wrapped it up. He noticed there was no impression of the button on the skin of the palm. Doc Hamilton took a few moments to run through a checklist in his mind—nothing overlooked. He placed a horse blanket over the body and said yet another prayer for the young man's soul.

Doc Hamilton stepped out into the sunlight and rubbed his eyes, as the sheriff arrived. Calderon was riding his horse and trailing a horse in case the doctor needed it to make his way home.

By the way Hamilton's brow furrowed, the sheriff knew Bathers had been telling the truth. Sheriff Calderon had few experiences with murder; he was most used to petty arguments between farmers, or transient thieves stealing from the locals. He understood he had to take charge of the situation, not a role he accepted readily.

Doc Hamilton said, "Looked at the body; Simms was killed." He coughed a bit to clear his dry throat. Calderon dismounted and stood beside the doctor; he scanned the farm for any other people.

Calderon asked, "Any idea how?" He noticed Doc Hamilton's eyes were red, and wondered when he had last slept.

"Looks like a blow to the head, something blunt. He may have been stabbed, as I found this knife next to the body. Didn't see any knife wounds, but I'll know better when they prepare the body for burial."

"Shame when a man's life is ended this way, most unnatural." Calderon took the knife and placed it in his saddle bag.

"There's one other thing," said Doc Hamilton.

"What's that, Ambrose?" asked Calderon.

Doc Hamilton took the copper button out of the cloth and showed it to the sheriff. He said, "Looks like Jeffrey was able to take something from his killer. I found this in his right hand."

"I find who this belongs to, and I have the man who murdered Simms." Calderon took the button and examined it closely before placing it in his vest pocket. He said, "Don't worry, Ambrose, I'm going to bring in the killer. Kingston will have justice."

Sheriff Calderon hitched a horse to Simms's wagon. Doc Hamilton climbed up into the wagon and headed down the road. He planned on stopping in to see Jacob later in the day, to make sure he was resting. Doc Hamilton had his own way of dealing with the death of a patient; he took care of others.

*　　*　　*

With the first light, Jones kicked the boots of the other three men. Kingman turned away from him and pulled the blanket over his head.

Jones wanted to pour coffee down on the sleeping Kingman, but stayed his hand. He kicked Kingman's boot again, while the Clemmons twins stood stretching. Jones knew the best quality these twins brought to the hunting party was the way they followed orders.

Kingman roused himself from beneath the blanket. He grabbed the cup of coffee and sipped while groaning about his headache. Jones turned away to check on his horse.

Kingman was irritated with Jones, as he asked, "You got a reason for waking me?"

Jones turned quick and stared into the eyes of Kingman. He knew Kingman hated staring more than anything Jones could say to him. Jones was tiring of his companions.

Kingman sipped the hot coffee and relented, saying, "I know we need a good start to get to them slaves."

"Need to get ahead of them," Jones said while looking at the road.

"So you think it's best to ambush them?"

"Don't know where they might be on the road. Just beyond Kingston is a good place, road narrows," explained Jones. Kingman took the calico neckerchief from his pocket.

"Jeremy found this in the woods; them slaves were by here yesterday," said Kingman. He handed the Calico neckerchief to Jones, who studied it.

Kingman continued, "We can check wagons along the road. I suspect those slaves won't want to travel by foot if possible.

Jones smiled and said, "Not as far off as I thought. Good day's ride will put us ahead of them."

The Clemmons brothers paid no mind to the conversation at hand. They just carried on packing up the camp, sipping coffee, and peeing in the brush. These boys knew life wasn't much to think about, planning was left for others. Jesse grabbed a piece of stale bread from Jeremy's saddlebag and dipped it in the coffee. Jeremy watched for a moment and then dunked his hard bread in, softening it to chew.

Kingman took his bedroll and tucked it under the edge of his saddle. He returned his twin rifles to the holsters on the saddle as well, but something was amiss. He noticed the loose strap on his bags, then feverishly searched the saddlebags and the ground near where he had slept. Jones wasn't certain what kind of bug had crawled up Kingman's pant leg and wasn't about to ask. He tightened down his gear on his horse.

Kingman shouted, "He stole it! That son of a bitch stole it!"

Jones looked at him in shock, while the twins looked bewildered.

Kingman's face reddened with his rage. He blurted out, "Oh, if I find that bastard, I'm gonna string him up by his balls and piss on his head!" Kingman kicked his coffee cup clean across the camp and into the woods. Coffee sprayed his pant leg, but he paid it no mind as he stomped around. He screamed gibberish for a minute and then blurted, "I'm gonna kill that son of a bitch!"

Jones had never seen Kingman this angry. He wondered what Willis and Davis had done. His first thought was the two of them had taken off with their share out of Kingman's money roll. If they'd done that, Kingman would have them jailed for stealing.

"He was here last night," yelled Kingman. This latest revelation confused Jones, and he was feeling a little bit like the twins looked most days.

Jones felt obligated to take the brunt of the anger, as he knew they wouldn't ride until this storm blew over. He asked, "Who was here?" Kingman's eyes burned with rage.

Kingman stepped towards Jones and said sternly, "The man who stole my money; that's who!" Jones didn't care for his tone, but stood his ground and awaited the explanation.

Kingman continued, "Man's name is Parker, and he's a thief, a lying thief! He rode in last night and shared our whiskey and apparently helped himself to my money. Parker was telling me about the people on the road coming south, but none of them was with slaves."

Jones desperately wanted to know if this Parker was dressed in black, as the deputy had told him, but he dared not ask. Kingman would blame him for the stolen money. Jones listened, well to be honest half-listened, while Kingman ranted about ten ways of castrating or killing Parker. To Jones this was a distraction from the task at hand.

Kingman was slow to break camp. He figured Parker would continue south, because as far as he knew, they were headed north, to buy a farm. Kingman felt that if his legs were long enough, he'd kick his own ass twice for thinking up a story like that.

He muttered to himself, "Of course someone looking to buy a farm would be carrying cash." Jones didn't understand the statement. The twins busied themselves with smacking mosquitoes off each other. Kingman finally seemed to be letting it go, and Jones didn't want to get him riled again.

Jones slowly mounted his horse, and the Clemmons twins did the same, almost simultaneously, which made Jones look twice. Jones didn't rush

Kingman, who was waiting for a fight. Jones was tired; he couldn't take any more abuse. Kingman searched the camp one last time for his money, saddled up, and they rode out.

Jones could tell Kingman was thinking about the thief, but he wasn't exactly sure. He wanted to tell him about the deputy sheriff's search for the thief; give him hope of getting his money back, but he knew what the consequence could be.

After another hundred yards of road, Kingman asked Jones, "Don't you think we could take half a day to catch that bastard and still get to Kingston?" Jones kept his mouth shut; he knew better than to whack a beehive.

Kingman answered his own question, "Guess we'd run the risk of losing them slaves. I should'a known he was up to no good, riding by himself like that."

"Don't kick yourself too hard, anybody could'a made that mistake," Jones said. "Who knows, we might get lucky and run across him again. What did the man look like?" Jones would get his answer.

Kingman was quick to describe a thin man with dark hair, dressed in black, riding a brown horse with white patches. He added that the man had a scab on his forehead and scrapes on his cheeks. Jones got the information he needed.

*　　*　　*

Sun peeked over the trees as Penn and his passengers continued along the road. Penn had some distance from the nightmare. They had a good start on the day and most likely wouldn't meet as many travelers. He wished he could rest his eyes for a moment, but knew he couldn't have Smitty seen with the reins. If he had only asked, Smitty would have told him that he often drove the wagon for his master. Penn had trouble thinking things through. He wondered if Miss Alice was coughing less, or he was just used to hearing the muffled coughs.

Penn needed to talk if he was to stay awake much longer. He chewed on a bitter coffee bean that raised his eyelids, but left his mind numb. To his embarrassment, he had no choice but to spit out the disgusting bean. He wiped his mouth with his sleeve.

Penn asked Smitty, "You have a difficult journey?"

Smitty replied honestly, "Yep."

"What has been the worst part?"

"Worstest part was in de swamps."

"When you were with Mister Keagle?"

"Yes sah, dat was de wors', cause I seen dem."

Penn was a bit confused, "Who?'

Smitty looked out into the dawn and said, "I seen de pattyrollers chasin' us."

"Did they see you?"

Smitty said, "I don't rightly recalls. I was hidin' in dem reeds. Squitoes bitin' e'ery part o' my body aboves de watah and my feets slowly sinkin' deepah an' deepah inta de mud. My hearts beatin' so loudly, I figures dey could'a jus' finds me by dat alone. But I's standin' still. One o' dem devils comes walkin' down de embankments jus' six feets from me. A squito lands on my nose. I cain sees him drinkin' up my bloods, but I cain't move. Dat man, he was wiry wid dark hair, an' eyes dat looked through de trees, I swears."

Penn was focused intensely on Smitty's story. He asked anxiously, "Then what happened?"

Smitty said with a straight face, "He caughts me and done takes me back ta Souf Carolina." Penn stared at Smitty for a long moment, as if he was chewing on a hard piece of dried beef waiting to swallow it. Smitty let out a hoot; burst out laughing. He couldn't help himself, but Penn believed him. Penn started laughing as well, realizing Smitty had just pulled his leg about as best as it'd ever been pulled.

When the laughter died down and all the tears were wiped away. Penn waited for the truth to come forth. Smitty didn't have him wait long.

Smitty said, "Must'a been the hand o' God pushed one o' dem pattyrollers inta de swamp. Man cain't swims an' was hollerin' 'bout gators, so de one lookin' for me has ta leave ta saves his friend. Yep, must'a been de hand o' God gived dat man a push. I stay't still fer a long whiles makin' sure it weren't no trick."

"I'd a been scared, real scared."

"Yep, reckon I was," assured Smitty.

In the sunshine, oak trees along the earthen road provided spots of shade. The two men sat quietly again as the sun continued to rise. For a moment, Penn wondered what it would be like to be neighbors in Canada. He kept returning to a feeling of hope with these passengers, a sense that no matter the trials in their lives, God would see them through. Penn wanted that same feeling for his own life. He longed to think his life would become hopeful again.

*   *   *

Sheriff Calderon entered the barn and saw the body of Jeffrey Simms covered with a horse blanket. He wouldn't move the body, let the mortuary take care of that. He peeked under the blanket and saw the skull wound. Gazing at the lifeless form, Calderon was struck with the peacefulness of the man's appearance. He stood up and checked the animals. All had been fed and were with water. He took the horse out the back of the barn to let him run in the paddock. Several cows needed milking, but the sheriff had no time for that. He had recognized the knife.

Calderon hesitated in his task, but knew what had to be done. He stepped out of the musty barn; his eyes adjusting to the bright sunlight. He saw a familiar figure sitting near an old elm tree.

Calderon stepped over to him and asked, "What are you doing here?"

Bathers replied, "Don't rightly know, came back to see if there was anything I could do to help." Low, long mooing came from the barn while chickens pecked at the odd remaining kernel of corn strewn on the ground.

"There's a few cows to milk in the barn. Everything else has been taken care of, just waiting for the men from the mortuary. They take the body." Bathers ignored the notion of him milking cows.

"Any idea who done this?" he asked off-handedly.

"Well, I have my suspicions, might have been Penn after all." Tom Calderon mounted his horse and began to turn. "Still don't have a reason for it."

Bathers quickly asked, "You planning on going out to see him?"

"Heading out to his farm now," said Calderon.

"Best take a few men with you. Man who killed can be pretty dangerous." When Calderon didn't respond, Bathers added, "I'll volunteer to bring in the man who killed my friend." He started toward his horse.

"Guess you're right," Calderon conceded. He mounted his horse. "Should go with a few men. You can come along as long as you promise not to shoot. I want this man to stand trial." Calderon had the nagging feeling he had just made a mistake.

Bathers appeared puzzled, and said, "I wouldn't shoot anyone without you telling me to." Bathers mounted his horse and pulled on the reins.

"Barnaby, you and I have known each other for years. Your temper has always gotten the best of you. I couldn't see anything making a man angrier than seeing a friend killed."

Bathers sat silent for a moment and then handed his gun over to Calderon. The sheriff waved him off, but said clearly, "Just remember the man stands trial."

CHAPTER XII

A Wanted Man

Sheriff Calderon was thankful he had put Bathers in his place. The man had a way of making his needs known and then intimidating others into meeting those needs. The sheriff wanted to have his deputies present in case anything went wrong. Above all else, Calderon wanted justice. He wanted a trial so the folks of Kingston could be reminded of the workings of the judicial system.

With the completion of the canals, Kingston was growing by leaps and bounds. People were pouring into the city to move cement and other building materials along the river. Businessmen came to invest money, seeking profits. Most of the folks coming into Kingston had little, if anything—they were just trying to make better lives for themselves.

Tom Calderon was used to keeping the peace, but murder would keep townsfolk awake at night. The killing would shatter the notion that a locked door made someone safe. Tom thought most folks could regain that sense of safety if they saw the justice system work, so there had to be a trial. He reminded himself to wire Albany for a judge once Penn was in custody.

Sheriff Calderon rode into the center of town, past the Dutch Church, which was recently finished to house the Dutch reformed Church. Aside from chirping birds, the town green was quiet this early in the morning. Calderon thought the town wouldn't be this peaceful again until the fall. He glanced at the cemetery surrounding the church, filled with old Revolutionary War veterans. He rode to the county courthouse and hitched his horse to the fence.

The sheriff entered the side of the Ulster County Courthouse, where the jail was located. Wooden plank flooring creaked beneath his feet, as he stepped up onto the front porch. He wanted to sit in his rocking chair and greet townsfolk as they walked past to go shopping, but not today. Behind metal bars, the four windows were full open to let in the cool morning air. He hoped Hank had opened the window in his hope-chest of an office. Calderon preferred the cramped space to the spacious office of his counterpart in Albany; there wasn't as much space for people to gather.

Calderon recalled a time when the Butler sisters were all but ready to tar and feather each other. Each of the beautiful but quite temperamental sisters had brought several friends to speak with him, standing room only. The women gathered in his office and spoke nonstop for what seemed like an hour. Calderon smiled to himself as he recalled wanting to fire a shot in the air just to get them to shut up, but the county courthouse had been in session upstairs. When they left, Hank said he had thought about throwing corn on the ground, the women were cackling so much.

A tiny bell tinkled as the door swung open. Joseph had fixed the squeaking hinges. Calderon was relieved that the cell along the back wall was empty. Hank had stepped up on a small box to check the dust on the rifle rack on the far right wall, not that he would dust it, but he felt compelled to check it. Calderon walked past Joseph, whose long legs were stretched into the space next to the wooden desk. He checked his office to see if anyone was waiting for him.

The two deputies watched Calderon walk on through in silence. This meant trouble of one kind or another. Calderon walked back over to the door and closed it, the bell tinkling again. His deputies paid more attention to him when he closed the door. Calderon hated the heat, and his office became an oven without the cross breeze. Hank always joked about frying eggs in the morning when he first came in, as Joseph was always in a bit later.

The sheriff spoke plainly, evenly as he said, "Jeffrey Simms was killed during the night." Joseph's usual baby-faced smile faded into a shocked look. He glanced at Hank for confirmation. Hank just stared blankly; nothing ever changed the serious look on his face except his laughter. Hank lifted a boot up to cross his legs. Calderon continued, "We think we know who killed him, and I plan to bring the man into custody" Hank sat up straight, attentive. "Before I give you his name, I want you both to be damn sure you are ready to bring this man to justice. I'm talking about keeping the peace in Kingston, by letting a judge decide this case. No matter what you think about the man, we are going to lock him in that holding cell over there until he can get a fair trial. Do you understand?" Joseph felt insulted; Hank knew better.

Hank replied, "Yes sir."

Joseph said, "Yes sir, I understand." He sat up straight, causing the captain's chair to creak a bit loudly.

"Some of the townspeople may be asking for a hanging, but that isn't going to happen in my town," continued the sheriff in a commanding voice. "Over to the Roggen house there is a beam with worn areas where hangings took place, but that isn't going to happen here, now." Hank knew the sheriff was practicing on them for when the townspeople got out of hand. Joseph wondered who among the townspeople was the killer.

Hank asked, "Who done the killing?" He spoke his mind when he felt the time was right.

Calderon said, "The man we suspect is, um, James Penn." The name almost caught in his throat. Penn had always been one to stay away from trouble.

Joseph asked quizzically, "The farmer?" Penn was a close friend. They shared suppers, spent time painting barns for the older folks, and gathered up the apples for the fall cider pressing.

"Yes," said the sheriff, "We have a witness to that effect, and evidence found on the body points to Penn."

Joseph said, "Sir, I will certainly bring James Penn to the jail, but I have known him for seven years and I know he would never harm another man, let alone a friend like Simms." Sheriff Calderon looked at his deputies. He wondered about Joseph's loyalties.

"That's why I want the man to have a trial," said Calderon, "then we won't have doubts. We need to bring him in now, before the whole town gets hold of the gossip and he's even worse off."

Joseph said, "I was by his place first thing this morning, and he wasn't there. My sister had some blueberry muffins for me to take to him, so I did before coming in to work."

"Any idea where he might be?"

"No sir."

The men gathered their hats and a couple of rifles and headed to the door. Bathers met them there with Luke and Pieter.

Bathers said, "Brought along a couple of extra hands just in case." Pieter stared at Hank; they had had words a few nights ago at the saloon. Hank just gave him a blank look and thought about hitting him in the face with a pewter tankard the next time he mouthed off. Luke was a tag-along sort of man, and would be no trouble without the others.

"I think we have enough men, without Luke and Pieter," replied the sheriff.

"Suit yourself," said Bathers, "but if anything goes wrong, it's on your head."

Sheriff Calderon didn't care to be in this position, but if anything did go wrong at the Penn farm, then Bathers would tell everyone Calderon had failed them.

Sheriff turned to his deputies, "Nobody shoots Penn unless I give a direct order." He pointed to the three men joining the posse. "If one of these three men takes out his pistol, you have my permission to shoot them." He stared at Bathers, who glared back. Sheriff Calderon waited for Bathers to back down and step aside before he went to his horse.

The ride out to the Penn farm was uneventful. The sheriff and posse rode down the dirt road leading up to the old white farmhouse and freshly painted outhouse. The posse cooled off as they rode up to the house. The house and barn were framed by ancient oak trees, which provided shade on humid summer days. The dirt road forked twenty-five yards from the house, the other branch leading to the barn. Calderon looked across the grassy field to his left and didn't see anybody, although anyone could have been in the cover of the trees. Sheriff Calderon walked with Joseph and Bathers up to the front door, while Hank watched the back door. Calderon stopped for a moment and gazed at the corn stalks flowing in the slight breeze in the fields behind the house. He looked at Bathers over his right shoulder, waited for him to back up a bit, and knocked.

Luke and Pieter ran off toward the barn. Calderon called out for them to come back, but they ignored him. If he chased after Pieter and Luke, Bathers might enter the house without him.

Bathers planned to distract the Sheriff from Luke and Pieter. If Penn was in the barn his friends knew what to do. He secretly hoped to catch Penn in a room by himself; no sense in letting the man get to trial. Bathers tensed his right calf muscle and felt the handle of the knife in his boot. The knife he would place in Penn's dead hand, if given the chance.

Calderon opened the door, called out, and stepped over the threshold. Bathers almost tripped over Hank as they walked through the doorway at the same time. Hank's small stature often had him at the ready to use his strong voice to meet his needs. Bathers looked down at the deputy. The sheriff led the search through the house; nobody was home. Calderon wondered if, by the face he was making, Bathers was more disappointed than he was.

Luke and Pieter searched the barn, looking behind the cluster of plows and in the horse's stables. Pieter used a pitchfork on the piles of hay scattered around the long plank flooring of the barn. Luke jumped when barn swallows scattered from the hayloft. Pieter noticed loose planks along the back wall of the barn. He shifted two planks aside, recognized the space was big enough for a man, but only saw the apple orchard beyond. Luke and Pieter settled on taking tools back to their horses.

Calderon went to the barn and hollered through the open door for Luke and Pieter. The men came toward him with tools in hand. Sheriff Calderon shook his head back and forth at the men and they put the tools back.

Pieter said, "Just thought we might need tools to get into a locked room."

Calderon said, "That's what I thought, otherwise I'd be taking you in for stealing." He glanced at Bathers, who was staring at the two men. Luke and Pieter shrugged their shoulders and joined the others.

"Hank, you'll stay here until Penn comes back, or I come and relieve you," the sheriff continued. "Joseph and the others will join me in searching the rest of the farm. Anybody finds Penn, they come and get me."

The sheriff and the others went into the fields. Calderon was uneasy as they wandered through the stalks of corn. He was troubled by Bathers and his band of thieves, but it was more than that. He couldn't shake the feeling that Penn wasn't a murderer. He knew every man had his breaking point, but there was something about the situation that was pestering him, like a fly during a Sunday picnic. He struggled with his thoughts, trying to make them clearer, but nothing was there save the feeling. He focused on getting through the fields as quickly as possible. Bathers suggested burning them down, but Calderon would have nothing of it.

The fields were as empty as the farmhouse. Calderon sent Bathers and his friends home, then paced the front porch of the farmhouse; the only sound was the creaking of his boots on the planks of the porch. He was thinking, and the deputies knew not to disturb him.

Finally, the sheriff came over to his men. He stood next to Hank and across from Joseph. Hank smoked on his pipe and rocked in a chair, while Joseph chewed on a long piece of grass.

"Men, we have a problem. In about two hours, word of the murders will be passed around on Main Street like biscuits at Sunday dinner. Bathers will be bragging about his role in trying to capture Penn. I worry about people shooting at one another, thinking a murderer is on the loose. Whenever you hear anything, and I mean anything about this murder, I want you two to have the townsperson speak to me. Anybody taking the law into his own hands will spend time in the jail. We need to maintain order, so people feel safe enough to let us do our job." Hank tried to act even more relaxed to offset Calderon's worried tone.

Joseph said, "If I knew where he was, I'd bring him in; safer in the jail than out here with Bathers and his friends." Joseph turned his head to spit out the piece of grass.

"You want me to bring Bathers in?" asked Hank. Sheriff Calderon knew their history, and didn't want to aggravate the situation. He did get a kick out of the mental image of Hank bringing Barnaby in hogtied.

"Not yet," he said, "but if he starts stirring up people, I'll be the one to bring him in hogtied."

"That I'd like to see," laughed Hank.

The men shared a laugh on the porch of the Penn farm. Joseph had retrieved the blueberry muffins, and told them he'd get his sister to make more. He passed the basket around and the lawmen snacked on them in the warm noontime sun.

CHAPTER XIII

Express to Kingston

Just past noon, under a bright sun, Penn pushed on past the fork in the road leading to New Paltz. He and Smitty had come across more travelers than Penn had counted on. With each passing wagon or rider, Penn bid them good day and Smitty stared at the ground. Penn felt cold stares from a number of travelers, but that was his fate for the moment. He wondered what would happen if he met anyone from Kingston. Penn's thoughts bounced from one reason to another for having a slave with him. His plan was to return home under the cover of darkness, but his nerves were too frayed to wait. He feared getting caught more on this journey than any before.

Penn took a long look at Smitty's dark face. His brown skin hid the wrinkles that covered the corners of his eyes. Penn thought the man looked rather serene for a slave on the run. If he wasn't so fatigued, Penn would have realized he was staring. Smitty turned and looked Penn straight in his brown eyes.

Smitty smiled and said, "You figures yer horse knows bes' way to git home." Penn appeared to almost wake up, as he turned to face the road again. His fingers clenched the reins as he gathered his thoughts.

"He's been getting me home from the tavern for the past three years." Penn gave Smitty a quick smile.

The men shared a laugh. A couple rode by in a surrey. Penn tipped his hat to the young man, then his girl, and bid them good day, while Smitty stared at the road. The well-dressed man in the surrey bid him good day, but the woman stared at Smitty.

After they passed, Penn said, "I get nervous every time we pass people. Even though I know they're looking at us out of curiosity, I still get worried they'll be on the lookout for you."

Smitty asked, "Is dat why you's gettin' us straight ta Kingston?"

"I guess so. I don't want to be your undoing," admitted Penn.

"Undoin'?"

Penn thought for a moment and replied, "I don't want to be the one to get you caught."

"Not likely Misser James; we's making good time."

"Others may need a break. We're coming up on a side road that takes the back way up to western Kingston, closer to my farm. We can stop along the road." Penn pulled on the reins, turning the wagon to a narrow road forking off just west of the main road.

"Misser Penn, I gots crampin' fierce, I gots to go now or I'll bus'. Minds if I hops down an' catches up wid you's?" asked Smitty plaintively. He was embarrassed at the request.

Penn could see the anguish in Smitty's face. "Of course," he said. He slowed the wagon just far enough into the side road so as not to be seen from the main road. Smitty jumped off. Penn said, "Smitty, we'll be up the road about fifty yards in a clearing on the left." Smitty nodded an understanding as he bounded up a hill on the left side of the road. Smitty crested the hill, pulled down his trousers, and passed gas. Penn continued on the bumpy road, unaware of the eyes peering at the buckboard from the fork in the main road. He shouted to the passengers that they would be stopping soon for a break.

*   *   *

Jones was the first to bolt down the side road. He was followed closely by Kingman and the Clemmons twins. Kingman was the only one of the three wondering where Jones was heading. The horses were tired from the day's travels, and responded slowly to the spurs in their haunches. Kingman thought Jones wanted to travel up past Kingston before nightfall.

Kingman cursed aloud, "This sprint will cost us Kingston!"

Jones saw the buckboard with the tarp covering the back. They'd passed a number of surreys and lone riders. Those with wagons were searched; he wasn't going to let this one slip away. Kingman had those with wagons believing they represented the law in this county, so if they saw the slaves they'd tell him.

Penn continued on in his slow progress toward the clearing. He knew Smitty could find them easily. Jones appeared by his side, startling Penn. Jones noted the shock and wondered why. Penn let out an audible gasp.

Jones grabbed the tack to the horses and pulled them up short. He stared at the middle-aged farmer on the buckboard, and glanced at the supplies.

Jones demanded, "What's in the wagon?"

Penn panicked. He slapped the reins as he foolishly attempted to outrun Jones. The horses pulled against Jones's arm, causing him to groan and yank back. Jones quickly grabbed the reins from Penn and pulled hard to halt the struggling horses.

As Penn's horses raised front legs into the air at the abrupt stop, the Clemmons brothers rode up alongside; Penn feared for his life. Kingman arrived a moment later, and Penn quickly became aware Kingman was in charge.

Kingman ordered, "Lift the tarp!" Penn's hands were shaking and his heart raced. He knew the four men weren't lawmen. Penn opened his mouth to ask a question, but his tongue was dry and he coughed, choked.

"Who are you?" he managed to rasp, nervously. Penn exposed the sacks of grain and dry goods.

Kingman said, "We're searching for runaway slaves. Now, lift the tarp off!"

Miss Hattie and the others froze in place. Miss Dorothy squeezed Trent's hand so hard, he barely felt the ache in his leg. When the wagon had first stopped and they heard the horses, Calvin had shifted his arm enough to shove a neckerchief into Miss Alice's mouth in case she coughed. He saw the fear in her eyes. Calvin wished he could lay his hand on her cheek to try to ease the fear. All of the slaves listened intently to the horses and the harsh words of the men around the buckboard.

Penn had a hard time swallowing. His mouth was dry; he felt his heart pounding out of his chest. He couldn't think. He tried to create enough saliva in his mouth, but it remained dry. He slowly reached for a jug of water. His hand was a few inches from the jug when he heard the click of Jones's pistol.

Penn turned to look at him. He squeaked out, "I'm thirsty." Jesse Clemmons passed Penn the jug at Penn's feet to him. Penn drank a bit of water to his great relief. He was able to think up only one excuse for being so nervous.

"I thought you were going to rob me," he eked out. "I don't have much of anything left. Thief already got most of my money; with providence I had already bought my supplies. He stole some of the dry goods as well."

Penn lifted the tarp to show the slave catchers his supplies. Jones used his stirrup to hoist himself up into the buckboard. He kicked the bags of grain and rolled the three barrels in the corner. The thump of Jones's feet scared the slaves. Nobody could see that even Calvin's eyes were filled with fear. Miss Hattie mouthed a silent prayer to God, "Let dese devils be gone." The slaves awaited the prayer's answer.

Kingman said, "Man who robbed you, what he look like?"

Penn described the stranger in black. He said, "Well, he was a bit stocky with dark hair and dark clothes."

Kingman asked, "He have any scrapes?"

Penn answered honestly, "I don't remember." He realized Smitty had hit the stranger.

"Wait, on his face, there was a scrape." Penn saw Smitty come back down onto the road, behind the slave catchers.

"Same bastard that got my money," Kingman declared. Kingman wished he had taken them south before coming up here.

Smitty saw the strange men clustered around the buckboard; he slipped back up the hillside. Penn sat quietly looking at Kingman as Jones mounted his horse; Jones studied the farmer.

Penn said, "You aren't robbers, thank God."

Jones asked tersely, "What's your name and where you headin'?"

Penn tried to swallow, but what little spit was in his mouth refused the effort. He said, "My name's James Penn, and I have a farm in Kingston." He wiped the dry corners of his mouth.

Jones pointed toward the road to the east. He said, "Road over there goes to Kingston."

"You men must not be from around here," Penn observed. "This road leads to the western edge of Kingston, my farm." Smitty hid himself deep in the brush beyond the road.

Penn looked at each of the men awaiting the next question. The Clemmons brothers didn't appear threatening to Penn, save for their size. He thought they looked rather simple. Kingman stared down at Penn from horseback; he had his right hand on his holstered gun. Penn glanced at Jones, who had a drawn gun in his hand. He fought back the tears, but failed.

"I told you I was robbed," he pleaded. "I have nothing left, please don't take the horse and wagon, it's all I have."

Jones hissed, "We're not thieves; we want them slaves."

"I don't know about slaves; I'm a farmer. I have a few hands, but they aren't slaves. If you want, you can come back to my farm with me and I'll show you."

Kingman said, "We've seen enough." The Clemmons brothers shifted their horses to follow Kingman in whatever direction he was heading. Jones took another look at the buckboard, knowing he would draw a severe tongue from Kingman for this "waste of time." The men rode off back to the fork in the road and then onto the main road. The slaves remained silent and Penn knew better than to look under the boards; he still felt watched. He flicked the reins, and the wheels slowly turned, moving them closer to Kingston. He wondered when he would see Smitty again. Jones watched Penn's wagon slowly roll down the road, as the slave catchers sped along toward Kingston.

"Got a strange sense from that farmer," he hollered to Kingman.

Kingman replied, "Man was scared enough to crap his pants. Been robbed and then the four of us ride up on him. He doesn't know a damn thing."

"Maybe he was frightened of robbers, but something isn't right about him," Jones countered. "I think we should follow him."

"We decided not to follow the thief who robbed me, but you want to follow some dirt farmer who was robbed by the same man." Kingman shook his head. "You're not thinking, Jones; you're distracted. Get back to the hunt!"

For a brief moment, Jones thought Kingman might be right. He was well aware his thoughts were unfocused; even now they wandered back to his wife, the day she left. Jones couldn't trust his instincts, and that affected the hunt. He understood a moment of hesitation could cost them the slaves. He wasn't aware of how true that was on that side road.

The Clemmons brothers stared off down the main road as Jones and Kingman took a last look back at Penn rolling casually away from them along the dirt side road. They traveled north toward the point of ambush. Kingman's thoughts focused on the thief who was robbing people along this road, and his strong desire to make his acquaintance again. Jones was thinking about his distraction and struggled with staying focused on the hunt. The Clemmons brothers were discussing their favorite meal, both eventually agreeing on Sunday dinners with mother.

Penn stopped the buckboard around the second bend of the road, in a clearing near a cluster of trees. He acted as if he was watering his horses, much to the delight of the horses. Penn sat there feeding the horses a few of the Jonathan apples that had been badly bruised on the journey. When Penn turned back to the buckboard, Smitty was crouched down with only his eyes poking out from under the tarp.

Smitty said, "Don't looks at me. Acts as if I weren't here." Penn understood and stepped up into the buckboard and continued his travels.

Smitty wouldn't join him on the seat of the buckboard for the remainder of the journey. Smitty said to Penn, "Dat man who jumps into the buckboard. Dat was de man in de swamps." Penn nodded his head to show an understanding of the information. Penn thought he might start breathing normal again in another few hours. Beads of sweat trickled down his temples and onto his soaked shirt.

CHAPTER XIV

Kingston Station

Hank watched the robins peck at the damp grasses for grubs. Rain had fallen on and off for the past two days and finally cleared out. Waiting for someone to return home left a man to think. He couldn't believe Penn killed Simms. A man had to have a reason to murder, plain as that. Of the few people he knew that had murdered, most did it for passion. Penn and Simms had no arguments. Penn was known in most circles as a man of reason. Of all the people who might kill for passion, Hank had Barnaby Bathers at the top of the list. A man with a temper as evil as his was bound to be behind bars sooner or later.

Hank was a patient man, but he didn't like sitting on another man's porch, waiting to arrest him for murder. Hank had seen murderers before, mostly men at the docks, blind with rage, killing someone they knew. He never felt anything for those men, because they created their own fate.

During his long career, he had taken three women into custody for killing a violent spouse. He felt sorry for the women, but like his cousin Gladys, they had had a choice to make and they made the wrong choice. Hank let the sheriff know, but nobody else. He hoped this Penn situation would be over before September, as that was his next scheduled visit to her. Hank worried that someone in the jail would recognize him and Gladys would come to harm. He recalled her face when he first saw her in jail, all bruised and swollen. Herman got his licks in before Gladys pulled the trigger. Hank knew what he would have told his cousin to do, if he had been given a chance. He didn't have that chance. He watched the birds pecking at the grass, as sunlight poked through the clouds. A lone horseman rode down the path.

Hank moved inside the house and watched from a window near the door. The lone rider rode out to the barn. Hank slipped out the back door and headed to the barn. He found the rider's horse tied to the building near a trough. Hank peeked inside, his lungs filling with the musty scent.

He could barely see inside the dark space. A figure stepped aside and then back out into a shaft of light coming through a crack in the wall. Hank took his hand off his pistol and relaxed a bit.

He called out, "Luke, you best get out here." Luke stepped out toward Hank; he had tools in his hands.

Luke said, "Just searching the barn, can't be too careful."

"Decided the tools needed to be taken into custody?" Hank knew Bathers must have sent him after the hardware.

"Heard you coming, and thought I'd be less likely to kill you with one of these. That is when I thought you were Penn." Hank just took the tools and tossed them on the floor of the barn.

"Best thought I was Penn," he said. "You can get back on your horse and ride out." Luke set the tools on the floor of the barn. He stepped closer to Hank.

"Still don't have Penn?"

"You asking?" Hank said.

"Yeah, I'm asking."

"You're asking for Barnaby," challenged Hank. "One of these days, that man is going to get you in trouble." Hank wanted to run Luke off the property, but didn't want any more trouble from Bathers.

"I ain't waiting on a murderer, Hank," said Luke. Luke left the barn, got on his horse, and rode down a side trail toward Bathers's place. Hank's nerves started acting up. He understood more clearly why his boss was anxious to get Penn into custody. Hank walked back to the house, without noticing the buckboard coming down the road.

*   *   *

Penn saw the figure moving from his barn to the house. He wasn't able to identify who it was in the shade of the oak trees. Penn stopped his buckboard, and Smitty was already slipping out from under the tarp and dropping down from the back. Penn stared straight ahead.

He said loud enough for Smitty to hear, "I'm heading to the barn. There's a trapdoor just this side of the stall. You'll have to move a couple of bales of hay to find it. You can go down there, like being in a root cellar. I don't know who is on my porch, but I wasn't expecting anyone." Penn added ominously, "God be with you."

Miss Alice felt Trent gently squeezing her hand. The passengers understood the slow pace toward the barn. Miss Hattie silently spoke yet another prayer for God's guidance, as the wagon creaked through a slow turn toward the barn. Smitty darted across the road, hidden behind the buckboard. He raced through the apple trees by the back of the barn. His hope was to be inside before Penn, so he could watch what happened. The figure on the porch wasn't moving. Smitty rushed from tree to tree toward the barn.

Hank decided to continue rocking in the chair. He watched the buckboard stop momentarily and then continue toward the house. If Penn had thought about running, he thought better of it. At first, Hank considered that a sure sign of guilt, but a moment later was giving the man the benefit of the doubt. He realized Penn couldn't see who was sitting on his porch.

Penn rode closer to the house and barn. He finally recognized Deputy Hank Stratton on the porch. His breathing returned to normal, and he relaxed. He waved to the deputy, and Hank returned the wave. Penn drove the wagon up to the barn doors and hopped down.

He turned and yelled to the deputy, "Just need to put the horses in the stall and I'll be right there." Hank waved again. Penn slowly led the horses and buckboard into the barn. Once inside, he said to the empty buckboard, "Stay in the back. A deputy is sitting on my porch. I have to see what the deputy wants, probably something about stolen property, but to be safe, stay put. If need be, Smitty will release you. God be with you."

Miss Hattie said, "God Bless you, Misser James."

Penn replied, "He has, Miss Hattie." Smitty watched Penn leave the barn and walk toward the farmhouse. Smitty slowly slid down from the hayloft, then stepped over to the buckboard and shifted one of the planks. The five passengers stared at him wide-eyed.

Smitty said, "Jes' me." He slowly removed the large planks, beginning with the one over Calvin. Calvin eased himself out of the back of the buckboard. He tried to stand, but his legs gave out on him. Blood flowed slowly to his extremities, easing numbness into a prickly pain. Smitty had removed all of the planks by the time Calvin joined him on the barn floor. Smitty gently tossed aside the three bales of hay beside the horse stall.

Smitty turned to Calvin and said, "You's gits de res' o' dem out o' de buckboards. Start wid Miss Alice, so's she kin help you's put de boards back once e'erybody's out." Smitty felt the cool of the barn as his sweaty clothes clung to his body.

A whispered, "Yes sah," was all Calvin said. Smitty's eyes had adjusted to the darkness of the barn. He felt for a crease in the planks on the barn floor. He finally felt the smallest of gaps and used a horseshoe nail to pry it open. A scent of mold wafted upward as he moved the wooden panel that hid the underground space. Smitty stepped back over to the buckboard.

All but Trent were out of the buckboard. Calvin was in the back of the buckboard, helping his brother to his feet. Smitty waited at the edge of the buckboard to help him off. As Smitty lifted the slight, young man over the edge on the buckboard, his lame leg struck hard on the wall. Smitty stared into Trent's eyes, as Trent winced, moaned in pain. Tears flowed from the corners of Trent's eyes, but he barely uttered a sound. Smitty continued to stare as if giving the boy his own strength.

Smitty and Calvin helped Trent to the ground. Trent held the side of the wagon as the others moved toward the space below the barn. The earth was damp and cool under the barn. They had about a four-foot high crawlspace, roughly the size of a root cellar, that could easily accommodate the six.

Miss Hattie was the first into the space. She placed a couple of horse blankets down to keep the cold earth from their bones. Miss Dorothy joined her and put up a small crate of supplies in a corner of the space. Miss Alice brought down an unlit kerosene lantern, as she settled in next to Miss Dorothy. Calvin stood above him and Miss Alice below for support, as Trent hobbled down the earthen steps.

The four heard the footsteps of Calvin and Smitty in the barn as they worked quickly, quietly putting the planks back on the buckboard. Upon finishing, Calvin took a sack of supplies into the root cellar. Smitty grabbed the map and headed down. As he pulled the platform to land on top of them, he threw a huge handful of hay in the air to land over it. The hay fluttered down over the wooden platform; below Smitty hunched over with his eyes adjusting to the scant light.

The six waited in the near darkness for Misser James to come into the barn, each having enough space to sit comfortably and stretch out their legs some. If need be, they could lie next to each other and sleep. The earth was packed hard, sturdy.

James Penn stepped up onto his porch to greet Deputy Stratton.

"Hi, Hank, what form of misfortune brings you to my doorstep. Hank Stratton's face was serious, not the look Penn had envisioned with his jovial greeting. Penn awaited the worst, possibly the loss of some of his dairy cows.

The deputy's face didn't change as he said, "James, a man you know has been murdered." That's when Penn noticed Hank was holding his gun on his lap. Penn still hadn't grasped the seriousness of the situation.

Confused, he asked, "Who was murdered?"

Hank couldn't tell if Penn actually was unaware, or simply pretending so. He reflected that life would be a great deal easier if Penn would simply break down and admit his guilt. He said bluntly, "Two nights ago, Jeffrey Simms was murdered on his farm." Penn's knees buckled; he leaned against a post on the porch.

Stunned, he muttered, "Simms murdered?" He looked at Hank with a lost, faraway look, and muttered again, "Simms murdered." Hank didn't respond, but watched Penn's reaction to the information. Penn repeated, "Simms murdered," as if by saying the words somehow they would become the reality he couldn't comprehend. The expression on Penn's face shifted to horror, as he leaned more heavily into the post.

Hank couldn't believe the man he was looking at had killed anyone, but he had his duty to perform. He stood up from the rocker, returned his gun to his holster, and told Penn he was being taken in for the murder of Jeffrey Simms. Penn stood there, as if the words were spoken in a foreign tongue. Hank repeated himself, but Penn was cold, ice cold; too numb to hear another word. The deputy physically moved Penn's unresisting body in the direction of the barn.

Once in the cool of the barn, Penn stood before his horses, thinking they needed apples. For some reason, he felt the horses needed apples. He reached into a cloth sack beneath the seat of the buckboard. Deputy Stratton instinctively took a step back and drew his revolver. If Penn had turned to face Hank, his life would have been lost.

Penn didn't turn. He stepped forward with the four apples and fed them to his horses. Hank returned the revolver once again to the leather holster. He let out a breath held a moment too long and watched the horses chew on the juicy snack. Hank recalled the conversations he had had with Luke and Bathers. He began to worry not for his own safety, but for that of his prisoner. Hank felt it strange to think of James Penn, a man caring for his horses, as a prisoner.

He stepped over to Penn and said, "You have to get up on the buckboard. I need to take you in to the jailhouse." Penn looked confused, but Hank didn't believe there was anything he could say to clear up Penn's thoughts.

Penn climbed up on the buckboard. Hank jumped up next to him and took the reins from Penn's shaking hands.

Smitty and the others could hear the wheels of the buckboard leaving the barn. Soft earth sifted through the floorboards and glistened in the brief rays of sunlight that poked through between the slats of the barn wall. The passengers of the Underground Railroad were silently suffering as a lawman took James Penn away. Calvin rushed over to a tiny opening in the barn wall that extended down to the earth pit. He could barely see, but he glimpsed Penn and the lawman riding the buckboard down the long dirt road, leading the lawman's horse.

As Calvin turned back toward the cluster of bodies, all eyes were on Smitty. He said, "Misser James weren't hisself. Somethin' powerful bad is happenin', but if'n it were us, dey'd be lookin' all o'er this place. We's needin' to make plans if'n he don't comes back." Smitty looked into the eyes of the lost travelers, and didn't have the heart to tell them he was just as lost.

Miss Hattie sat in the corner of the earthen pit and prayed, "Our fathah, who art in Heaven, hallow't be dy name . . ."

CHAPTER XV

A Charge of Murder

Hank had Penn hide under the tarp in back of the buckboard to get him to the Ulster County Courthouse. Penn felt the heat of the sun, his breathing a bit harder. He wondered about the passengers in his barn, sharing their experience for a moment. He'd know what it was like to lose his freedom.

They had to ride through town in late afternoon, a busy time. Hank knew Penn wouldn't try to run. Hell, where would he run? He thought it best not to parade a suspected murderer down John Street. If Bathers saw them, he'd certainly stir up a crowd, causing all kinds of grief.

The deputy drove the buckboard past the Kingston Academy along John Street. The stone structure took up most of the block. In the afternoon, the students often sat beneath the shade trees for a lemonade and a breath of fresh air. The buckboard rode along the cobblestone streets toward the smaller avenue by the court house. He glanced over at the Roggen House and recalled the words of Sheriff Calderon, "the marks on the beam from the hangings." Hank took a quick glance at the lump under the tarp behind him, while he waited for a wagonload of furnishings to pass by. Women carried boxes from shopping while the men socialized by the stone fountain in back of the house. He followed John Street to Main and made the right-hand turn onto Main Street. Hank bid good day to a number of people crossing Main Street during an afternoon shopping trip. The center of town was busier than ever, but a world away from the docks on the canal.

He reached the courthouse and pulled the wagon onto the lawn outside the jail. He stepped down as Joseph and Calderon came out of the jailhouse. Sheriff Calderon stepped within two feet of Hank.

"Penn didn't come home yet?" he asked in an anxious tone. Hank pointed to the movement under the tarp.

"He's under the tarp, Sheriff. He's in shock; he thinks he's here because his friend was murdered. I don't think he understands he's the one accused of killing Simms."

Calderon began to redden from frustration. He asked Hank, "You told him why you were bringing him in, right?" His index finger crossed over his mustache.

Hank explained, "I told him everything, but I don't think he heard a thing after I told him Simms was murdered. He's in shock. If I wasn't so concerned about his safety, I would have taken him to Doc Hamilton's place." Hank lifted the tarp, but Penn just lay there. He looked up at the sheriff with a bewildered expression. Calderon turned to Joseph and motioned for him to help Penn.

Calderon said, "We better get him inside. Wrap him in a blanket and get the man some coffee."

Hank and Joseph hopped up into the buckboard and pulled the rest of the tarp off of Penn. Penn's eyes closed for brief periods as they adjusted to the sunlight streaming through the clouds. He stepped off the buckboard and almost fell, misjudging the height. Sheriff Calderon caught him before he hit the ground. Penn stood up and looked at the sheriff.

"Much obliged, Sheriff," he said. Calderon looked on as Penn entered the jail, not realizing he might never leave. Hank tied the horses to the railing outside the jail, where they dipped their snouts into the watering trough. Joseph could tell they had had a long day's journey and were more than fatigued. He'd take them to the stables next to the Flint place near his boarding house. Hank walked beside Penn into the jail.

The front and back doors had been left open to allow an afternoon breeze ease the summer heat in the jailhouse. Penn walked with the others until he noticed the iron bars were missing from the jail cell. A moment later, he realized the door to the jail cell was open and it was expected he enter. He looked at the sheriff.

Calderon, in a quiet, gentle manner that Joseph and Hank had never witnessed before, said, "James, you need to go in now." He took Penn by the elbow and led him into the cell. He sat Penn down on the straw bed and left the cell. Joseph slowly closed the iron bars; the door clanking shut.

"You caught the bastard, very good, Sheriff", said Bathers, who suddenly stood in the doorway. "You treat all your murderers that well?" Calderon walked over to Bathers to prevent him from taking any further steps into his jail. Hank slid his right hand down to rest on the butt of his gun.

Calderon said, "Barnaby, you got business here?" Joseph and Hank stood silently behind the sheriff with their hands on holstered pistols.

"Tom, I just wanted to see justice served, by that man being behind bars." Bathers pointed his finger at Penn. Calderon raised his hand to bring Bathers's arm down, but Bathers pulled away quickly. Penn looked at Bathers, but most likely wasn't quite hearing his words.

Calderon said sternly, "You've seen him jailed, now get on out of here."

Bathers said, "I'll be back in the morning to find out what you're going to do with him."

Calderon asserted, "James Penn will stand trial for the murder of Jeffrey Simms. I will be requesting that a judge come down from Albany for the trial." Penn heard the words; for the first time, he heard them. He was in jail for the murder of Jeffrey Simms.

Penn wondered aloud, "Simms was my friend, why in God's name would I kill him?" He was confused, but he understood exactly why he was in jail and didn't know what was going to happen next. His first thought was of the slaves hidden in his barn. How was he going to get them out of there? They needed to get on their way, but they needed a conductor. Penn was lost in his thoughts about the people hidden at his home. He didn't hear the remainder of the conversation.

Bathers said, "You know he done it. What we need a trial for?" Bathers tried to take a half step closer, but Calderon blocked his path and wouldn't retreat. Bathers shifted uncomfortably due to his proximity to Calderon.

Calderon said, "If you were in his boots, you'd want a trial."

"Yeah, if I killed someone, I'd try any trick I could to get out of the hangman's noose." Bathers tried to glare at Penn, but he was facing the far wall. "I'll be in the first row at the trial."

Sheriff Calderon watched Bathers leave the jailhouse, get on his horse, and ride off. He turned back toward the deputies, but made eye contact with James Penn. Penn's face couldn't hide the confused fear he felt. Tom Calderon was left speechless. He went into his office and closed the door; the heat quickly became stifling.

CHAPTER XVI

Awaiting the Signalman

As the last of the sunlight clung to the tops of the trees, the chill in the barn forced the slaves to huddle on one side of the earthen pit. Trent was smack dab in the center, to prevent him from suffering the chills. If given half a chance, Smitty would have moved the corner of the army blankets and lit a small fire in the opposite corner of the cellar, using his hat to force smoke out the thin cracks between a few of the slats of the barn's wall at the top of the earthen space. Smitty wouldn't get that chance. He used the last of the sunlight to study the maps.

An unspoken restlessness gradually grew among the slaves; the cluster of six feared the loss of freedom. Each was doing his or her own to keep from climbing out of the trap door and running into the woods. Smitty knew if the six split up, at least half would be brought back south, out of dumb luck, a lack of knowledge about the woods, or trickery. He figured he had the best chance to make it north, because most folks wouldn't pay no mind to an old nigger, thinking him either free or not worth the price to send back.

Smitty traced his finger across the Catskill Mountains and northwest to Oneonta. A faraway place with a name he could scarcely pronounce. He traced his finger north through Albany to Canada. A quicker route by far, but Penn had said something about Oneonta on their way to Kingston, and slave catchers near Albany. Penn spoke of safe homes along the route, those that left a ribbonned lantern by the roadside, or a quilt on the fence. Smitty felt a great weight on his shoulders, far greater than his massah's whip.

Trent looked up beyond his brother's shoulder to his face and quietly asked, "How come we's stayin'?" Calvin's eyes betrayed his fatigue. Trent wanted to prop himself up off his brother; his mind was willing but his body was not. Calvin replied, "We'se waitin' on Misser James." His eyelids drooped, aching for sleep.

Miss Dorothy echoed the sentiment, saying, "We has to git outta here. Dey gonna come back fer us." She hated waiting ever since the raid in Virginia, two were caught.

Smitty kept studying the map, squinting in the dim light. He said, "Where's you plannin' on goin'?"

Trent blurted out impulsively, "North to Canada." Smitty took his eyes off the map, studied Trent, and looked back at the maps. Calvin, Miss Hattie, and Miss Alice turned to Smitty, waiting for him to put Trent in his place. Smitty just kept looking at the map.

Trent said, "All we's needin' is dese here supplies an' de maps."

Smitty said calmly and with utter command, "You cain takes yer fair share o' dem supplies, but dese here maps is goin' wif de rest o' us when we's leavin'." Trent and Miss Dorothy stared at Smitty. Trent didn't utter a word.

"Go on chil'en," Smitty added. "You cain gits on yer way. I ain't holdin' you's here and I ain't 'bouts ta let you's git de rest 'o us caught. Trent tried to shift his weight, move toward the trapdoor.

Calvin stepped in, saying, "My brothah be happy ta listens ta you's, Misser Smitty." Trent was angry with Calvin for doing what he did best, keeping him from making a mistake. Trent glared at the far wall; Smitty waited for him to say something. Smitty looked at Calvin and nodded; Trent felt like he was being treated as less than a man. Calvin wished his brother understood more about life and the consequences a man could face.

*　　*　　*

Calvin lost himself in a memory from their childhood, when a neighbor caught them stealing a handful of her apples. The two boys had picked them from a bountiful apple tree, but the tree was closest to her home. Miss Louisa claimed rights to the apples, and most everyone on the plantation respected that situation. When Miss Louisa caught them, she took them to a tree, picked a switch, and gave each of them several whippings on their bare backs. On the way home, Calvin told Trent to keep quiet about Miss Louisa.

Trent's anger got the best of him. When they got home, he tattled to his mother about the whipping from Miss Louisa. When their mother found out why, she told the boys to collect up a switch from the tree out back.

Calvin never spoke to his brother about the second whipping, as he figured not speaking about the whipping was worse than hitting his brother. After that whipping, Trent had listened to Calvin most times.

*   *   *

Everyone in the cellar froze in place at the sound of horses' hooves outside the barn. The cluster of panicked slaves stared at Smitty. Words were held on the edges of their lips, as Smitty held up a large, scarred hand to keep them quiet. He looked at Miss Alice, who was letting out a soft cough. He handed her his neckerchief and motioned for her to put it in her mouth. She obliged and the cough was muffled.

The horses sounded as if they had stopped just outside the barn. Miss Hattie's eyes lit up; Smitty figured she thought it was Penn. Smitty shook his head from side to side, as he knew it wasn't. The light faded from Miss Hattie's eyes. Smitty knew Penn would have returned with his buckboard.

The door to the barn creaked open, and muffled voices could be heard—two, maybe three men. Smitty looked up to the floor of the barn, as if he could see right through the planks. His eyes followed the footsteps in the barn. Miss Hattie sat motionless between the two couples of young folks. Smitty held up his hand to make sure nobody uttered a word. The men came close to the stall.

Pieter asked, "You need any tack? Penn has an extra set." He held up the leather and metal works.

"No, got what I need. I came for tools," Luke said. He placed the plane and hammer on the floor of the barn, and took down a scythe from the barn wall. There was a brief scraping sound—metal on wood. He asked, "You sure Penn is in the jail?"

"Course I'm sure," Pieter reassured him. "Bathers saw him there in the cell; said he looked like a lost dog." He grabbed a leather pouch full of ten penny nails.

"You'd look like a lost dog, too, if you got caught after killing a friend."

Miss Hattie placed her hands over her mouth. Smitty just stared at the planks above him. Nobody in the cellar saw Smitty's right hand clenching a long metal pole he'd brought down with him.

Pieter said, "I wouldn't be foolish enough to get caught. Stabbing a man with your own knife and then leaving it there."

"I figure he got the jitters and ran off, not realizing his knife was there," Luke replied.

Pieter said, "Wasn't him anyway." The slaves heard metal on metal clanking, as tools were placed in a cloth bag.

Luke asked, "How do you know that?"

"Angela told me Bathers's girlfriend Jenny was with him last night. He told her he had done it the night before last."

"Who in their right mind would tell a girlfriend such a thing?" Luke challenged.

"Jenny was talkin' about goin' to his wife and tellin' her everything. Tellin' his girlfriend he killed someone would be enough to keep her mouth shut."

Luke was dumbfounded; he said, "Why would Bathers kill Simms?"

"It was over them water rights," Pieter said. "Now, we ain't gonna talk about it again."

A loud thud shocked the slaves, as a heavy object fell to the barn floor. Pieter said, "I want this plow, but I'll have to come back for it." He leaned the long structure against the wall of the barn.

Luke said, "I got what I wanted; we best git outta here."

Smitty's eyes followed the sound of the two men's boots, as they walked out of the barn. Calvin shifted his body to the barn wall. He spied through a small knothole in one of the wooden planks at the top of the earthen wall. Calvin watched the two men slowly ride away on the dirt trail on the far side of the house.

Miss Hattie said with worry, "Misser James is in terrible troubles. Dat man said he been 'cused a murderin' somebody."

Smitty added, "Worse dan dat, dey knowed who done the killin'."

"He gonna be hanged?" Miss Alice asked. She wrung her hands in worry.

Trent replied, "Some white folks been hanged fer killin'." He bit into an apple.

"If'n he was colort, he'd a been hanged," said Calvin soberly.

Smitty said, "Mos' white folks doesn't meet de hangman's noose." His thoughts jumped to their journey north without a guide.

Miss Hattie grunted, knelt on the earth, bowed her head, and said, "Dear Lord, please takes Misser James inta yer han' an' he'p him through dis here trial. You's knowed he weren't de man what done dis murder. He's a good man, Amen." She looked up to see the others with bowed heads. Each muttered an "amen" as they looked up.

Trent said, "Now we doesn't has a choice, Misser James ain't comin' back." Smitty just sat in thought, trying to figure out what to do. The others sat quietly staring at him. He knew their eyes were on him, but he wouldn't look at them until he knew what to do.

*   *   *

Jones, Kingman, and the Clemmons brothers rode into town as the sun was providing a rosy glow to the stone and wood houses along the street that held the wall of the first settlement here. Tired from the long day's journey, they proceeded down Main Street to a boarding house. Once the horses were tied up to a post in front, the men headed into the house.

Kingman asked the proprietor, "Do you have two rooms?"

Proprietor Everett Tappen said, "I can let you men have two rooms for the night for three dollars." Kingman searched for the money from his own pocket, remembered he'd been robbed, and accepted the three dollars in Jones's hand. Tappen said, "Rooms are the second and third on the right at the top of the stairs."

The Clemmons twins had never paid a dime along the hunt, as it was far less confusing to settle up at the end. Jones never paid, because he was worth it. Kingman knew he'd have to pay him back. Kingman nodded to the three men. The Clemmons brothers started heading to the room they'd share for the night. They'd wash up before supper the way their mother had taught them. Jones wanted his choice of bed, as he preferred to be away from the window.

Kingman asked the proprietor, "When is the evening meal?" He'd have to get the Clemmons twins for supper.

"In an hour in the dining room," responded Tappen. "We'll be having chicken and dumplings." He glanced at the twins and wished he had asked for more money.

"Very good." Kingman followed the others up to their rooms. Kingman and Jones took the first room; the Clemmons twins the second. Kingman washed his face in the white metal basin on the worn dresser. Jones lay down on the wooden-framed bed, feeling the comfort of a featherbed. He felt just as comfortable on a bedroll under the stars, but the bed reminded him of his wife's warmth.

Jones said, "We'll make good time in the morning and find a spot on the road to Albany."

Kingman said agreeably, "Hit the trail at first daylight." Kingman knew it was a lie, but he had to give Jones hope or he'd never get laid.

"Clemmons'll want breakfast." Jones was thinking ahead, and testing Kingman's conviction to an early start. He reached out to the chair next to his bed, grabbed his saddle bag, and drew it up under his pillow.

Kingman asked, "You believe that man heading south. The one who said he hadn't seen any slaves pass him by?" He wanted to change the subject. He placed his bag under the mattress out of habit, rather than necessity.

"Yes, I do, because he was from Alabama, and any man from Alabama traveling in the North isn't about to lie to fellow Southerners."

Kingman said, "I need to get to a bank in the morning to get money for the rest of the trip." He had found the answer to hitting the trail at a reasonable hour.

"Should get the money tonight, want an early start," Jones urged. He wasn't about to let go of this one. He wanted to be sure of getting to that ambush point before the slaves.

"Might have enough time to get a wire to my bank. I'll be back." Kingman left the room, and Jones was left to his thoughts. He wished he could be more like the Clemmons twins, simple-minded. He'd like to be able to think of anything but his wife, but that wasn't possible. He forced himself to focus on the hunt, trying to think of every possible action the slaves could take to escape destiny. His thoughts wandered back to the image of her at the doorway, his wife. Standing there, looking into his eyes, saying something that he didn't hear until she was well out the door and gone into the night. Her words continued to haunt him.

Jones got up off the featherbed, threw on his boots, and stepped out of the room. He left the boarding house and crossed Main Street. He found a saloon. Tonight he needed the whiskey to keep his mind from remembering. The comforts of the boarding house were too great for him to stay focused on the hunt.

Jones didn't hear more than bits and pieces about a murder of one of the farmers in Kingston. He drank the first whiskey quickly. The second whiskey could be sipped; he could feel the warmth trickle down his throat, chasing the burn of the first drink. Jones wondered why anyone would murder a farmer. It wasn't his business, but it was a distraction. He joined the conversation at a nearby table. The locals welcomed a visitor's point of view.

CHAPTER XVII

Runaway Engine

Fried eggs and Canadian bacon would have satisfied Penn on any other morning, but today he was in jail for the murder of his friend. Penn felt hollow inside, as if he no longer needed nourishment or sleep; he needed to lie down, breathe, and exist in the pain. He pushed the fork across the plate in a vain effort to spark an appetite. Joseph had brought the breakfast for Penn from his boarding house. Joseph knew Penn well, so well he didn't talk about the death of Jeffrey Simms. Joseph was puzzled, as he knew Penn hadn't committed the murder, but Penn didn't speak of an alibi.

Penn took a bite of bacon and chewed much longer than necessary. He didn't want to talk to his friend. He stared through the bars at the open jailhouse door. The early morning breeze was fresh after a light evening rain. Penn stared at freedom, a freedom he hoped his passengers would enjoy. Joseph looked at Penn, at the doorway, and wondered who he was waiting on to walk through the door.

Penn couldn't stop thinking about the slaves hidden in his barn. He knew they'd be fine in the small space, but how long could they stay down there while he waited for the sheriff to find the killer? He remembered Quaker Jowett helping him build the small pit under his barn. The earthen room could hold about ten people squatting side by side, giving them room to move about if necessary. Penn thought about Jeffrey Simms being in the earth; his friend was gone. He had an urge to pay respects.

He recalled the last time the two had spoken, and thought about it being the "last time." Simms had talked about plans to expand his corn crop this season with the land purchased from Bathers. He wouldn't have to worry about maintaining grazing pastureland this year, limiting his crops. Penn remembered Simms's smile when they spoke about the thousands of people moving to town since the completion of the canals, causing an ever-rising demand for crops. The two had toasted the completion of the canals and the hope for a bumper crop year. Penn remembered that smile.

* * *

The soreness in Miss Hattie's knees left her, as numbness moved in. She held her hands close to her body, palms facing one another; fingertips pointing toward the Heavens. She knelt in the cold, dank cellar, praying. Miss Hattie prayed to God to help them find safe passage to Canada. She paused, let out a moan as she shifted her weight to a sitting position, and gazed at the group. Smitty spoke softly to the others.

Smitty said, "We's got ta un'erstan's dat Misser James mos' likely won't be comin' back here. So, we's got ta makes a choice betweens stayin' an' waitin' on he'p, or leavin'."

Trent blurted out a little too loudly, "How's he gonna send he'p?" Calvin sighed as Smitty let this one go.

Calvin glared at his brother, and Trent settled back. Calvin said, "I know'd dey's got a whole lot o' white folks workin' dis here un'erground, but I don't sees how Misser James is ta let dem know we's down here."

Miss Hattie chimed in, "De Lord, He done works in myster'us ways. He know'd we's here an' He'll be showin' us what's ta do." Smitty didn't know how to respond to Miss Hattie. If he said she was right, he'd be following God's plan. Smitty was a Christian, but worried about listening to God, because sometimes he didn't hear so good. He drank a bit too much at times, cursed often enough, and rarely made prayer meetings on Sunday. Smitty just let her words stand out there.

Miss Alice coughed softly and took a swig of water from a jug. She passed it to Miss Dorothy, who waved her off, as she began chewing on an apple, the juice dripping onto her hand. She enjoyed the sweetness of the apple. Mice scurried through the barn with what sounded like a cat not far behind, above the huddled travelers.

Trent gently pulled up his pant leg and moved his calf over with only a dull ache. He and Calvin looked at the swollen red bump just above his ankle. A crusty brown scab had replaced the oozing green puss. Smitty checked the wound.

"Comin' 'long nicely son," said Smitty. He pulled the small corncob pipe out of his coveralls, put the stem to his lips and breathed in. He could taste the stale burnt tobacco.

After a long pause, he said, "We's gonna heads north through de route Misser James done has fer us. We travels in de early sunlight an' de late afternoon, o'er dem Ca'skills mountains ta de Oneonta. Wif God's he'p, we's gonna fin' us dem friendly peoples Misser James spoke ta me 'bout."

Calvin asked, "What 'bouts headin' due north, ta Albany an' Canada?"

"I reckon dat looks good ta you's, but I figures dem bounty hun'ers would be lookin' dat way. Dem bounty hun'ers is gittin' paid good money fer a slave. Dey doesn't minds spendin' money ta finds us. I pray we's won't has ta worry 'bout dem bounty hun'ers, but we's bes' stays clear."

Calvin said, "Dat's one long walk." His tone was of concern, not a challenge.

"Yes son, dat's one long walks." Smitty leaned against the cool earthen wall and closed his eyes.

*   *   *

Barnaby Bathers wasn't used to repeating himself, especially with someone writing it down. But he could scarcely refuse Tom Calderon. The sheriff had asked him to the office for a late supper and to discuss the murder of Simms in his office. When Bathers had arrived, they ate a supper of roasted chicken, boiled potatoes, glazed carrots, and chocolate cake. Calderon wanted Bathers in a good mood when he had Miss Westcott write down what had happened the night Bathers found Simms. The sheriff wasn't exactly happy about doing this, but the judge from Albany had wired him to make sure he had a statement from the witness describing everything about finding the body of Jeffrey Simms.

Miss Westcott, a young, slightly round-faced, red-headed woman, looked at the blank pieces of paper before her on the corner of Sheriff Calderon's desk. She held her pencil ready to begin writing, as Calderon explained the purpose of writing down what happened.

Bathers protested, "Why can't I just tell the judge what happened?"

Calderon said, "That just won't do."

"You know I don't do anything in writing. A man is only as good as his word." Calderon had suspected Bathers was illiterate. Bathers didn't like writing; that left more room for changes in what was said.

"As I told you, the judge wants it in writing." Calderon thought for a moment, and, feeling he could benefit, said, "You'd be doing me a favor." He tried to look as pathetic as possible.

Bathers smiled and looked at the pieces of paper. He wondered how this could go wrong, but if the sheriff owed him a favor, all the better to influence him. His hesitation was being noticed. He said, "I just don't know where to start."

Calderon said, "Just think of it as talking to me." The sheriff motioned for Miss Westcott to begin writing. He felt a twinge of guilt, seeing her pleasant smile and sweet disposition, but she had volunteered to hear about the murder of Simms. "Bathers, tell me what happened the night Simms was killed?" Miss Westcott raised her pencil.

Bathers said, "As I told you, I was out at Simms's farm that night. I found him in the barn. He was lying there and I almost tripped over him. His lantern was by his side. He was bleeding. I told him I was gonna get him help. He just held on to me, my pants leg. He said, 'Penn done this.' I asked him if Penn was the one who stabbed him, and he said, 'yes'. He then stopped talking. I just ran out of there and ran to get help. I came across Jacob, and he went to get the doctor while I came to get you." Miss Westcott wrote in the shorthand she had learned, keeping up with Bathers.

Calderon said to Miss Westcott, "That would be Jacob Knufield and Doctor Hamilton." Miss Westcott smiled briefly and wrote down the names. She didn't want to think of Simms's murder. She tried to think of this as an exercise in dictation, like in Miss Humboldt's class.

Bathers added, "Well, yeah, who did you think?"

Sheriff Calderon asked, "Anything else you remember about that night?"

Bathers said, "There is one other thing. When I stooped down to listen to Simms, he opened his hand and there was a button in it. I tried to take the button, but he pulled his hand away from me, and clenched his fist real tight, like he had to keep it for something." There was a silent pause; Bathers leaned forward and took the glass of ice water off the sheriff's desk. He took a long drink.

Calderon asked, "Can you tell me what you were doing at the Simms's farm?" He tried to look bored, paying little attention to the details he was cataloguing in his brain. He'd think this through later.

Bathers said, "I was there to get my water rights signed. He told me he would sell me water rights for forty dollars, as long as I put up a fence to keep my sheep from his crops."

Calderon asked, "Did you see anyone else that night?" He glanced at the scribbling on the pieces of paper, reminded of a woman he had been sweet on a half-century ago. She had taught him shorthand while they courted.

"No, just Simms and Knufield was all I met."

Sheriff Calderon sipped a cup of coffee. He asked, "You know of anybody else who may have seen what happened that night?" He had the list of questions from the judge.

Bathers looked at the sheriff kind of funny and asked, "No I don't, do you?"

Calderon said, "Nobody else has come forward, yet. I guess that's all."

Bathers got up from his chair, and said, "That wasn't so bad." He tipped his hat to the sheriff and winked at Miss Westcott. Bathers stepped out of the sheriff's office. He paused for a moment in front of the jail cell, shot an angry look at Penn, and left the jailhouse. Penn sat wondering what the look entailed.

Miss Westcott, with youthful innocence, turned to Calderon and asked, "I don't understand one thing." She quickly reviewed her notes for accuracy.

"What's that, Miss Westcott?" asked Calderon. He was about to pick a piece of corn from between his teeth with his letter opener.

"Well, Mister Bathers said he took a contract for water rights to the Simms's farm, but if I'm not mistaken, earlier he said a man was only as good as his word, never wrote anything down." She looked puzzled.

Sheriff Calderon said thoughtfully, "MMhmmm, that's interesting. That's what I heard as well." The sheriff didn't want any further questions. He helped Miss Westcott to her feet. He said, "Thank you for your help tonight, Miss Westcott. You can come by tomorrow to write this out longhand. Remember this has to remain between us, as this is for court." Miss Westcott used her right hand to make the symbol of a cross over her heart.

"Swear to God and hope to . . .," Miss Westcott said uneasily. Calderon placed a hand on her shoulder.

"I'll have Hank see you home." Calderon studied Bathers's statement. There was something else that bothered him. There it was.

*　　*　　*

After Miss Westcott and Hank left the jailhouse, Calderon went over to the jail cell with a leftover piece of chocolate cake. He passed the cake through the bars. James Penn had a notorious sweet tooth, but he waved off the cake.

Calderon said, "Go ahead and take it, only go to waste otherwise."

"Better the hogs have it, get more out of it that way." Penn sat looking at the sheriff, but the sheriff felt he was looking right through him.

"Suit yourself." Sheriff Calderon gazed through the bars at the man in his mid-forties who sat on the straw rope bed. He looked so small in the jail cell. Not that Penn was large by any means. His dimpled, round face made him look younger than his years, but in the cell he looked small.

Calderon said, "Where were you two nights ago?" He set the piece of cake on Joseph's desk beside the "Deputy Bielk" sign.

Penn said, "I was home by myself." The sheriff took a bite of his piece of cake. He swallowed the piece.

Calderon said sternly, "Jim, I know you are lying, and if you keep lying, you will spend a better part of what remains of your life in prison."

Penn said plainly, "If you refuse to believe me, then I have nothing more to say." He really did want to be left alone; the better for the slaves to get away.

Calderon said exasperatedly, "Mister Penn, there is very little evidence that doesn't point to you for killing Jeffrey Simms. You understand in a few days you will have a trial and at that trial you will get a chance to defend yourself. If there is anyone who can vouch for you two nights ago, you best get them into that courthouse. Otherwise, you will be seeing plenty of me before transfer."

Penn quietly said, "I appreciate your concern Sheriff Calderon." He licked his dry lips, sipped cold coffee from his dinner, then continued with an emotional intensity, "A good friend of mine is dead and I'm being accused of killing him. I don't have any better alibi than my word that I did not kill Jeffrey Simms. Right now, I could jump around this cell throwing everything into the air and screaming my innocence, but that wouldn't change anyone's mind any more than if I sit here trying to figure out what has been happening over the past two days." He placed the cup on the metal tray, causing a thump.

Calderon said, "I understand, Mister Penn. If you are innocent, may God find a way to bring that to light in the courtroom. If guilty, may I hang you myself."

"Then if I hang, may God have mercy on both our souls." His even tone had them let the words hang for a moment between them.

The sheriff stood up, with the chair creaking out the shift in his weight. He walked back into his office, leaving the door open so he could hear Penn.

Penn knelt down in the jail cell. He prayed aloud, "Dear God, please forgive the sheriff and the others who believe that I have killed my friend. Please take care of my friends; find them safe passage. Please rid me of this painful situation. God, please take this rage from within, as it poisons me."

The prayer of James Penn puzzled Sheriff Calderon, but then again everything Penn did puzzled the sheriff.

CHAPTER XVIII

Man on the Road

Trent and Calvin woke about the same time, shivering in the cold of the night air. Trent's teeth chattered, while Calvin rubbed his arms and legs to get some kind of warmth in them. Soft moonlight illuminated the trapdoor, as Trent placed his hand on the underside of the heavy door. Trent tested the door and found it heavy. He moved a tad closer, kneeled to get better leverage, and came face to face with Smitty. Trent gasped and fell backward at the large face of the dark-skinned man. Smitty didn't say a word, just stared at Trent. Calvin touched the sleeve on Smitty's worn cotton shirt.

"He doesn't means no harm Misser Smitty; he's cold. Boy's been wif de sickness o' de devil."

Smitty's eyes softened, but his hand remained on the metal pole by his side. Calvin glanced down at the pole, too late to stop his words in defense of his brother's actions.

Smitty said, in such a way that the young men knew these words wouldn't be repeated and the punishment for forgetting them would be harsh, "Nobody done dare goes through dat doors widout e'eryone bein' awakes, as we's all might has to runs."

Trent said, "Yes sir," and his brother echoed the words. Trent and Calvin huddled up next to Miss Alice and Miss Dorothy. Smitty sat in the darkness thinking. He thought long and hard about the people he would be taking across the mountains to the promised land. He said a prayer to God, asking Him to look over the man he was to the man he was trying to become. Smitty asked God to look beyond his own soul to the five other souls that traveled with him and the good they could do. He prayed that God look over the three men who were killed in a barn fire Smitty helped set to save slave's lives. In a most humble way, he asked God to see them safely to Canada. Smitty hoped God was listening to this broken-down old mule of a man.

*   *   *

Jones lay awake in the early morning hours, angry at himself for the hangover and at Kingman for the woman in the room. In the bed next to his Kingman lay with a young prostitute, scarcely a woman. The two of them had had quite a night and had fallen asleep only a couple of hours before. Jones cursed the darkness, as the morning sun would burn away the chill in the air long before the four of them hit the trail. Jones wanted to get out of bed, dress, and head out into the streets of Kingston, but he was leery of the city.

Jones wasn't worried about handling himself; he was worried he might get into trouble with the law. Anybody trying to steal from him would quickly find a hunting knife sticking out between his ribs. Jones didn't mind anger, anger he knew well since he was a young man. He knew his anger helped him go above and beyond what others might do to survive. Jones felt lucky, no proud, that his body carried only three scars, two from bullets and one from a knife. Tonight, if he walked the streets of Kingston, someone else might not feel so lucky.

Jones could hear the Clemmons twins snoring in the room next door. The walls were too thin to keep out that loud growl. Jones thought about hitting the trail to keep his sanity. He could head north toward Albany, and they could meet up with him there. That way he'd get the opportunity to watch for the slaves. He'd lose a couple if they spotted him and scattered, but that was better than losing them all. Jones slipped out of the sheets and into his pants. The prostitute stirred, as if losing a coin, but quickly fell back asleep when she saw it was the one who had watched. She thought to herself, too bad she couldn't charge a man for watching.

Jones finished dressing and left a map of the road with a wooden match stuck into a spot just north of Kingston. He opened the door with a slight creak and stepped out into the dark hallway. Jones felt his way along the wall down to the parlor. A dim kerosene lamp lit the parlor.

Jones stepped toward the door. He heard a sound behind him, took his hand off his pistol, and slowly turned. The proprietor had been aroused by the noise. Jones gave the awkwardly smiling man a cold stare.

Proprietor Tappen said nervously, "Just looking after the place. Townfolks are pretty jumpy since that murder." He wished he were in bed, and that his wife didn't hear footsteps.

Jones said politely, "Heard about the murder, shame about that farmer. Somebody said last night they caught the man." He didn't know why he was chatting with this man; just curiosity.

Proprietor Tappen turned up the kerosene lamp to shed light on the parlor. He saw the stranger's pistol and tried to pay it no mind. He was eager to discuss the murder.

"Man they have in the jail is James Penn, not a likely killer," said Tappen. "I once saw him hit a dog with his buckboard. Dog ran right into the wheel. He picked that poor animal up and took him to Doc Hamilton. A man like that doesn't kill." He waited for a response from Jones.

Jones said thoughtfully, "No, I reckon he wouldn't." He recalled the name, James Penn, but didn't recall where he had heard it. Past couple of days must have been, possibly in the saloon? No, it was somewhere on the trail. Farmer with a buckboard, heading north to Kingston. He was alone, but surely the man he bought supplies from could say he was down south and couldn't have gotten back in time to do the killing. James Penn was in jail, but if he had the slaves, where could they be? They had searched the wagon, under the tarp. Jones didn't have all the answers, but he had enough to stay in Kingston.

Jones stepped outside, leaving behind the anger he had possessed on the stairs. He walked swiftly down Main Street, turning onto Wall Street at a fine stone house. A sign in front said "Johnston house." Jones traveled by moonlight, without another soul around. He arrived at the Ulster County Courthouse, then sneaked behind the building to the jailhouse.

He spied a small window with bars. He quietly stepped over to it and peered in. His eyes searched the lump on the straw bed, but the blanket was pulled up high. He stared in at the body, as if he was trying to will the sleeping body to move the covers aside. Beyond the cell, Joseph sipped at his cup of coffee and teased himself with the notion of an hour's sleep. Penn lay still, as still as a mouse in an open field. He heard the steps outside the building; he feared for his life. Covers pulled up to his head, he wished he could disappear. He thought of calling out to Joseph, but worried it could alert the man outside the window. After a long moment, Jones took back to the road. He headed back to the boarding house; along route, he thought up a plan to get to Penn. James Penn lay there for an eternity listening for footsteps other than Joseph's boots.

*   *   *

The tiniest rays of sunlight streamed through the slats of wood making up the barn wall. Miss Hattie awoke first of those still sleeping. She saw Smitty sitting by the wall staring out at the road.

Miss Hattie asked, "You been up all night?"

Smitty replied, "No, only de dark moments." Smitty chuckled, and Hattie was soon to follow.

She quipped, "You's may be in need o' soap, an' I doesn't just means yer mouf." They both laughed quietly.

Smitty asked in a serious tone, "Is God listenin'?"

Miss Hattie reassured, "We's ain't been caught, yet." There was a long pause; they listened to the songbirds chirping. Miss Hattie cleared her throat and continued, "We's got ta saves him." She sipped on the jug of water to rinse the dust from her throat.

"We's will, Miss Hattie, I's intendin' on savin' all o' us," said Smitty reassuringly.

"You's talkin 'bout Trent; I's talkin' 'bout Misser James," explained Miss Hattie. Smitty was perplexed.

"How we supposed ta saves Misser James? He's inna jail," he replied. Smitty looked at Miss Hattie as if she had asked him to turn white.

Miss Hattie stared straight into his dark brown eyes and said, "God works in myster'us ways, Smitty."

Smitty remarked, "Dat is mos' myster'us Miss Hattie, mos' myster'us indeed."

*   *   *

Midmorning arrived before Kingman stepped down the stairs. He smiled at the Clemmons brothers, knowing they'd respond with more than annoyance. The twins had eaten more than their fair share of breakfast, and the proprietor was only thankful these haystacks had woken late. Jones was dressed and reading the paper. Kingman knew of only three times Jones read the paper, all of them when Jones was waiting on him. Kingman wanted a warm meal, but knew he had delayed the party long enough. Jones would blame him if they missed the slaves.

Kingman stepped over to the velvet-lined chair Jones was sitting in. Jones pulled the top of the paper down, showing Kingman the article on the murder of farmer Jeffrey Simms. Kingman looked at Jones, and looked at the paper, unaware of the significance, other than that Jones had had to wait a couple of hours.

Jones said, "That farmer in the buckboard yesterday morning. That was the killer." Jones put the newspaper down on a small coffee table, and turned it so Kingman could see the story.

Kingman asked, "What killer?" He was a bit annoyed at Jones but didn't want to push it. Jones wasn't himself this trip.

"The man who killed Simms is sitting in the jail. He is the same man who had the buckboard on the side trail to Kingston. The farmer with the dry goods we stopped. The one who said he had been robbed once already," said Jones, putting all the pieces together. Jones showed Kingman the article. Kingman's thoughts moved slowly, but at least Jones could see the movement.

Jones said, "That farmer was heading north and was at least a day's ride from Kingston if he was getting supplies anywhere south". Jones smiled as he watched Kingman finally fit all of the puzzle pieces together.

Kingman said, "That farmer couldn't have committed the murder. He was too far away." Kingman put the paper down. Jones stood up.

"I knew there was something about him."

"Why wouldn't he get the dry goods supplier to alibi him?"

Jones smiled, and said, "I asked myself the same question last night. I went by the jail, but I didn't get a chance to see his face."

"We checked his wagon," Kingman replied. "There wasn't anybody there." He glanced at the newspaper.

"He said he was robbed along the way, but I ran into a deputy heading south and he didn't mention this farmer getting robbed. So I figured he never told the deputy."

While Jones nodded his head up and down, Kingman concluded, "You don't tell a deputy you've been robbed if you're doing something illegal."

Jones said, "Could be he's running rum, guns, or something else, but who knows." Jones was itching to see Penn.

"I need to report my stolen money to the sheriff and see how this . . ." Kingman picked up the paper and read the name aloud, "James Penn reacts to me."

Jones and the Clemmons brothers waited in the parlor of the boarding house for Kingman to return. Jones returned to his paper, no longer thinking about whiskey to distract himself. Kingman walked down a mildly crowded Main Street, past a group of students heading to school, and on to Wall Street. He entered the jail at the side of the courthouse.

Hank was tending to the business of the day, while Penn sat on the straw bed. Penn had a newspaper in his hands, but only glanced at it. Hank was listening to a gray-haired, stern-faced woman, Mrs. Samuels, complaining about riffraff, schoolchildren to everyone else, throwing crabapples at her old mule to get him to buck and run around the pen.

Mrs. Samuels reported, "Those Jameson twin's are nothing but trouble I tell you. And that Billy Rafferty, he's one of them, too. All of them throwing rock-hard apples and hitting that mule on the haunches. Makes him surly, and if any of them gets kicked, it's not going to be me and the Mister paying doctor bills. Asking for it, that's what I say." Hank's mouth opened and closed a number of times, having a hard time getting a word in.

"I'll take care of this Mrs. Samuels," he assured. "The kids won't be by today." Hank knew the kids and planned on talking to their parents, who scarce spared the rod.

"You best take care of it before my mule does." Hank pitied the mule for two reasons.

Mrs. Samuels walked straight out of the jailhouse with a promise from the deputy to get the boys to stop. Kingman walked over to the left of Hank, so he could be heard best by Penn.

He said, "I need to report a robbery." Hank didn't recognize the scruffy, tall man that stood before him.

He asked, "You from around here?" Kingman wondered if he should lie, but decided against it.

"No, but does that make a difference?" he asked.

"Not to me," said Hank, "except where to send whatever was robbed from you if we get it back." Kingman glanced at Penn who was staring at the small window in the cell.

"Fair enough. I was on the road heading north from Newburgh when a man came into my camp. He seemed friendly enough, but he must have come back in the night. He took over a hundred dollars, don't know exactly how much, from my saddlebags. I was planning on buying a farm with the money." He felt it better to keep the same story.

Hank asked, "Anybody see this stranger actually take the money?" Always the first question to ask a victim of a robbery. Kingman thought if he saw the man he would have put a bullet in him, enough said.

"Not exactly, but he was the only stranger in the camp. I checked the saddlebags of those with me." Kingman lied, but he trusted Jones, and the Clemmons twins just weren't smart enough to think such an evil thought.

"Tell me where you were again." Hank took out paper and pencil, starting the report.

"I was coming up from Newburgh with my three companions," Kingman repeated. "We're looking to buy a farm near Albany. This dark-haired man dressed in black comes into the camp. He left that night, but must have come back. I told him about buying the farm. So, he knew I had money with me. On the way here, my friends and I stopped anybody we ran into; checked to see if they knew where the thief was hiding."

Kingman expected Penn to move to better eavesdrop, but Penn just stayed on that bed, staring at the window. Kingman would have to get his attention.

"That man in there can tell you," he said. "I stopped him along the way." Kingman pointed to Penn in the cell. Penn slowly looked up at Kingman and recognized him, but tried not to show it.

Kingman said to the deputy, "He was on that road, getting supplies from Newburgh, I guess." Kingman looked straight into Penn's eyes as he spoke.

"That don't make any sense," replied Hank. "Townsfolk from Newburgh come up here to get their supplies. Barges bring the supplies to the port at Kingston Point." Penn wasn't sure exactly what to say.

He muttered, without much thought, "You must be mistaken. I was on my farm." Kingman wasn't about to allow Penn to evade him so easily.

"You weren't on that road yesterday? That's what you're telling me?" He sensed the fear rising in Penn.

Penn could feel his mouth dry up, his throat feeling strangled, but he said calmly, "I wasn't on that road you were traveling. You must be mistaken." Kingman noticed the rosy blush in Penn's face.

Kingman enjoyed the hunt, even when it was only a battle of wits. He enjoyed the kill even more. He stepped a little closer to Penn to face him. He wanted the deputy to be looking at Penn's reaction to the next statement. Penn swallowed hard as this stranger came forward. He had no place to hide.

Kingman said slowly and deliberately, "You weren't on that road, but a farmer who could be your twin was riding in a plain buckboard wagon drawn by two dark brown horses with a tarp on the back held down by burlap sacks and three barrels."

He looked into Penn's eyes and saw the recognition. Penn swallowed hard and tried vainly to moisten his lips.

Kingman put the pressure on, as he said, "Ain't that a coincidence, Mr. James Penn?" Penn wished he could disappear.

"Yes sir," he croaked, "that is a coincidence." Penn could say no more, and Kingman didn't push any further. He saw the doubt in the deputy's eyes. Hank thought to himself, a man, a stranger, comes in to alibi you and you deny him.

Kingman waited a few moments to let it all sink in with both men. He waited for the deputy to recognize that Kingman was still in the room. When Hank turned to him, he said "The name is Harold Kingman, and when the money is recovered, it can be wired in my name to the First National Bank of Georgia. Good day, sir."

Hank said a fairly feeble, "Good day." As Kingman was leaving the jailhouse, he gazed back to see Penn with his back to the deputy, who was staring right through Penn. Kingman planned to stay close to the jailhouse, after he and Jones visited the Penn farm. Penn's heart raced. The bounty hunters were here; they were here and they knew.

CHAPTER XIX

Spiritual Guidance

At times the fates play a hand in a person's destiny. Quaker Jowett walked down Crown Street toward the alley behind the courthouse. He saw a young woman, Miss Westcott, lose her grip on three books; they tumbled to the stone walkway alongside Kingston Academy. He crossed over and helped her retrieve the books. After a brief conversation about the unfortunate Mister Penn, Quaker Jowett walked back across the street. If he hadn't stopped to help Miss Westcott with her schoolbooks, he would have entered the jail just before Kingman left. As it was, Quaker Jowett saw the tall stranger leaving the jailhouse with a devilish smile on his face. He worried for his friend James Penn.

Quaker Jowett entered the cool jailhouse. His thin, black coat and trousers held the heat of the midday sun. He took off his coat and wiped the perspiration from his brow. He had wished Joseph would be behind the desk, but Hank was there, cleaning the dirt from beneath his fingernails. Hank looked up at him.

"What can I do for you, Benjamin?" he asked. Hank wondered about Quakers wearing only black and white, but didn't feel comfortable in the asking.

Quaker Jowett held up his bible and said, "I have come to provide your prisoner with spiritual guidance."

"He isn't a prisoner," Hank corrected. "He's waiting trial." He turned to Penn and asked, "You want spiritual guidance?" Quaker Jowett nodded his head up and down slightly, beyond the eyesight of the deputy.

Although he didn't believe it, Penn said, "Yes, I believe I am in need of spiritual guidance." He stood up and pulled his suspenders back up over his shoulders. He sat back on the bed and waited for his friend to pull up a chair. Hank stepped over to the door of the cell. He pulled a set of keys from his pocket, and Penn could swear he heard the clanking of the lock. The door swung open and Quaker Jowett was allowed in to join Penn. Penn was dumbfounded. After the door clanked shut, Hank sat back down at his desk.

Penn had a puzzled look on his face. Quaker Jowett opened the bible as if the two would be looking at the good book. On a piece of paper, Quaker Jowett had written "religious counsel is private." Penn smiled away the confusion.

He asked in a whisper, "Can you get me out of here?" Penn sat up straighter.

Quaker Jowett whispered his reply: "No, they think you killed Jeffrey Simms." He knew better.

"It saddens me that they think I could kill, let alone a dear friend of mine." Penn took a sip of coffee.

Quaker Jowett reminded Penn, "They have your knife, found it next to the body, and Bathers said Simms mentioned your name when he died. I know Barnaby has done some terrible things to you in the past, but I can't believe he would murder someone and blame it on you." Quaker Jowett felt despondent; he didn't want to hurt his friend.

Penn whispered, "I'm not blaming anyone, but I know and you know I didn't kill him."

"We'll do everything we can to get you out of here." Quaker Jowett turned a page of the bible slowly.

"You need to help my friends," pleaded Penn in a hushed tone. "Bounty hunters are here and I think they know."

Quaker Jowett asked, "Is the package safe?" This reminded Penn that unaided passengers were to be considered packages when discussed in the presence of others.

Penn said, "Yes, the crates are safe, but I'd get to them before they spoil. Peaches spoil so quickly in this sun." Penn remembered the crate of peaches on his back porch.

"Yes, I'll want to retrieve them within the next day or two."

"The sooner the better. There are six bushels of peaches in one crate. You can put them in the barn for safe keeping if you have to wait a day or two." Penn added a wink to emphasize the location.

Quaker Jowett felt relief in knowing that Hank had never worked a farm. He thought for a moment, wondering about his ability to move the six passengers from the barn.

"I fear I have gotten you into a terrible situation," he said finally.

"This is not your fault. I am a man, and made my choices. I decided to pick up those peaches" The two fell silent for a short period of time. Neither man would truly accept the other's point of view.

Quaker Jowett asked, "Who was that man who was in here a moment ago?" Penn leaned in closer to Quaker Jowett's ear.

"That I don't know, except that he's a man looking for a farm of his own," said Penn.

Quaker Jowett said, "Let us pray."

Penn whispered, "He was on the road up from Newburgh; his name is Kingman. He said money had been stolen from him and he was seeking to get it back. There was a thief along the road, one I had trouble with for a moment, but I knew better when Kingman and his boys searched my buckboard. These men are dangerous." Penn asked, "Did he see you?"

"With God's grace, no," said Quaker Jowett. "I will try hard to get to your farm undetected. I won't go to the barn until I am certain nobody is there."

"I overheard the deputies talking," whispered Penn. "Joseph is at the farm now, and three deputies from Newburgh will be arriving either tonight or tomorrow morning. You need to get them out tonight." Penn peered over at Hank, who had returned to reading his newspaper.

Quaker Jowett said, "I shall do my best," hoping to mask his uncertainty. They both declared, "Amen."

*　　*　　*

Barnaby Bathers felt the growing agitation in the town; people were in the mood for a lynching. He had carefully placed words of fear and outrage into the ears of drunken tavern patrons throughout the city, who shouted their demands of retribution for the killing of Jeffrey Simms. Bathers initiated the dissent, then disappeared once he heard the cry for a lynching. The entire city of Kingston was gossiping about Penn the killer; the city crackled like kindling just before a fire erupted.

Bathers wanted it to be over. He ran into Pieter and Luke at the Bull and Bear Tavern on Crown Street near the Bruyn House. Luke was finishing a pint of amber ale, with foam dripping onto his facial stubble, while Pieter began a pint of stout. Bathers approached their table, and Pieter pointed to the bar. Sheriff Calderon sat on a stool with a dark drink in hand talking with two shopkeepers. Bathers stepped over to him.

Bathers said, "Tom, should you be drinking while the killer of Simms sits in your jail?" Calderon sat still for a moment to give Bathers the time to turn to the crowd.

The sheriff didn't even turn around, but said, "Drinking iced tea, something you ought to try, keep you out of trouble." The patrons closest to Bathers let out a laugh.

Bathers replied with a half snarl, "I ain't the one in jail." Luke and Pieter laughed.

Calderon slowly turned round on his barstool. He took a long sip of tea and stared at Bathers. Bathers was talking with his friends. Luke cleared his throat and pointed to the sheriff. Bathers turned to face the sheriff.

"You want something?" he demanded. He stared at Calderon, seeing a weak man.

"Yes," said the sheriff, "You can keep me from throwing an old friend in jail." He finished his iced tea and put the glass on the bar.

"Now, who might that be, Tom?" asked Bathers contemptuously.

"Barnaby, you keep going around town getting people fired up for a hanging, and I'll put you in there with him. When they come for him, you'll be up for murder."

"You can't blame people for wanting to hang that killer. You can't blame me for what other people do." Bathers snickered.

"No, I can blame you. Your visits to the taverns end tonight. You want a drink, buy a bottle and drink at home." Calderon knew everyone within three barstools heard him and would tell the rest of the town.

Bathers sat down in his chair. He felt confident the sheriff could do little with one gun to his three. He sipped his beer and eyed Calderon.

"Tom, I just bought a pint."

Sheriff Calderon knew he had to pick his battles, and when Hank walked into the tavern, the time was right. The deputy could tell he had walked into trouble. He positioned himself off to the side of Bathers's table and awaited the hand signal. He gently removed his pistol from the leather holster.

Calderon said, "You need to take that pint with you. I'm sure Daniel trusts you to bring that tankard back tomorrow." While the three men at the table focused on the sheriff, he gave Hank the signal. Hank moved into position.

Bathers pushed the chair next to him over by Sheriff Calderon's legs. Hank lowered his pistol to Bathers's ear. Bathers heard the click and froze. Keeping his head steady, he looked out of the corner of his eye to see Hank smiling down at him. The only movement Bathers made was to keep air flowing in and out of his lungs while he looked at Hank out of the corner of his eye.

Bathers and Hank had a history, not a pleasant one for Hank. With the permission of her parents, Hank had been seeing Erin, a beautiful Irish lass. It turned out she wasn't one to be tied to one man, though, and Bathers was the other man. Hank found the two of them together one day, and he was lost. Bathers moved on, and often mentioned her to Hank. In the tavern, Hank held his pistol steady.

Bathers hoped nobody at the table would move too quickly. Pieter sipped his drink; Bathers would have slapped the tankard out of his hand if he could avoid being shot.

Calderon said sternly, "Now, take the tankard home and bring it back tomorrow, clean." Bathers slowly stood up from his chair and walked out of the tavern with his hands raised. His right hand held the tankard of ale.

The sheriff walked over to Hank, and the two lawmen left the tavern. Once on the street, Calderon slapped Hank on the back and started chuckling. Hank chuckled as well, imitating Bathers with raised arms.

Calderon said, "If your timing don't beat all. Bathers was really poking me with a sharp stick."

"I couldn't help myself," Hank replied. I've wanted to do that for years. And it really felt good." Hank had hoped he would see Bathers piss his pants.

Calderon suddenly appeared worried. "Who's watching Penn?"

"One of the deputies from Newburgh. He had been trying to track down a thief who was robbing people on the main road. That guy, Kingman, may have been telling the truth about being robbed." Calderon wiped the sweat from his brow.

"Makes me wonder about the rest of his story," he said.

"There is something strange about this whole situation that I just don't understand. Why wouldn't Penn let this guy alibi him if he could?"

Calderon thought about it. "James Penn did something two nights ago," he said finally, "but I'm not sure if he murdered Jeffrey Simms. But if he didn't kill Simms, who did?"

"Maybe Barnaby knows more than he's telling us. No offense to you, sir, I know you two are friends, but Barnaby Bathers could easily be blackmailing the real killer." The sheriff and deputy tipped their hats to townspeople passing them on the street.

"Wouldn't that get him killed?" asked the sheriff.

"Yes, I think you might be right," replied Hank.

*   *   *

Trent and Calvin had sneaked up into the barn. Trent's knees would have been knocking if he stood still long enough. Calvin had more experience sitting on fears, but was just as nervous. The young men searched the barn quickly for supplies and blankets. They grabbed everything they could find and threw it down into the hole. Miss Alice and Miss Dorothy grabbed each item and put it aside to await the next one to fall through the trapdoor. Smitty stared at the dirt trail leading up to the farmhouse and barn. He saw no movement on the road. He gazed back at the house and saw a figure on the porch. He rubbed his eyes and realized he wasn't making an imagined man from out of the shadows. He moved toward the trapdoor, and grabbed Miss Dorothy's mouth before the shout of alarm could escape. Smitty poked his head up through the trap.

He made a hoarse whisper that caught the attention of the men. They scrambled toward the trapdoor. Trent all but fell into the hole, and Calvin almost landed on top of him as he jumped. Trent rolled over onto Miss Dorothy as Calvin hit the packed earth. Smitty grabbed two handfuls of straw and threw it up into the air while he quietly closed the trap door. Straw gently drifted down to the floor of the barn.

Smitty didn't say a word. He pointed to his eyes and then to the porch of the farmhouse. Through cracks in the wall of the barn, Calvin and Trent could see the figure on the porch. When Smitty took a look, he realized the figure hadn't moved. His heart could slow down now, not that it would for another few minutes.

Smitty whispered, "Dat was a close ones."

Calvin asked, "Who is it?"

"Bes' guess, de law."

Miss Dorothy worried, "Misser James mus' a tol' him we's down here."

Miss Hattie declared, "Misser James ain't like dat. If'n he tol' on us, dat man on de porch woulda been down here taken us backs ta de Souf."

"Miss Hattie's tellin' da truf," said Smitty. "Misser James mos' likely spends time in jail, instead o' tellin' 'em where we's hidin'. We bes' sits here."

CHAPTER XX

Provisions and Plans

Calvin chewed on a piece of dried beef on the left side of his mouth, washing it down with warm water. From the cellar they could see the water pump, but couldn't get to it without revealing themselves. Miss Alice continued to cough, sounding worse than before. The cold nights and hot days had scarcely helped her cold. Trent shifted over toward Smitty, his leg not hurting him nearly as much as two days earlier.

"When does you thinks we's leavin' here?" he asked.

Smitty looked around at the cluster of worn-out souls. He said, "Bes' be movin' on tonights. Cain't see stayin' here wif dat man settin' on de porch. We's cain leave in de late night, jus' keeps headin' towards de mountains 'til we comes acrost a trail. Wif God's he'p it be de right one."

Miss Hattie heard the conversation, as her left eye opened up to look at Smitty. She opened both eyes and sat up straight.

"De Lord is gonna he'p us," she said.

Calvin questioned, "De Lord gonna guide us o'er dem mountains?" Smitty shot him a look reminiscent of the ones he gave Trent.

Miss Hattie said righteously, "If'n He sees fit, He will. Rights now, I's prayin' fer Misser James. He needs de Lord more'n we does."

Miss Alice took a swig of water and said, "You's'll forgives me, but I's be prayin' fer us. Nothin' we cain do fer Misser James, but fer us, we cain use de he'p gettin' ta Canada." She picked up a piece of dried beef and bit off a small piece.

Smitty worked on tying knots into a long twig he had found. He admitted, "I still doesn't know 'zactly what we's gonna do."

Calvin said, "Smitty, you tells me Misser James gave you a map. We cain finds dat trail an' git o'er dem mountains."

"Dat we cain," said Smitty, "but den where does we go? Lotta miles betweens us an' Canada. Misser James tol' me 'bout the lanterns wif blue ribbon bein' safe, but I doesn't rightly know." Smitty felt entirely inadequate for this job. He'd rather shoe a surly mule.

A storm was brewing in Miss Hattie's heart. She said sternly, "We gots ta worries 'bout today an' you all is talkin' 'bout tomorrah. We needs ta git some res' an' den sees if there's any ways we cain he'p Misser James."

Smitty said meekly, "I jes' doesn't sees how we can he'p Misser James. Who would believes us?" He stretched out his arms to include all of the slaves.

"I doesn't rightly knows," Miss Hattie replied. "All I knows is I got more questions than answers, an' I needs ta pray an' rests mah head." She leaned a little lower against the wall of the earthen room.

Calvin said, "I's'll checks on dem supplies ta see if'n we cain gets three or four days togethah." Smitty was mildly surprised at Calvin. When Calvin and his brother had joined them in Virginia, Smitty had wondered how two young men would do on the journey.

He remembered what his father had once said: "Life makes a man. Doesn't mattah how many years a man's been on dis earth, mattahs what's happened durin' dose years." Smitty saw Calvin growing into being a man.

Trent said remorsefully, "I doesn't think I's'll be much of a he'p. But I am feelin' a might bettah." He wasn't able to walk on his leg in the cellar, but he stretched every few minutes so it wouldn't stiffen up.

Miss Dorothy added, "His fevah's gone. I'm guessin' it done broke fer good." Miss Dorothy chewed on a piece of brown bread.

"Dat it done," said Miss Hattie. "Right now, bes' thing you cain do is gittin' yer rest. We'll be takin' cares o' e'erythin' else. Devil's done moved on ta torment Misser James." Miss Hattie feared the devil's hand in the world.

The slaves suddenly stilled, as if frozen for the moment; each one breathing slow and even, listening for the sound. Again came a scratching at the back of the barn. Smitty slowly moved toward the crack in the wall to see if other men were on the farm. He wondered why the lawman on the porch was still in his chair.

A creaking sound was followed by solid footsteps above the hiding slaves. Someone was in the barn above them. Miss Alice fought with her cough; she crammed Smitty's neckerchief into her mouth. Six pairs of eyes followed every step above them. Mice scurried in the wall near Miss Dorothy's left ear, and she almost shrieked from fear, fear that spread from one to another until all six were ready to jump out of their skins.

The footsteps moved to the center of the barn, turned in their direction and paced out the distance to the trapdoor. Smitty held up his left hand, palm facing the others, to signal them to wait. In his right hand, Smitty held the iron bar. Calvin and Miss Dorothy were closest to the trapdoor. They shifted to a crouched position, waiting, holding their breath. Scraping sounds from a shoe against the barn floor had the six looking at one another. Miss Alice was thinking, so far to have traveled for them to be caught here in this barn. Smitty glanced at the barn wall, wondering if he could pound his way through.

The scraping sound stopped for a moment, and Miss Hattie closed her eyes, as she silently prayed. More than one of the other slaves wished they could close their eyes, but they remained focused on the trapdoor. A rustling near the door tightened every muscle in their bodies. A voice startled them, as Trent jumped the highest of the bunch. The person spoke close to the door. Smitty raised the bar.

The voice said clearly, but softly, "My name is Quaker Jowett, and I was sent by James Penn. He said you'd be hiding in the barn. I know you can't trust many folks, but today, you're going to have to trust me. James Penn is currently in jail, accused of a murder he did not commit. He was transporting you from New Jersey through the Catskill Mountains to Oneonta, to avoid slave catchers up in Albany. The man on the porch of the farmhouse is a deputy, and I believe more are coming. I will return with Penn's buckboard tomorrow, the one with the false bottom. I wished I could sneak you out tonight, but the deputies will be traveling the roads into Kingston. But tomorrow, we'll be able to sneak you out of here and through the woods to a place where I can hide the buckboard. I can only take you as far as the mountain trail, because I am watched. Smitty, I'll have the supplies you need. I'm not sure why, but Penn told me to say I will treat you like a slave." Quaker Jowett stood up and waited in the silence.

The trapdoor moved slowly, as Jowett shifted his gaze back and forth from the trapdoor to the barn doors. His breathing increased, as well as his pulse. He looked down into the hole of the cellar, down into six pairs of weary, hopeful eyes.

Quaker Jowett glanced at the door to the barn. He said to the older black man, "I brought provisions to last through the night." Smitty stood up, his head poking out of the trap.

Smitty said, "Nice to makes yer quaintance Misser Jowett." He held out his large, scarred hand, and Quaker Jowett shook the rough hand. Smitty took the provisions and handed them to Miss Hattie.

Smitty asked, "How's Misser James doin?" Quaker Jowett had to think for a moment, then realized he was asking about Penn.

"His spirits are low, but will improve knowing you will be getting away from here. He worries most about you getting caught." Smitty looked to the ground, then back up at Quaker Jowett. Quaker Jowett could tell Smitty had a question on the tip of his tongue; he waited.

"What they going to do to him?" Smitty was uncertain of the answer, but felt it would help to know.

Quaker Jowett cleared his throat and hesitated. Smitty realized the answer wouldn't help him, but didn't want Quaker Jowett to suffer.

"He he'ped save our lives. We's in need of de truf." Smitty stood with his head and shoulders outside the cellar, awaiting bad news.

Quaker Jowett said slowly, "He is getting a trial, but it doesn't look good. If he's found guilty, he'll spend the rest of his days in jail."

Smitty said, "Don't seems right, him given his freedom fer our'n."

Quaker Jowett was quick to remind them, "He didn't trade his freedom for yours. Someone killed a man and blamed him for it. If anything, your freedom will get him through the dark days of prison." Smitty felt helpless.

Smitty asked, "Ain't dere anythin' cain be done?"

"We are doing what we can. The sooner you are safely over the mountains, the sooner he can tell the judge where he was when the killing took place." He looked at the heavy wooden door of the barn.

Calvin was watching the farmhouse through the crack in the wall. The deputy who was sitting on the porch had gotten up and was moving toward the barn.

Calvin whispered loudly, "Deputy's a'comin'!" Quaker Jowett jumped back as Smitty swung the trapdoor closed. Smitty heard the straw being pushed back over the trapdoor; footsteps scurried to the back of the barn. The creaking came again, the sound of a board or two being pushed aside.

Calvin just stared at the deputy, until he lost him behind the side of the barn. A man on horseback rode down the dirt trail. The rider waved a lanky arm toward the deputy by the barn.

Calvin whispered to the others, "Man on horseback coming; knows deputy, waved." Smitty nodded acknowledgment. Several in the cluster breathed a sigh of relief. Smitty looked at Miss Hattie, who wore an expression of fear.

Calvin looked back at the men on the grass outside the farmhouse. The deputy had the lead to his horse in hand as the men spoke briefly. The deputy rode down the road, and the other man walked up onto the porch.

Joseph Bielk had returned for another four-hour shift at the farm. He spent many a summer day with James Penn, playing chess of all things. Penn had taught him to play the "game of kings," as he liked to call it. Penn was better than Joseph, but Joseph rose to the challenge and had beaten him in a game or two. Joseph wondered about his friend's fate and the oddity he had just now spoken to Deputy Kluuth about.

Joseph thought about the murder, Penn's knife and button, and the man who had come in identifying Penn as a man on the road from Newburgh, describing his buckboard and all. He hoped the judge could figure it all out, and get Penn freed.

He saw the apples on the trees in the orchard just beginning to turn red. He remembered how he and Penn would sit on the porch wondering when the first of the apples could be picked for pressing. They'd get a bunch picked and press out ten or twelve gallons of cider. Fresh, sweet cider cooled them down on the hot Indian Summer days of September. Then, on a fall Saturday, Penn's tradition was to bring in the children and their folks to picnic on the farm, picking apples, pressing them, and sharing in the previous batch of cider. Joseph wondered if they'd again see cider in the fall.

A thunderstorm brought a quick downpour. Joseph watched the deluge from the porch, rain pouring down from the roof. Riders, at least three, quickly traveled down the dirt road toward the farmhouse. Joseph moved into the shadows, watching the riders. The four of them rode over toward the farmhouse, then at the fork in the path, shifted direction to the barn. Joseph thought the men to be looters. Rain slowed to a drizzle, as the deputy gingerly picked up his rifle and followed quietly toward the barn. The four strangers opened the barn doors and walked in.

Jones and Kingman stepped into the barn with the Clemmons twins following. The coolness of the barn would have been refreshing if not for their wet clothing. The men glanced around the barn searching for a hiding place. Jones had the nose for finding runaway slaves. He spotted the loft, but thought nothing much of it. Kingman showed Jones the concern he had for him this hunt. In the past, if Jones didn't take a liking to a hiding place, Kingman left it alone. Kingman headed to the ladder leading up to the hayloft. He walked up with each rung creaking as he went. He searched the loft finding nothing but bales of hay. He felt a reassurance in Jones, even though Jones's face had a twinge of disappointment when Kingman joined him again on the floor of the barn.

The disappointment may have come from the rifle the deputy held at Jones's back. Joseph was none too pleased with looters.

The deputy said, "I can shoot you right now for looting." He hoped they understood that he would shoot, if necessary. Kingman and Jones raised their hands, and the Clemmons twins followed suit. Joseph didn't show fear and didn't back down, leading Kingman to believe there were other lawmen about.

Jones replied, "We haven't taken anything," his hands still raised in submission. Jones knew he could take the deputy, but wondered if they could find the slaves in time. He wasn't about to kill a lawman.

Joseph demanded, "What's your business here?" He didn't recognize any of the men, and was more than a little concerned about the two giants in the crowd, hell that made up a crowd.

Jones said, "We're looking for a man called Bathers. He owes me money and said to meet him here." Joseph was taken aback a bit.

"Bathers said to meet him here?" he asked. His rifle barrel pointed at Kingman.

"Yes, sir," said Jones. As he lowered his arms, the deputy said nothing. Jones continued, "He said he'd have the money he owed us."

"Owed for what?" asked Joseph suspiciously. Jones knew he had the deputy's attention and they could get out of this without raising suspicion.

"We were playing cards," added Kingman. "Bathers lost." The deputy began to lower his rifle.

"That figures. You men need to clear out of here." Joseph thought the men weren't moving fast enough.

Jones asked, "Couldn't we stay a bit and wait for Bathers?"

"No sir, you need to leave now." Joseph raised the rifle again as Jones looked at the Clemmons twins, the ones closest to the deputy. Kingman was getting a little nervous with the building tension.

"Fair enough," said Kingman, "you've got the gun." The four men walked out of the barn, as Joseph let out a long, slow breath. He watched the men get on their horses and ride off down the road. As he stood there, Joseph thought he heard a cough, but when he turned, no one was there. He stepped back out onto the wet grass and smelled the earthy, damp world. He reminded himself to tell the sheriff tonight about the four strangers.

*   *   *

The Clemmons twins ate well that night, finishing off the last five pork chops on the platter between them. Proprietor Tappen found Kingman and Jones in the parlor, the former smoking a cigar.

Jones was saying, "I bet they are hiding out there. That's the last place Penn was seen."

"We'll go back out in the middle of the night, tomorrow," replied Kingman. The two looked up as Tappen cleared his throat to gain attention.

Tappen said, in a voice more of a request then a demand, "I'm going to need more money to feed those two men."

Kingman replied with annoyance, "Room came with board."

"I understand, the room came with a standard meal, but those two are eating enough for three people each." Kingman looked at the proprietor with disdain, embarrassing Jones.

Kingman said, "All right then, I'll give you an extra fifty cents a day, no more." The proprietor took the money with little argument. The next day's supper would consist of baked beans and brown bread. Hell, every supper would consist of beans and bread until they left.

CHAPTER XXI

Justice of the Peace

Sheriff Calderon sat in his wooden rocking chair in front of the jailhouse, enjoying the chirping of evening crickets. He was finishing a last bite of peach cobbler when Hubbartt and Dillancy came strolling up to the jailhouse. The sheriff took a napkin to his face to wipe away any crumbs, though a few rested on his shirt. Fireflies lit and then disappeared into the darkness.

The sheriff asked, "What can I do for you gentlemen?"

"I was at the tavern that night Simms was killed," Hubbartt said. "Penn wasn't there, but Bathers and Simms had an argument. Bathers was upset about the water rights."

Dillancy added, "That's right. Bathers was threatening Simms at the tavern. Nate, the tavern owner, took him outside to keep the peace."

Calderon wanted to pick his teeth with a toothpick, but he didn't have one handy, so he gently sucked in saliva on the speck of peach caught between his teeth.

Hubbartt said, "Bathers never came back in." He leaned against one of the wooden posts on the porch.

"So, Bathers had an argument with Simms," the sheriff summarized. Hubbartt and Dillancy glanced at one another.

"Bathers was asleep outside the tavern," Hubbartt admitted.

"He had too much to drink," Dillancy explained, feeling Hubbartt hadn't described it well enough. "But he was angry with Simms over the water rights, and I know Simms wasn't going to sign anything over to Bathers."

Calderon finally picked the peach bit free with the corner of the telegraph reply for a judge that was in his pocket. He said, "I know there was a problem with water rights, but they worked it all out. Bathers showed me the deeded water rights. He was going to get Simms's signature on it when he found Simms dying."

"Dying?" asked Dillancy.

"Yes, apparently Simms said Penn's name before he died."

Dillancy was surprised. "Bathers was with him when he died?"

"Yes, Barnaby came directly here to get me, and we went out to Simms's farm." Calderon swept away the crumbs from his shirt. "After that, we set out to Penn's farm to arrest him."

Hubbartt said, "Tom, this doesn't make sense. Why would Penn kill Simms?"

"Don't know yet, but we'll find out at the trial. I've got to check on Penn." Calderon stepped into the jailhouse. Hubbartt and Dillancy took a few steps along the porch to the jailhouse. Bathers crept out of the alley behind the jailhouse, and slipped quietly up behind the two men as they stepped into the damp street.

"William, Brett, how are you?" he snarled. Hubbartt and Dillancy started at the words. Bathers laughed aloud.

Hubbartt collected himself and said, "Barnaby, what are you doing sneaking up on us like that?" Bathers continued to laugh.

Dillancy added, more out of fear than anger, "Man could get hurt doing that." Bathers took a step forward to stand directly in front of him.

"Who's going to hurt me, you?" he challenged. Dillancy awkwardly stepped backward to maintain a comfortable distance from him.

Bathers turned on Hubbartt. With flecks of spit flying from his mouth, he snapped, "That's Mister Bathers to you! I was just walking down the street minding my own business, when I heard two friends of mine questioning what happened the night I found Jeffrey Simms. Penn killed him! Simms told me."

"Anyone else there?" Dillancy asked from a safer distance.

"Why no, I didn't realize that a close friend of mine was in the process if dying."

"Close friend?" cried Hubbartt. "You hated Simms for buying that land from you." He wished the sheriff had returned to the porch to witness this conversation.

Bathers said intimidatingly, "You know what I learned. A man can't be too careful. I plan on getting a dog for my place. You two may want to think about how you will keep safe."

"That's true, the killer is still on the loose," Hubbartt shouted to Bathers as he walked away. Bathers turned slowly, scowled at the two men, and

disappeared down the dark alley. Hubbartt and Dillancy remained in front
of the jailhouse thinking about his last words to them.

As they stood there wondering whether that meant Bathers might be
coming after them, a stocky man with curly brown hair stepped past them.
He walked into the jailhouse with determination, and stepped into the
sheriff's office.

Calderon asked, "Can I help you?" The man didn't exactly look lost.

"I'm Judge Markette, and I'm here for the trial," he said plainly. "You
the sheriff?"

Calderon stood up and walked toward the judge. "I'm Sheriff Calderon.
If there is anything you need, just give me a holler." He had imagined that
the judge would be a bit taller. Judge Markette removed his jacket, checked
the time on his silver pocket watch, tucked it back into his vest pocket, and
looked back up at the sheriff.

He replied, "I'm not one to holler. Which is the best inn in town?"
Calderon realized this would be a formal relationship.

"Well, we have a nice boarding house around the corner, but if you'd
like to stay at my place, you are more than welcome." He felt courtesy called
for him to make the offer, even knowing the response.

"Thank you all the same, Sheriff," said the judge, "but I'm better off
alone. I'm a bit of an insomniac." Markette gazed over at Penn sitting on
the straw bed in his cell. Penn's barely eaten dinner remained on a stool in
front of him. The judge stepped over to the cell and looked through the
bars; Penn didn't move.

"My name's Judge Markette," said the broad-shouldered man. Penn
looked up at him.

Penn said softly, "Name's Pe . . ." Penn cleared his throat, sipped at his
glass of lemonade. He said, "Excuse me, my name is James Penn." The judge
studied Penn's round, sad face. Penn realized he was being disrespectful,
and he stood up.

Judge Markette said, "You'll get a fair trial, Mister Penn." Penn looked
down and nodded. The judge continued, "You don't look like much of a
murderer." Penn looked Judge Markette straight in the eye, as his father had
taught him many years before.

"I'm not a murderer," he said plainly. He continued to look into the
judge's eyes. The man had cold eyes, the kind that never betrayed a thought.
Judge Markette stepped away from the bars, and Penn was struck with the
thoughts about his father, a man who didn't have to hit a child to get him
to obey. His father had had a way of talking that put someone, especially a

child, of a mind to do as he was told. When Penn was a boy, his father had told him that when telling the truth, he should look a man in the eyes to show him he meant what he said. Penn wished his father was still alive to advise him now.

* * *

Sweat dripped from Bathers's strong arms and chest onto Jenny's slender naked body. The once clean sheet clung to them as they rested in each other's arms. Bathers rolled to his side, dragging most of the sheet with him. Jenny pulled at the white cloth to cover her nakedness, but he refused it to her. Bathers enjoyed the control he had with her.

He said, "I like to see you naked." He stared at her breasts, and she felt a wave of shame.

Jenny replied, "Let me have the sheet." She felt the shame of a woman with another woman's man.

Bathers chided, "You don't need to cover yourself. I was just inside you." He grabbed at her body; she felt dirty now. She didn't enjoy his crude ways, but still held out hopes of becoming his only woman.

Bathers leaned in to kiss her, and she turned away. He grabbed her jaw with his left hand and forced her to look at him. He kissed her as she tried to pull back.

"You know I done killed a man, ain't much more to kill a woman," he reminded her. "Don't look at me that way." She turned away. "I don't like it when you look at me that way." Bathers took a swig of whiskey. Jenny wanted to leave, but if he caught her arm, he'd smack her. Jenny wished she hadn't angered him.

Jenny thought of her children and the friend they were staying with that night. She enjoyed being with her three children, but could barely keep them in food and clothing. The Reformed Dutch Church provided shelter at times of need. Bathers provided more for her than most of the men she knew. She had to settle for him going home to a wife. Jenny understood the hope was like that of her children, hoping their father would come home.

Jenny's thoughts were momentarily interrupted by Barnaby pressing against her flesh. She wished to return home, gather up her children in her arms. She knew he wasn't finished with her yet. His sweat dripped on her limp body. Bathers didn't like her in these moods; he'd be done soon.

CHAPTER XXII

Judgment in Kingston

Judge Markette said, "I'll need a few things for the trial. I want to see the courthouse. I'll need a fresh pitcher of lemonade at my bench every time we convene. I want pitchers of water at the two tables for the solicitors and the accused. Don't want them to get too comfortable. Some solicitors prefer white wine; I don't like a solicitor who drinks in my court." He paused and may have been thinking, but Calderon wasn't sure.

The sheriff said, "We don't have many lawyers in Kingston, mostly work on commerce contracts."

Markette thought for a brief moment, then said, "I'll speak directly to the witnesses."

"Let me show you the courtroom." Calderon grabbed a kerosene lantern, and the two men went through a doorway into another section of the building. Penn had seen the door, but was unaware it exited into the courthouse. Judge Markette followed the sheriff down the narrow hall.

The two men went up one flight of old creaking steps to the courthouse. The judge's bench was against the far wall. Judge Markette took a few steps forward and heard the echo of his footsteps. Light from the lantern threw shadows on the rows of wooden benches that led up to the judge's seat. The stars shone throw the large windows on three of the four walls.

"I don't understand why they build the ceiling so high in courthouses," he complained. "Makes any noise seem louder, echoes every word spoken, and the cold drafts on my feet chill me to the bone." He walked toward the bench, with the sheriff trailing.

"I'll have Miss Westcott make your lemonade for you and bring you a foot warmer from the boarding house."

"That's mighty kind of you, Sheriff. I'll tell you if I need the foot warmer." The judge smiled for a moment, but then returned to his rather dour countenance. He said, "Sheriff, I am hoping to get through this trial quickly. I will hear all of the evidence that is relevant to the case. How many deputies do you have available?"

Calderon wished he had gathered a few more. He said, "I have six deputies in all, three of my own, and three from Newburgh."

"I looked at that man's hands, they are rough from a plow. Man works that hard, he makes friends in a city like this. I don't want any trouble, but I will not allow disorder in my courthouse."

"I understand, sir, um I mean, your honor," Sheriff Calderon said sheepishly.

"I carry a pistol wherever I go. Your deputies and you will also have pistols in my courtroom, but nobody, and I mean nobody else gets in with a gun. Do you understand?"

Calderon could tell by the judge's tone that he had had a bad experience in a courthouse. He said, "I'll make certain of it, Judge."

Judge Markette looked around the empty, lifeless room. He said, "Anybody who I want to hear from in my courtroom that decides he doesn't need to come to my courtroom, I want to see them in your jail."

"You want me to put them in jail?" Calderon wasn't too keen on this idea. Farmers needed to tend crops, shops had to be open.

"Yes, because there is nothing more important than justice. I want you to give me the names of everyone who had anything to do with the murder, like Barnaby Bathers, Doctor Hamilton, and Jacob Knufield. Get James Penn to give you the names of anyone who can speak on his behalf."

Calderon said, "He doesn't have anybody. The man doesn't want to put up a fight."

Markette turned to him. "What kind of a man doesn't put up a fight? He knows he's fighting for his life."

"He thinks he's going to prison."

"No sir," said the judge in a most serious tone. "If Penn is found guilty, we'll be hanging him on the town green." The sheriff looked at Markette in disbelief. He had known James Penn for a number of years; the man was not an outlaw. Judge Markette read the sheriff's face well.

"You got a better way of stopping a man from killing?" he asked.

Calderon took a deep breath. "No, your honor," he said in a resigned tone. As the men walked back down to see Penn, they could hear yelling and screaming coming from the alley. The sheriff quickened the pace. The yelling could be heard through the walls, as the mob outside followed a parallel path down the alley. Calderon broke into a run. He rushed through the door to the jailhouse, just as Joseph jammed the wooden beam into the brackets on the middle of the jailhouse door. Hank stood sentry at one of the barred windows, a rifle in his hand. Judge Markette noticed that Penn just sat on the straw bed, paying little attention to the commotion outside.

Shadows on the walls twisted and turned with the movement of torches in the crowd, as thirty or so people gathered in the alley outside the front of the jailhouse. Penn felt the sharp sting on the side of his face, sweat trickled down his cheek. He touched the cheek where the bug had bitten him and saw that it was red, blood. Two stones flew past his head. He saw the stone that had struck him on the floor, as he crawled into a corner below the barred window in the cell. Calderon thought about handing him a pistol, but knew the judge would put him in the cell too.

The sheriff moved over to the window by the door and gazed out at the crowd. He saw Bathers throwing a rope into a nearby hawthorn tree. A shiver ran up the sheriff's spine. Hank leveled his rifle's aim on Bathers's back. Calderon put a hand on Hank's shoulder; Hank lowered his sight.

Voices in the crowd grew steadily louder. A number of the men shouted. "Hang him!" "Don't let the killer go free!" "An eye for an eye!" Calderon worried about the torches getting too close to the jailhouse. Judge Markette stepped up behind the sheriff and gazed at the crowd.

"You're going to need more than six deputies," he said. "I've seen this before, and it has turned ugly. You need to get control of the situation."

Calderon motioned for Joseph to remove the wooden two by eight from the door and to put it back once he was outside. He went out to face the crowd of his fellow townspeople.

Shouts and yelling continued as the mob set up the hangman's rope. The men inside the jailhouse watched the sheriff stand on the porch for what seemed like several minutes. A man in the crowd spied the sheriff, pointed at him, and said, "Look, it's the sheriff! Let's get Penn." The mob turned attention to the sheriff, and their voices grew louder as they drew closer.

The sheriff watched for a moment longer. He tried to speak, but the voices in the crowd were too loud. He waited, but the crowd was edging closer. He held up his hand as he looked out over the crowd. Voices shouted out angry words; his voice could not speak over the din of the mob. He drew his pistol and held it in front of him, barrel pointing to the ground. The volume of the crowd began to diminish.

The sheriff shouted over the indistinguishable voices in the crowd. "Gentlemen, you will not be allowed to hang James Penn. He will stand trial beginning the day after tomorrow, as tomorrow is the Sabbath."

A voice in the crowd shouted, "Don't waste time, hang him now!" Behind the farmer who shouted stood Jones and Kingman. They began edging themselves to the right side of the crowd, opposite Bathers.

Calderon said, "We all want justice, for the killer of Jeffrey Simms to pay for his crime. Hanging is not justice; it's revenge. You killing is the same as what was done to Jeffrey Simms."

Bathers could tell the men were beginning to lose their fight. Two large men emerged behind him, as people in the crowd stepped aside for them to walk through freely. The crowd had quieted enough to hear the sheriff.

Calderon continued without shouting, "Most of you men work on the docks or farm the land. You're not killers. Let justice serve you; let the court decide his guilt. Then your hands are clean. You can . . ."

Bathers interrupted, shouting at the crowd, "You can see Penn go free, because this justice is blind. Who's he going to kill next?" Kingman took off his hat, and the Clemmons twins stepped up behind Bathers and took him to the ground. The angry mob pushed in three directions at once. Those nearest the fight pushed to move away, while those farthest pushed to get even closer, and a third cluster from the mob pushed to get inside the jailhouse.

Sheriff Calderon took a step backward, and instinctively raised the barrel of his pistol toward the crowd. Inside the jailhouse, Hank shifted to leave the jailhouse, once Joseph removed the wooden barrier. Judge Markette took up a position in the corner of the room that was in the shadows. Penn watched everyone leave the jailhouse. A shower of rocks pelted the floor of the jail cell. Blood continued to trickle down his neck and drip on his shirt, as he felt throbbing pain from the rock that had hit his cheek.

The Clemmons twins beat down Bathers, and quickly disappeared into the middle of the crowd. Barnaby Bathers was swinging wildly as he got to his feet. Several townspeople who tried to help him up were hit with errant blows. He hit one farmer in the eye and a dockworker in the crotch. These men retaliated as the three lawmen struggled to reach Bathers.

Jones and Kingman slipped into the jailhouse. Kingman waited by the door as lookout. Neither man noticed the judge in the shadows of the corner of the room. Penn stayed crouched on the floor of his cell. Jones splashed Penn with the glass of lemonade. Penn's cheek stung, as he looked up at Jones. Penn was frozen with the fear he'd be shot.

Jones said in an angry tone, "Remember me, farmer?"

Penn saw the judge in the corner; he shook his head slowly from side to side.

"If I could get my hands on you, you'd remember me," Jones continued. "I want my property back." Judge Markette's eyes opened wider as he waited to hear more. Kingman stared out the door at the brawl. The sheriff was close to grabbing Bathers. One of his deputies was hit dead on the nose and fell back into the crowd. The other deputy was close to the fray.

Kingman reported, "They're almost to Bathers, hurry."

Jones said, "We know you didn't kill Simms, because you were busy on the road from New Jersey. You have something of ours and we'll get it back. You better hope they hang you, because if you don't tell me what I want to know right now, I'll make you beg for death." Jones didn't like threatening any man he couldn't reach. He always liked to bring home the reality of the threat with a smack or two.

Penn said evenly, "You have me mistaken for someone else. I was not on that road. I was at home on my farm." Penn put his arms up to cover his head as another barrage of rocks came flying through the window. Three rocks fell close to Jones. He reached through the bars, gathered up the rocks and threw them at Penn. One struck his forehand, causing it to bleed. Judge Markette tensed, but was in no position to help.

Kingman reported, "They have Bathers and they're bringing him in." Jones looked at the doorway, and then back at Penn.

Penn muttered through tears, "I don't know you, please leave me be." He curled up even tighter in the cell. Jones wanted to shake him, to get his answer.

Jones and Kingman pushed through the doorway as the sheriff entered with Bathers in tow. Joseph and Hank, with pistols drawn, watched the angry crowd.

Calderon got Bathers settled into a chair, and Hank shackled him to it. Joseph watched the door as the angry mob settled back into disgruntled farmers and dock-workers. The crowd slowly drifted toward the nearest saloon.

Calderon was livid, as he said sternly, "Barnaby, if you hadn't been bruised up by the crowd, I swear I'd take you out back and beat the daylights out of you."

Bathers lisped, "Couldn't beat me without the thhackleth on." Blood dripped from the corner of his mouth. His right eye was half closed "I warned you not to get people stirred up, damn vigilantes. Now what do I do with you?"

Bathers smiled a painful smile, and said, "You can alwayth put me in wif Penn. I'd kind of like that." Calderon steamed. Hank knew that if the judge hadn't been standing behind him, the sheriff would have cracked Bathers in the mouth himself, friend or no friend.

Judge Markette came out of the shadows. Bathers was surprised; he hadn't known anyone else was there.

"This man needs to stand trial after Penn," Markette said evenly. "We can't have them in the cell together, so he will have to be let out." He turned to Bathers. "However, the sheriff will hold the deed to your property until you appear for court." Bathers began to protest, but the judge shook his head back and forth.

Judge Markette moved within inches of Bathers's face. He said, "If you don't appear in my court, I'm going to take your land."

Bathers protested vehemently, "You can'th do thath!"

"I can and I will."

Hank looked at Sheriff Calderon. The sheriff nodded, and Hank took the shackles off Bathers's arms. Bathers stood before the sheriff.

Bathers said, "I'll thee you out back one of theethe dayth." Calderon had to keep himself from laughing. Hank saw the curl on the sheriff's smile. Hank let out a cough to stifle a chuckle. Bathers pushed past them to step outside.

Judge Markette stepped closer to the sheriff and said, "Something strange happened here a moment ago. We need to talk about it, but I think that man is involved. You should have a deputy from Newburgh, someone he doesn't know, keep an eye on him."

"Sounds like a good idea," said Calderon. He was curious to find out what had happened when he stepped out of the office. Hank wished he could be the one to watch Bathers. That man needed tending to, like a spoiled child needed the rod. Penn wanted to sit in the corner and cry, but knew he couldn't or the others might think the strangers were right about him. He choked back the acid in his throat when Joseph came into the jail cell and removed the numerous stones.

Joseph said, "Town has gone mad; people throwing stones at the law. Who'd save them if they were in trouble?" Joseph started to toss a stone out the window, then realized it might come back at a later time. He tossed the stones into a bucket near the desk he shared with Hank.

Penn said, "They're not thinking about the consequences of their actions. Feelings of rage are hard to control." He dabbed at his cuts with a handkerchief.

Joseph looked over at Penn and said, "You must be pretty angry at them."

"Not really. They're angry about the death of a friend. I'm upset too, but I'm in here." Penn wiped away another trickle of blood. Moonlight shining through the window helped Joseph see that it wasn't sweat.

Joseph said with urgency, "Sheriff, Penn's been hurt." Calderon came over to the jail cell, while Hank grabbed his hat. Judge Markette felt he might be in the way, and he quietly left the jailhouse.

Hank blurted out, "I'll get Doc Hamilton. He was having supper at the Fitch house."

Calderon said, "Hurry back, I don't want you to be gone too long. I need to talk to the judge." Hank left the jailhouse. Calderon went to step into the jail cell, then turned around and placed the wooden barrier across the door. He returned to the open cell and took a look at the gash above Penn's left eye. Blood trickled down his cheek, as well. The sheriff took a pillow from the bed, stripped off the cloth cover and wrapped it around Penn's head. The sheriff moved Penn's hand to apply pressure to the wound.

Calderon said, "Penn, put pressure on the wound, it will slow the bleeding. Are you okay?" Penn looked as if he had lost a fight.

Penn said flatly, "Fine, thank you." Joseph and Calderon looked at one another and then at Penn.

The sheriff wondered what else could go wrong this evening. He hadn't been one to worry, but tonight would be different. He knew that he and his deputies would be in the jailhouse for the night. He couldn't wait for the light of day.

Penn worried about the slaves under his barn, and whether the vigilantes would go to burn his home. He bit down hard on his bottom lip, the pain keeping the thought from his mind. He prayed, while the others spoke about his head wound; he prayed to God for the safety of the slaves. Six lives for one he kept telling himself, "six lives for one."

CHAPTER XXIII
Morning After Madness

Hank and Joseph cleared the burned-out torches away from the porch of the jailhouse. Save for trampled flowerbeds and a few broken boards on the porch, everything was as it had been before the mob gathering. A few of the men who had been in the crowd the evening before, passed by to apologize to the sheriff. A swift lecture and the promise from the offender that he would tell the sheriff if Bathers got out of line again sent each on his way. Calderon wanted a peaceable solution to the problem at hand, getting Penn to trial without the town exploding. Penn sat in his cell, eating the eggs and bacon this morning. He needed his strength; he needed to have a clear head.

Quaker Jowett turned the corner off Crown Street to the alley by the courthouse. He saw the deputies clearing out the old torches and wondered about the events last night. On Main Street, everything from "the mob had him in the tree and the sheriff had to cut him down" to "the sheriff came out with guns blazing" was heard. Quaker Jowett knew neither of those tall tales was believable, but he wondered if his friend was well.

Quaker Jowett approached Joseph and said, "Good day to you, Deputy Bielk." Joseph held three burnt torches in his right hand.

Joseph said, "Good day to you, Quaker Jowett. James Penn is inside having breakfast." Quaker Jowett couldn't help but find humor in the way Joseph spoke, as if Penn was just visiting.

"May I ask of the events last night?" he asked.

"A mob came to take Penn out and lynch him, as far as I could tell," said Joseph. "Sheriff stopped them. May not be safe for Penn to stay here; you may want to recommend the Fitch house." Joseph watched Hank pick up a torch tossed behind an old elm tree.

Quaker Jowett was puzzled, and asked, "Why the Fitch house?" He took his hat off to further cool himself in the breeze.

Joseph stepped in close and said, "Fitch house has a tunnel underneath it that leads to the Dutch Reformed Church. Penn can request sanctuary." Joseph nodded knowingly. Quaker Jowett nodded in response.

"He won't go," he said. He hoped the night's events would encourage Penn to change his mind.

"I don't understand him," said Joseph. "He won't defend himself, and he won't find a way to escape the gallows."

Quaker Jowett looked at Joseph with surprise. He brushed a handkerchief across his forehead and asked, "The gallows?"

"Judge Markette said if Penn is found guilty, he will face the hangman. Only way to keep a man from killing again."

"James must have his reasons." Quaker Jowett knew the reasons, but didn't want the deputy following him.

Joseph asked, "What could a man trade his life for?" Quaker Jowett didn't like where the conversation was heading. He reminded himself that if James Penn wanted Deputy Bielk to know, he would tell him. He saw the sheriff leaving the jailhouse and quickly went over to him.

"May I provide spiritual guidance to James Penn?" he asked.

Calderon replied, "Do as you like, but I think there are about thirty men who need it more than him." He walked away. Joseph followed Quaker Jowett into the jailhouse. He opened the cell for the Quaker to visit and then stepped over to the desk.

"James, you've gotten your appetite back, and a couple of lumps on the head to boot," Quaker Jowett observed. Penn looked up at his friend.

"I need my strength. Lumps were from rocks through the window last night." Penn sipped his lemonade, as the morning sun warmed the cell.

Quaker Jowett sat close to Penn and whispered, "We leave tonight." He said in a normal voice, "I'll get those peaches off your place tomorrow morning. I'll need your buckboard for the job." Quaker Jowett saw the words register with Joseph.

He smiled in relief. Penn said, "That would be fine. I don't want them to spoil." He whispered, "God bless you, Quaker Jowett." Penn took a few bites of toast; a calm came over him. Quaker Jowett noticed the peaceful look in Penn's face.

Penn whispered, "They need to be on their way. I know it would be better if they had a conductor, but if they stay, they will surely be discovered.

Three deputies from Newburgh are watching over the farm." Joseph stepped into the sheriff's office.

Quaker Jowett said, "I saw two more looters at the farm, taking tools. I think I recognized one of them; we'll get the tools back when you get out of here."

Penn said solemnly, "I won't be getting out of here. I will not give up six lives for my own. I would rather stay in prison the rest of my days than give up those people. That's why I wanted them to leave as soon as possible." Penn sipped his lemonade again.

Quaker Jowett said, "They refused to leave. Miss Hattie is praying and the others are staying put until she gets a sign." Penn set down the lemonade.

"Tell her I did the praying and God told me this was the way it had to be," he said insistently. "I understood the consequences when I started working on the railroad three years ago. I understood it might come to this. Maybe in my heart, I even wanted this to happen." Quaker Jowett didn't understand how to respond to the last statement.

"Wanted this to happen?"

Penn explained, "Not being imprisoned, but since I lost my wife and child, I have felt there was no meaning to my life. The railroad gave my life meaning. That if I died the very next day, at least when I arrived at Heaven I could say that my life held value, some virtue that guided my existence, no matter how misguided I was in believing that. The railroad gave purpose to my life." Penn looked in Quaker Jowett's face for any sign of understanding.

Quaker Jowett failed to grasp Penn's explanation, asking, "But coming to this end?" Penn wondered if any other man could truly understand him.

He continued, "Coming to this end allows me to tell the world I had been helping escaped slaves gain freedom for the past three years. That I am willing to suffer imprisonment for my beliefs."

Quaker Jowett continued to probe. "But if you don't tell anyone about the slaves at your farm, how will anyone know of what you have done?"

Penn said with confidence, "We know and eventually we will be able to tell the world. I will not have survived my wife by three years without merit." Quaker Jowett wondered if the grief was too much, but he felt Penn should know the truth about his fate.

He said solemnly, "Then it will be my task to tell the world." Penn looked puzzled for a moment. Quaker Jowett saw the understanding come to Penn's mind as Penn's face became ashen and sad. There was a silence between the two men.

Penn finally took a deep breath, slowly let it out, then asked, "How do you know?"

"Deputy Bielk told me the judge said it would be so," said Quaker Jowett. He placed a hand on his friend's shoulder, as much for himself as for his friend.

"I must get my affairs in order," said Penn, as if he were home readying his place for visitors.

"I shall tell them to travel."

"It is the only way." Penn sipped once more, and almost missed the table when he put the glass back. Quaker Jowett wished he had words that could comfort his friend.

"Bless you, Brother James," he said.

Penn said with a crack in his voice, "He, um, he already has, Brother Benjamin."

*   *   *

Sheriff Calderon looked about the immaculate room in which Judge Markette was staying. Even the bed had been freshly made. The judge stared out a window at the city of Kingston. He was unaware of the city's growth within the past few years.

Calderon was uneasy with the silence between them, too many things not being said. He said, "I've been hearing all kinds of stories about the murder." The judge turned to face the sheriff.

"So have I," he said. "In fact, several people are questioning Mr. Bathers's story." He looked for a reaction from the sheriff, wondering if he'd defend his friend.

"I've known Bathers for a long time. He can be pretty mean . . ." Calderon had few regrets, but befriending Bathers was one of them.

Markette was quick and deliberate in his interruption, as he said, "Pretty mean? This man once came close to drowning a man in a horse's trough, because the other man didn't stop and let Bathers ride through. Bathers isn't mean, he's a menace to the community. I saw what he did last night." Calderon felt like a child being reprimanded.

Sheriff replied defensively, "Well, as I was about to say, Bathers has been a bit of a problem around these parts. I have tried to get him to see the error of his ways . . . ."

Judge Markette didn't have the tolerance for a sheriff without a spine; he asked, "How many?"

Sheriff Calderon was confused and said, "Excuse me?" He wasn't sure what had been said.

"How many days has that man spent behind bars?"

"Well, he's spent about a dozen days in jail over the past three years. Yes, I can rightly say he has spent a dozen days there." The sheriff felt vindicated.

The judge was not as sure. "How many of those days have been to sleep it off?" Calderon wanted to sit down, but dared not. Actually, he would have preferred to leave the damn room!

"Sleep it off?" He knew very well what the judge was asking him, but he didn't want to give an honest answer. He felt he had had a rough evening until this moment in the judge's room.

Markette said with disdain, "Playing possum doesn't make you look any smarter, Sheriff. How many days has Barnaby Bathers been in jail to sleep off too much whiskey?" The sheriff was quiet. In a sarcastic tone, the judge answered the question with, "let me take a wild guess, about a dozen?"

Calderon said sheepishly, "I wish I could say it wasn't all twelve, but I can't." He'd been caught.

The judge said matter-of-factly, "I know he's a friend of yours by the way you've been treating him. But he's got to be put in his place or he will continue to be a threat to this community. I don't have any proof that he killed Simms, but I do believe there are a number of people who would like to see him in jail."

Calderon said, "Some people hold a grudge against him."

Markette added, "Too many people. Sheriff, you are the law. You should be the one that people hold the grudge against, not him." The judge took a sip of coffee, and his mood changed. Calderon breathed a short sigh of relief.

"I will be holding court tomorrow," said the judge. "Everyone who has something pertinent to say will get a chance, except Nigel Johnson and Theodore Grimes."

"Johnson and Grimes?" He wondered if they had been in the crowd last night.

Markette explained, "They came in here this morning and tried to alibi Mr. Penn. Said they were with him the night of the murder. I spoke to them separately and was told two different stories." He looked out the window again, then said, "There's something else. Last night, in the jail, two men came in while you were outside getting the crowd under control."

"Yes, we didn't get the chance to discuss them."

"Yes sir", the judge said, "One of them threatened Penn, something about being on a road heading north to Kingston when the murders took place and having something of theirs." He took another sip of the coffee. He continued, "Puzzles me when a man is facing the hangman and would rather hang than take an alibi. You should find out why."

Calderon asked, "Tall, lanky fellow with blond hair and blue eyes?"

Judge Markette admitted, "I didn't get a good look at him."

Calderon said, "A man came in day before yesterday and said he saw Penn on the road. Penn denied it, but the man described his buckboard. I'll check on it." He took a step toward the door and put his hand on the doorknob.

"Don't forget what I said," reminded the judge. Sheriff Calderon touched the brim of his hat and stepped out of the room.

*   *   *

Barnaby Bathers was buying a second round of drinks for Luke and Pieter. He threw a couple of copper pieces down. The three tankards of ale thudded onto the table. The men clanked them together, then sipped simultaneously.

As Bathers put down his tankard, he saw the face of Harold Kingman staring at him. Bathers shifted forward in his chair to stand, but two large hands prevented him from rising. He looked up to see the men that dared to lay a hand on him. He saw double, the Clemmons twins.

Kingman said, "Now, Mr. Bathers, I understand you want to see Penn punished for his crime. I also know you were the only one to be with Simms the day he died. Now, I want you to help me get Penn out of jail." Bathers was confused by this stranger, as his blood boiled.

He shrugged off the hands on his shoulders, but didn't stand. "Why the hell would I want to do that?" he exclaimed.

Kingman leaned in toward him. "Think of it as insurance. Penn gets out of jail, you have the chance of living a long, healthy life." Bathers glared at Kingman.

"You have big balls coming in here threatening me in front of witnesses," he challenged. Luke and Pieter sipped their ales and watched the hands of the strangers.

Kingman said in a calm voice, "Much bigger than you'll ever know. You see, Penn has something I want back, and if I don't get it back, I stand to lose a great deal of money. Now, I am well off, but these boys behind you, they aren't so lucky. These were the guys who jumped you outside the jailhouse . . . ." The twins smiled.

Bathers interrupted and sneered out, "Good to know, I'll remember them." Kingman nodded, and the Clemmons twins placed their hands on his shoulders and held Bathers down again. The weight from the two became painful; Bathers had trouble catching his breath.

As Bathers gasped, Kingman said, "That beating was just the way these boys say hello. You don't want to make them mad. Get Penn out of jail."

Kingman nodded again, and the boys let up. Bathers caught his breath, as Kingman and the Clemmons brothers left the saloon.

Bathers stared at Luke and Pieter. He said angrily, with spit flying from his reddened face, "Why didn't you pull your guns?"

Luke and Pieter pointed to a corner of the room behind Bathers. Bathers turned to see Jones sitting at a table with a rifle pointed at them. Jones tipped his hat to Bathers and smiled.

Bathers said sternly, "I've got to do something about those men."

CHAPTER XXIV

Day of Rest

Judge Markette rested comfortably on the porch of the boarding house. He sipped a glass of iced tea, cool and comforting on the hot summer afternoon. He watched the carriages pass along Main Street—families returning home from Sunday services. The judge had thought about attending, but felt it might not be seen as impartial. He read his bible for two hours that morning and prayed to the Almighty for guidance.

His thoughts roamed to James Penn. He wondered about the man, and what other kind of troubles he might be in. Townfolks brought the judge good will and almost always a Penn story, about times when the man accused of murdering a friend had helped that person out in one way or another. The judge had seen it before, a pillar of the community committing a heinous crime, but this seemed different. Penn potentially had an alibi that put him on the road heading north. Penn might feel guilty for killing his friend, but guilt usually faded when a man was facing the hangman. Some of these kinds of men, Markette knew, attempted to kill themselves as a means of avoiding the law, but not Penn. He had a secret, a secret the judge wanted desperately to know.

The judge took another sip of the iced tea. He gazed at children playing along the street, being chased by mothers who wanted to salvage their still fairly clean Sunday clothes. He thought the law was much like the mother, always chasing afterward to prevent something worse from happening.

"Judge Markette, my name is Dillancy and this is my friend Hubbartt. Your honor, may we talk to you?" asked a man from the edge of the street. Hubbartt stood to the left of Dillancy, making him look a little smaller in stature.

The judge quickly asked, "Does this have to do with James Penn?" Hubbartt removed his hat, even though he was not inside.

Dillancy said, "Yes, sir, but it is important." The judge picked up a finger sandwich, then placed it back on the plate. He asked, "Are you wanting to tell me about his character?" Two children in white shirts and pressed knickers raced past with a haggard-looking mother a step behind.

Hubbartt said, "More than just his character. We know something about that night." Dillancy stepped up the wooden step and stood on the porch. Hubbartt followed.

"Does the sheriff know about this?" Judge Markette wasn't certain about the friendship between the sheriff and Bathers.

"Yes, sir", said Dillancy, "we told him a few days ago." The two men stood for a moment while the judge was thinking.

"Gentlemen, I want you to come into court tomorrow and testify before the eyes of God as a witness to what you know," said the judge. Dillancy and Hubbartt looked at one another.

"We will be there, your honor," Hubbartt said. The two stepped back off the wooden porch and out onto the busy street, chatting with one another. Judge Markette wrote down their names on a slip of paper. He wanted to hear what they had to say, but it was far more important to have statements brought into court.

*   *   *

Penn sat on the bed, staring at the floor. He'd respond to the sheriff and his deputies, but otherwise made no comments. At times he would kneel and pray, or lie down and nap. He made no requests for food or drink. Sheriff Calderon was perplexed by his prisoner. He wanted the trial to begin, but understood the need to honor the Sabbath.

The sheriff walked over to the jail cell. He opened his mouth to speak, but thought better of it and turned. Turning back, he pulled over a chair. The scraping sound of the legs of the chair on the wooden floor attracted Penn's attention.

Calderon said, "I'm worried about lynch mobs. I've never seen the town like this before." He saw the scabs on Penn's face.

"Jeffrey Simms was a good friend, a good man. People are angry at the loss. I'm angry, too." Penn looked away. He moved too quickly, and his head throbbed.

"One of my deputies had a good idea; we ought to move you to another place for protection. Sneak you out of here."

"Where would you take me?" Penn had immediately thought about losing contact with Quaker Jowett.

"To the Fitch House," said the Sheriff. "We could have you stay there through the trial. I worry that one of the vigilantes may shoot at you."

Penn looked at the sheriff and said, "Sad that people get so angry they'd rob the hangman a day's bread." Calderon looked down at the floor, searching for words that just weren't down there.

He said awkwardly, "You'll get a chance to defend yourself. You can have people come forward and speak on your behalf. Tell me their names, and I'll have Hank and Joseph fetch them in the morning." He waited with pencil and paper ready.

Penn said in an even tone, "I'm not sure who could come forward to help me."

"Well, anyone who could testify on your behalf," the sheriff explained, "like a friend who could tell the judge what kind of person you are, your character. Anybody who may have seen you on the night of the murder, who could say you weren't at the Simms farm." He looked at Penn's face and could see the lost look in his eyes, as if the sheriff was asking him to do something he could not do. Penn didn't speak for five or six breaths.

"I don't think there was anyone who saw me that night," he said finally.

Calderon asked, "Well, where were you?" The questioned had been answered at least a half dozen times before this.

"I told you before," explained Penn, "I was at home resting. When I arrived to meet your deputy at my farm, I had just finished hauling firewood to the house to get ready for next winter." Penn looked down at the floor of the jail cell.

"I don't believe you," the sheriff challenged. Penn looked up into his eyes. "If nobody was there," Calderon continued, "then the judge will know and will make a decision."

Penn said, "I didn't kill him. I would never harm anyone, especially a good friend like Simms. What reason could I have for killing him?" Sheriff Calderon wanted to smile; Penn was talking.

"Maybe you and he had an argument, had an old grudge, maybe you wanted his land?"

"Or water rights?" Penn snapped. Calderon swallowed hard.

"Don't make matters worse by trying to blame someone else," the sheriff said, irritated. "That won't work in Judge Markette's court. Be honest, that's the best you can do for yourself."

Penn retorted, "I've been honest and look where I am. Not a pleasant view from in here." The sheriff saw the fire in Penn's eyes. He wished he hadn't been angry, but the damage was done.

"Trial begins tomorrow after breakfast," he said. "You best get ready."

"I don't think I'll sleep tonight. I'll sleep enough from the hangman if some people get their way." Penn faced the back wall of the jail cell. He wished he had three more walls and a door.

"Well, you know the fate that awaits you if you're found guilty. You'll get a fair trial." Sheriff Calderon stood up and walked toward his office.

Penn said quickly, "Then I know I shall be released. I can sleep better now." Calderon wasn't certain if Penn was being sarcastic.

The heavy wooden door to the jailhouse slowly moved open. Sheriff Calderon realized he hadn't barred the door after Joseph left that morning. He drew his pistol, as Judge Markette walked through the doorway. A moment's pause for recognition; the sheriff holstered the pistol.

"Good afternoon, your honor," said the sheriff, relieved. Markette closed the door.

"Good afternoon. Interesting way to greet people, Sheriff." The judge stepped forward, pointing to the sheriff's holster. He said, "I have a few last details for tomorrow. We should speak in your office."

Calderon placed the large block of wood in the metal slats on either side of the door. He followed the judge into his office. He hoped he wasn't in for another lecture on Bathers.

Once inside, Markette said, "I'll want Penn in shackles inside the courtroom." Calderon thought the request unusual.

"What if he's attacked; he can't defend himself?"

"Every prisoner that comes before me wears irons and if not irons then ropes," the judge replied. "I had one prisoner jump out of the witness box and over the bench. He tried to strangle me in court. It happened so quick, I had to shoot him in the belly with my own derringer. Prisoner took two days to die, and I had to wait around to see what would happen." The judge sighed and for the first time looked weary.

"All right, Penn will be shackled," Calderon consented, although he felt sad about the idea.

"Something even more important," continued the judge. "Tell me what Dillancy and Hubbartt told you about the night Simms was killed." The judge's eyes were full of life. Calderon felt like he had that morning with the judge. He swallowed hard, and then swallowed hard again as the saliva disappeared from his mouth.

He said, "Two of Simms's friends who came to me. They said Simms and Bathers had an argument the day Simms died. Bathers argues with almost everyone and then works it out later. He showed me a deed to the water rights, so I figured they had worked it out." Markette didn't say anything for a moment. He found it hard to say anything; was the sheriff just bungling things, or was he involved in this mess?

Finally he said, "This is evidence in the trial. I want these men put on the list of witnesses. You may not think it's relevant, but anything that has to do with this case is important for me to hear. I want to hear from anyone who has something to say about that night. I have to put the pieces of the puzzle together to determine if Penn killed Simms. Hell, Bathers may have a motive for killing Simms."

"Water rights aren't much of a reason for murder."

"What motive did Penn have?" retorted the judge. Calderon couldn't answer that question.

*   *   *

Dusk had passed and stars filled the night sky. Quaker Jowett arrived at the boarding house of Deputy Joseph Bielk. He entered the house, noticing a collection of china dolls in a hutch on the far wall. He spoke with the proprietor, Mrs. Johanson.

"My name is Quaker Jowett, and I'm here to collect the buckboard of James Penn." Mrs. Johanson looked at him and smiled, nodding her head.

"Yes, I have a room," she said.

"I do not need a room," replied Jowett, slightly confused. "I'm here for two horses and a buckboard." He wished Deputy Bielk could have handled this part of the transaction, but he hadn't wanted the deputy to get suspicious.

"She's a trifle deaf," said a boarder. "I spent the better part of my first day here explaining to her my allergies to strawberries, and she gave me strawberry shortcake with dinner."

"Oh, I see." The Quaker leaned in closer to Mrs. Johanson and said, "I'm here to collect the buckboard of James Penn." Mrs. Johanson smiled at him and nodded again; he worried he hadn't say it loud enough.

But before he could repeat himself, Mrs. Johanson said, "I have them in the stables. I will show you." Quaker Jowett, with the assistance of the boarder, was able to have the horses rigged to the buckboard within minutes.

Shortly, he was rambling along the western road out of town, past Crown Street. He thought about the six slaves that would again be on the train to freedom. He wished he could journey with them to Oneonta, but if he were to leave town for longer than a couple of hours, it would draw attention. He hoped his journey this evening would go unnoticed.

As he rolled along, the creaking wheels and chirping crickets were the only sounds. He stopped and listened for anyone else on the trail. He gazed up at the stars. He stared at the Heavens, wondering about the fate of men. Beneath the Heavens, the railroad would be on track again.

CHAPTER XXV
All Aboard

Quaker Jowett passed the turnoff to Penn's farm and continued down the dirt road to a path heading into the woods. The dirt path would lead him back to Penn's farmhouse, to the other side of the barn. He had known of the trail, but had only walked it once, since the deep snows of winter. This time he would be leading others back.

As he continued past Penn's place, he peered through the woods and spied the flickering of light along the road to the house. He thought about stopping, but knew better of it.

Three kerosene lanterns lit the main dirt road leading to Penn's farmhouse. Quaker Jowett had taken that road not but two weeks before, bringing word of the slaves coming up from New Jersey. The underground informants had provided valuable information about slave catchers waiting in Albany and Buffalo. Routes had been blocked, as if trees were felled along the tracks. This route through Oneonta was most treacherous, as the slaves would be in New York for a long journey.

Quaker Jowett recalled the eagerness with which Penn had accepted the task. He wondered if Penn's idealism had blinded him to the realities of the situation. He pulled the buckboard over to a clearing off the road. At the head of the clearing was the path to the barn.

Quaker Jowett moved slowly through the darkness, until he reached the last fifteen yards of the path, a clear patch to the back of the barn. If he was spotted, he had little recourse but to allow himself to be caught. He could run, but then the slaves would be in greater jeopardy. He trotted as quickly as his legs could carry him.

He stood for a moment at the back of the barn, trying to calm his breathing, as well as his beating heart. He felt for the loose boards on the back wall of the barn, then said a prayer and moved the slats to the side, causing a creaking sound. He entered quickly and stepped over to the trapdoor. He heard voices outside the barn and froze.

Deputy Sanders walked past the front of the barn on his way back from the outhouse, and greeted Deputy Briarton, heading the opposite way. Fireflies flicked on and off in the dark summer night.

Sanders said, "We should just pee off the porch, ain't nobody around." Sanders's stern facial features didn't match his boyish zeal.

Briarton replied, "Never know when the sheriff will come round. If he sees us peeing, could cost a day's pay." He didn't much care for nonsense.

"You been in the house?"

"Yeah, nothing but a bit of hard cider. Townspeople say he's quite virtuous." He stroked his clean-shaven face.

"There was a riot in town yesterday; lynch mob wanted to get Penn and string him up. If they did we could have been on our way back home."

"You think he done it?" asked Briarton. He slapped a mosquito on his neck.

"Yep, I think he done it. Should be a quick trial." The men separated, moving away from the barn door. Quaker Jowett took a few deep breaths. He stepped over to the trapdoor and scraped away the hay.

"Smitty, it's Quaker Jowett, Penn said to treat you like a slave," he whispered loudly.

The trapdoor opened. Jowett saw the large face of Smitty looking back at him. One by one the slaves came up out of the cramped cellar. Miss Alice coughed, but drank water to ease the rasp. Trent stretched his stiff leg, checking the scabbed over wound again. Smitty had a few supplies in hand.

Quaker Jowett said in a low voice, "We will be leaving out the back of the barn. We can crawl through the loose boards. We have about fifteen feet to the protection of the woods. It's best to travel one at a time. I want to go first, to show you, but then each one of you will watch the person before you to know where to run to in the woods. At least two deputies are watching the place, but both are on the opposite side of the barn." Quaker Jowett turned to find the place in the wall.

Miss Hattie said, "I ain't goin' ta leave." Quaker Jowett looked at Smitty. Smitty stepped over by Miss Hattie.

Smitty said, "Miss Hattie, I doesn't want ta go aginst God, but we has ta leave. If'n you stays, dey'll know we's been here."

Miss Hattie said, "I prays an' I cain't leaves Misser James ta de fate I knows ain't rightfully his." Smitty wondered if he and Calvin could carry

Miss Hattie to the woods, while Miss Hattie considered climbing back down in the earthen room.

Quaker Jowett stepped forward and said in an urgent tone, "The longer we stay here, the more likely we'll be caught. We can make arrangements at the buckboard for those who want to stay." He turned to Miss Hattie and said, "I promise you, I'll do as you wish once the others are closer to freedom."

Miss Hattie said gruffly, "I'll goes wid you all, but if'n you lies, God will be de one ta asks fer forgiveness."

Quaker Jowett moved to the back of the barn with the six following. Trent's leg had stiffened while down in the cellar. He hobbled along with Calvin's help. Quaker Jowett moved the wooden planks at the back of the barn and listened. He stepped out into the darkness, then ran quickly across the open patch of grass. He ducked into the trailhead and looked back at the barn.

Miss Alice was already running through the grass toward the woods. Miss Dorothy followed her and almost tripped on her dress as she ran. She reached the trailhead, breathing heavily. Miss Hattie held her dress up off the ground and came running on through the patch of grass, faster than any would have expected. The women hugged as Quaker Jowett scanned the dirt road for any signs of life.

Without warning, horses appeared suddenly on the road; three or four, it was hard to tell from the distance. Quaker Jowett raised his hands to stop the next runner. Trent and Calvin were outside the barn and lay flat against it. Smitty remained in the barn. The men on horseback continued up toward the farmhouse. Trent hobbled away from the barn with Calvin's supportive shoulder.

Shots rang out. The two young men jumped into the clearing. Quaker Jowett looked for the source of the shots, but wasn't able to tell.

He whispered to the slaves, "Take this trail to a clearing. The buckboard is there. Leave now, it will be better for all of us." The slaves took to the trail without question.

Quaker Jowett turned to see Smitty looking out from the plank-hole in the barn. More shots were fired, and Smitty ran as if he was the one they were shooting at. He ran past Quaker Jowett and down the trail. Quaker Jowett ran after him. The two men quickly caught up to the others.

In a forever moment, as Quaker Jowett liked to refer to them, he and the passengers arrived at the buckboard. The others climbed into the back and covered themselves with the tarp, while Quaker Jowett sat alone up front.

He took the reins and shook them to get the horses moving. Calvin was helping Trent get into the buckboard when the wheels to the buckboard turned. Trent fell forward into the wagon. Calvin chased after the wagon, finally jumping up into the back. The slaves made it to the road.

Quaker Jowett took the buckboard up another half mile to a turnoff. He stopped at the clearing to determine exactly what would happen that night. Moonlight shone down on the tattered cluster in the buckboard.

Quaker Jowett said, "I need to know who will be traveling on to Oneonta." He worried that any of them might want to return after the shooting.

Smitty said sternly, "All o' us."

Miss Hattie chimed in, "No, I won'ts be goin' ta Oneonta." She gathered herself and moved to the back of the buckboard as if to jump off. "I has ta he'p Misser James."

"Wait, stay in the buckboard, I'll bring you back with me," said Quaker Jowett. Miss Hattie sat back down.

Smitty eyed Miss Hattie. "We's all done spoke yes'erday durin' yer prayers," he said. "We's decides you has ta come wid us."

Miss Hattie said with unfailing dignity, "I done tol' you all, I would be goin' ta speaks ta de judge on Misser James behalf." Miss Hattie sat straight up in that buckboard, with great inner strength.

Quaker Jowett solemnly said, "I'm afraid it won't help. The judge won't believe you, and Mr. Penn will suffer the same fate he is destined to suffer now." Smitty picked up three pieces of straw and wove them together.

Miss Hattie spoke as if she was being asked to break a Commandment. She said, "But de dream, I has de dream. It were a sign from God dat I needs ta he'p Misser James." Miss Hattie appeared to be on the verge of tears, although her dignity wouldn't allow it.

Quaker Jowett added, "I must agree with the others. The best way to help him is to leave for Canada. His hope, his life is focused on the six of you making it to freedom."

Miss Hattie said plainly, "I ain't gonna go."

Miss Dorothy chimed in, "Remember when we done lef' de plantation? You doesn't wants ta leave den, but we done makes you leave. You was set on spendin' yer remainin' days on dat plantation."

"Den I were foolish, thought I'd slows you down, gits you caught. Didn't realize how slow de rest o' you is." She looked down at her hands, then back up. "Dis ain't nothin' like dat. I needs ta he'p a man who has done he'ped me." Miss Hattie wished she had jumped off the buckboard. Smitty was still worried about the gunfire. Quaker Jowett was sure the gunshots weren't aimed at them; otherwise there would have been horses on the road.

Miss Alice tried to reason with Miss Hattie. She said, "But if'n dey wasn't believin' you, how would that he'p Misser James? He'll be sufferin' seein' you taken 'way in dem chains ta be returnt ta de plantation. He'd be sufferin' knowin' you all're sufferin'." Miss Alice rubbed Miss Hattie's left forearm.

Quaker Jowett added, "He knows the fate that awaits him and accepts it. He wouldn't want you to suffer his fate for anything."

Miss Hattie said in an irritated manner, "I needs ta git back ta Misser James. He done needs me, dis I knows." She sat in the back of the buckboard, away from the others. Quaker Jowett and Smitty looked at one another. Quaker Jowett turned and faced the road.

"We'll need to leave so I can get back before dawn, otherwise you'll all be in peril," he said. He snapped the reins and the horses moved out onto the road.

Smitty asked, "Will you be sendin' word 'bout Misser James?"

"You'll get a message through the railroad." The passengers climbed back under the tarp.

*   *   *

Deputy Sanders fired back at the two riders on the road coming up to Penn's farmhouse. He wished Deputy Briarton had pissed off the porch. Rifle fire again burst into the night. Sanders got a bead on the muzzle fire and shot into the dark.

Bullets zipped past the head of Jeremy Clemmons, as he and his brother dodged for cover. While the boys drew fire from the lawmen on the porch, Jones and Kingman were slipping toward the barn. They'd heard from Bathers that Penn was in his barn for a moment before he was taken to the jail.

The Clemmons twins shot at the porch a few more times. Soon shots were coming from another direction, and they saw dark figures running from the back of the barn. The brothers figured they were being surrounded, so they did as they were told and high-tailed it out of there.

Jones and Kingman barely made it into the barn. A deputy had been in the outhouse and ran past them to the porch of the farmhouse. The two men slipped into the musty building and began to search quietly.

Jones checked the stall, and behind the feed sacks, but there wasn't any space large enough in which people could hide. Kingman looked up to the rafters, while Jones inspected the floor as best he could in the dim light. Jones appeared to be pacing as he walked throughout the barn. Kingman thought Jones had lost it; was trying to clear his mind. Jones was listening.

As Jones approached the horse stall he heard it. The sound of his boots on the floor changed. He walked across the area three more times, and each time heard a change, a hollow sound. Kingman continued on up a ladder to try to see if there were boards across the rafters.

Kingman was unaware of Jones crawling on his hands and knees, brushing away the hay. Jones tapped the floorboards of the barn and found the area. He was able to map out the space on the floorboards that coincided with the hollow sound. Kingman came down the ladder and stepped over towards Jones. He watched as Jones took out his jackknife and pried at the floorboards. Kingman thought it would take a great deal more effort to get the planks up.

Kingman whispered, "Shooting has stopped."

Jones said, "I am aware of that fact. We have a trapdoor." Kingman fell to his knees and tried to assist Jones. Jones was able to get the trapdoor open an inch. Kingman placed his fingers in the opening, as Jones lost his grip on the knife. The door fell onto Kingman's fingers; he bit his lip to keep from shouting. Jones quickly pushed up the trapdoor and Kingman exhaled. Kingman massaged his fingers and Jones jumped into the dark pit. Jones' nostrils flared as he took in the scent.

Jones said, "They were here, I swear it." Kingman continued to massage his fingers.

Kingman said, "Any idea how long ago?"

Jones said, "I'm not that much of a bloodhound. But I'd bet my life they were here." Kingman helped Jones out of the hole.

"That means Penn was involved, and he's passed on the information to someone else. We need to find out who's visited Penn." Kingman helped Jones brush straw off himself.

Jones said, "Answers the question of why Penn wouldn't say anything about being on the road. He knew if he alibied himself, we'd come after the slaves."

Kingman had an idea. "What is important to Penn?" he asked. Jones wondered if Kingman had listened to what he had just said, but decided to play along.

Jones said, "The slaves."

Kingman said, "So let's have him think we have one of the slaves and are willing to torture the woman if he doesn't cooperate."

"It'll be tough to get in to see him. But we can think of a way."

Kingman said, "We'd better get out of here." The two men crept out of the barn while the deputies were searching the road for the source of the shooting.

CHAPTER XXVI

Shots in the Dark

Penn chewed on the boiled red potato and let the mush slide down his throat. He wasn't eating; he was sustaining himself. Sheriff's deputies came in and out of the jailhouse, gathering munitions and providing reports. Joseph Bielk coordinated assignments as volunteers came in to assist the sheriff. Calderon was at Penn's farmhouse, where gunfire had been reported. Hank Stratton was with him, out on the dirt road near Penn's house, tracking the gunmen. Word came in that Sullivan, a man who worked on the newspaper, had been sent out two days ago to find Deputy Briggs and Deputy Everett on their fishing trip up north. He had found them and was bringing them back.

Joseph had three armed civilians assisting him in keeping Penn safe. However, there had been no lynch mob, no mob at all at the jail. Joseph would have thought it any other night, save for his having to send men out to a gunfight. Reports had come in about shots fired and a deputy being hurt. Doc Hamilton sent word that the deputy had tripped coming out of the outhouse with his britches down, suffering a shin-length wound to his leg and a deep bruise to his dignity.

Joseph wasn't about to speculate as to the dangers; he merely handled the volunteers in nondiscriminating fashion. The first three men who walked through the door were sent to the sheriff at the farm. The next two were sent to help Hank on the western road. Then three men were to remain with the deputy, while a fourth was sent to protect Judge Markette. When Calderon had given the order to protect the judge, he told Joseph to make sure the volunteer said the order came from the sheriff and was not refusable. Joseph sent Phillipe, a good-tempered, jovial man who had three well-behaved teenage children at home.

Joseph spent a couple of hours coordinating the efforts to maintain order in Kingston. He gave the three volunteers two badges to wear as two at a time patrolled the streets around the jailhouse. The third volunteer maintained watch at the front window inside the jailhouse.

With everything thus arranged, Joseph turned his attention toward Penn. "As you know," he began, "shots were fired at your farmhouse. So far, nobody has been really hurt. As far as I know, they haven't caught the men doing the shooting, but Hank is out tracking them."

Penn cleared his throat. He said softly, "Thank you, I appreciate knowing what has been happening." He said a silent prayer for the slaves, then asked, "Who was hurt?"

"A deputy from Newburgh. He'll be fine." Penn looked relieved. Joseph continued, "Have you any idea why men would want to take over your farm?" Penn shook his head back and forth.

"I really don't know why. I don't have much there, fifty dollars hidden in the fireplace cache." Penn appeared perplexed.

Joseph said, "Men don't shoot at lawmen for fifty dollars. James, it's time to tell the truth." He stepped closer to the jail cell and sat down near Penn.

Penn looked the deputy in the eye and said, "I am. There is nothing there." Joseph sighed his frustration and walked back over to the porch. He gazed out at Carlos, a volunteer leaning against a post watching the road. Joseph sighed again and went back to the cell.

"James, I know you, I know you didn't commit this murder. I want you to go to the Fitch house for your safety." Penn thought only about the six slaves at his farm. Were they safe?

Joseph's legs were a bit wobbly due to his nerves; he braced himself against the bars. He continued, "The Fitch house has a tunnel to the Dutch Reformed Church. You can go there and ask for sanctuary until we find the killer. I will press Sheriff Calderon to send you there for your safety."

Penn said, "It matters not." He wanted to lay down on the straw mattress and close his eyes, but he was too polite.

"James, we are talking about your life! I understand you'll be able to see your beloved wife again, and maybe that fills your heart, but think of your friend, think of Simms." Joseph's knees began to ache and he knelt on the floor as if in prayer. He felt as if he were praying for a man's life, only the man himself didn't care.

Penn asked, "What about him? What about Simms?" He worried that he hadn't thought of his friend.

"If you give up your life, you allow the man who murdered Simms to go free." Penn stared at Joseph as he considered the words, then swallowed hard. He wanted to turn away, but couldn't; he realized that Joseph was right. Penn could not allow the man who had murdered his dear friend to go free.

Loud voices on the porch caught Joseph's attention. He grabbed a rifle and ran to the window. Carlos was saying something to Bathers, Luke, and Pieter.

Bathers shouted, "I have a right to protect my community. We want to volunteer." The men had had a few ales before arriving.

Carlos retorted, "Orders are to keep you out, by any means." Carlos raised his rifle, as Luke and Pieter grabbed pistol butts. Joseph jammed the barrel of his rifle out the window.

"Enough!" he yelled, catching everyone on the porch by surprise. They all froze.

"Joseph, I only want to volunteer," Bathers shouted. He held his hands up in the air to show he wasn't going for his gun. Luke and Pieter relaxed, though Carlos remained at the ready.

Joseph shouted, "Bathers, you and only you can come up to this window. Pieter and Luke, you fellas need to disappear." Pieter and Luke looked at Bathers and then decided it would be best to leave. Bathers stepped up on the porch as Carlos watched the others walk away down the street.

Bathers came in close and bent down to speak to Joseph, who lowered his rifle. Bathers said indignantly, "You got farmers out there; I'm one of the best in town with a gun."

"Sheriff said no. Said if you put up a fuss, to put you in shackles and leave you on the porch for him in the morning." Bathers' temper burst forth with a loud grunt and he considered rushing the door, but Carlos stood blocking it with his rifle at the ready. Joseph thought, if steam could come out of a man's ears, he would be seeing it.

Bathers shouted, "That bastard, he is no man to be sheriff. His mother mated with a horse to birth that ass." Bathers glared at Joseph through the bars, then placed his hands on them and screamed as he pulled with all his strength. Joseph jumped backward as if Bathers actually had a chance to pull the barred window off. Penn was startled and slid the straw mattress over his body, as a child pulls the covers over his head to keep away imaginary monsters. Carlos leveled his rifle at Bathers' head. The only other time he had witnessed such fury was from a wounded bear. He had had to shoot the bear in the head to stop him.

Bathers strained, releasing anger from every muscle in his body. He screamed into the night, "That bastard, who the hell does he think he is? I should chop his balls off with an ax." Bathers let out one last scream and ran off into the night. Joseph opened the door, and Carlos jumped into the jailhouse. The bar was replaced, and the men sat down, exhausted.

* * *

Sheriff Calderon lit the last of fifteen kerosene lanterns placed on the road to Penn's farmhouse and the surrounding property. He wanted to be able to see any movement near the farmhouse. In the hayloft sat Deputy Briarton, not the best shot with the rifle, but he had a bum leg. His eyes were focused on the road to the farmhouse. He knew the signal to shoot if anyone were to come down the road. In his mind he marked the fourth lantern in as his farthest accurate shot. Deputy Sanders and one of the volunteers walked the perimeter of the farmhouse-barn area. Calderon watched the night and wondered what the hell was happening.

He thought about James Penn and wondered what he had gotten himself into. Men starting fights to distract the law, while Penn was too threatened to accept an alibi? It all didn't make sense. Now Penn's property was being fired upon; people were shooting at the law. Calderon wanted answers. He wanted to be able to take those answers to Judge Markette and say, "This is what it's all about." The sheriff had more questions than answers, though, and he hoped Joseph was making some progress speaking with Penn.

Deputy Sanders came around the corner of the house. He made a "cluck" sound twice as he rounded that corner, letting the sheriff know it was him. The volunteer made a "click" sound twice with his wedding band on his belt buckle.

Sanders stopped for a moment to keep his pace random. He said, "I don't know who shot at us, but it was more for distraction than to take the farm." The deputy's voice sounded tired.

Calderon asked, "How do you know they weren't trying to take the farm?" The sheriff took out a pipe and pouch and started packing the pipe.

Sanders said, "It's none of my business, but you sure you want to be lighting that pipe out here with people shooting at the place?" Calderon realized what he was doing and put the pipe away. Sanders continued, "I was on the porch about here, and Briarton was in the outhouse. If they were watching us, they would have started shooting while Briarton and I were talking near the barn. If they happened across the place, they would have come a good deal closer, like pretending to be friendly and then ambush us. It just didn't make sense, until I came around the house that last time when I figured it had to be a distraction. Don't know if someone got in the house or the barn."

Calderon took a long sigh and said, "You have a point. If they went into the barn or the house, they'd be long gone by now. I still don't know what they were after."

Sanders asked, "That prisoner say anything?"

"I have my deputy asking him now," said Calderon. He paused for a long moment, staring at the ground. He looked into the sky and said, "I just hope this whole thing wasn't a distraction; we almost had a lynching last night."

Sanders said, "None of us would feel the worse if you decided to get back to the jailhouse." He heard two clicks and awaited the volunteer's jovial face poking out from around the corner of the old farmhouse. The lanterns flickered along the dirt road.

"You may as well have Deputy Briarton come down from the hayloft," Calderon decided. "The three of you can guard the farmhouse. I'll send one of my deputies by in the morning. When Deputy Stratton comes back, have him return to the jailhouse."

"Will do," said Sanders. Calderon preferred a "yes, sir" from his men when he gave an order like that. He saddled up and rode along the lit path toward the road back to town. He wished the clouds wouldn't hide the road so much from the light of the moon. Along the dark road, he heard crackling tree branches behind him and pushed the horse all the harder.

*   *   *

Quaker Jowett rode the buckboard north and west away from town, up toward the mountain trail. He knew the slaves would need all the help God could give them to make it to Canada. Along the route, the slaves lay low in the belly of the buckboard; all but Smitty, who rode under the tarp. A rider came up quickly from behind them. Quaker Jowett didn't look until the rider was nearly on top of them. His breath quickened and his heart raced, but he dared not appear nervous nor look back too early.

The rider came to his side. Quaker Jowett looked to find the familiar, stoic face of Deputy Hank Stratton. Hank slowed his horse to match speeds with the buckboard.

Quaker Jowett said, "Hank, nice to run into you." Hank looked at Quaker Jowett and the buckboard.

"What are you doing on this road at night?" he asked.

"I told Penn I would get his peaches to the Gilles. They'll be making pies for the August fair. Never can tell where a favor will take you."

Deputy Stratton said, "That man may not see the August fair." He looked further down the road, avoiding eye contact with the Quaker. He asked, "You seen anybody on the road?"

"No, I haven't. Guess most folks have better sense than I do." Quaker Jowett looked at the deputy sheephishly.

Hank said, "You best be careful on the road this evening. There was shooting at the Penn farm, and we haven't caught the men responsible, yet."

"Do you know why they were shooting?" He glanced back down the road.

"Don't know as of yet, but I fear it has something to do with the murder. Keep to the roads, and if you see anything . . ." Deputy Stratton's voice fell off. He looked at Quaker Jowett with consternation and said, "I know you don't carry a gun, so I guess you'd best holler as loud as you can and run away fast." Hank didn't understand why any man would be without a rifle, let alone never own a gun altogether. He thought to himself, "Some folks take religion a might too far."

Quaker Jowett smiled and said, "Now that I can do." Hank touched the brim of his hat, and Quaker Jowett responded in kind. The deputy rode on up ahead. Quaker Jowett slowed a bit as he came across the fork in the road that led to the base of the mountain trail. The tree-lined path was a bit darker and slower than the main road. Creaking wheels joined the crickets again.

Long journeys do find an end, and for Quaker Jowett he had found it. Awaiting him was his own surrey provided by his friends in the underground, tucked a bit back in the woods. If Hank came across him in the surrey, he would tell the deputy that the Gilles planned on using the buckboard. Smitty crawled out from under the tarp, then hopped out of the buckboard and began helping Quaker Jowett with the removal of the wooden planks.

Smitty asked, "What was you gonna do's if'n dat deputy wants one o' dose peaches?" Smitty looked at Quaker Jowett's face; he was stumped.

Quaker Jowett said, "I hadn't thought of that possibility." He laughed along with Smitty. Together the men removed the remaining five passengers.

They'd have to go alone, go with God. Quaker Jowett said a silent prayer for their welfare. Smitty and Calvin replaced the wooden planks in the buckboard and put back the supplies.

Quaker Jowett said, "Time for us to part ways. God speed to Canada." He shook Smitty's hand, to Smitty's surprise. He then hugged Miss Alice and Miss Dorothy. Miss Hattie was coming back out of the woods after taking care of nature's business. Quaker Jowett shook Trent's hand and then Calvin's hand. He arrived at Miss Hattie and opened his arms to give her a hug.

Miss Hattie said sternly, "An' what pray tell does you thinks you's doin'?" Quaker Jowett took a step back, with his arms still open for a hug.

"I was planning on hugging you good-bye," he explained.

"What's you doin' that fer?" She appeared mildly upset with Quaker Jowett, who did not understand how he had insulted her.

He put his arms at his side and said, "Good-bye Miss Hattie."

"Taint right," Miss Hattie blurted out. "I's goin' wid you. I un'erstan's God wants me ta tell de judge what I done seen, and Smitty, you cain't stops me." Smitty glared at her for a moment.

Calvin said, "Beggin' yer pardon Miss Hattie, but if'n you tells de judge about us runaways, den dey comes lookin' fer us."

Miss Hattie reassured the young man with the sparkle in his eyes, "Son, I doesn't wish ta hurts you; I doesn't has ta tell de judge today. Ain't dat right, Misser Quaker Jowett?" Quaker Jowett thought about the question.

"No ma'am you don't have to tell him today," he answered. "We can wait a couple of days, I'm sure. I'm not sure where to hide you, though."

Miss Alice asked Miss Hattie, "Is you sure dis is what God's intendin' fer your life?" Miss Alice looked worried, and Miss Hattie placed a hand on the child's arm.

"I knows child, I knows in my heart. For'n we stepped on dis trail north, I has a dream. In dis hear dream, dere was six baby blackbirds in a nest. One by one, dey tries ta fly and each one makes it inta de air. Spreadin' wings and flyin' away. Til de las' one, and dat one falls ta de earth. I's de las' one." The cluster of weary travelers looked at one another, and then to Smitty.

Again the weight was on Smitty's shoulders. He, as well as the others, knew Miss Hattie's fate. Leaving her behind was like leaving family behind. Miss Dorothy started to cry. When Miss Alice turned to comfort her, she in turn began to cry. Trent and Calvin attempted to comfort the young women. Smitty tried to talk, but his voice wouldn't come to him. He just stood there staring sadly into Miss Hattie's soulful eyes.

Quaker Jowett was moved. He would ensure her safety, even with his life if necessary. When a person does right, strength shines from within and forces those around them to do right as well.

Smitty, choked up, finally said, "If'n dat's whats you want den dat's what you does. Dat is freedom." The young ones hugged Miss Hattie; the kind of hug only their Mommas knew before this night. Smitty thought Miss Hattie was powerfully strong; not one tear did she shed. Miss Hattie looked to Quaker Jowett.

Quaker Jowett said, "You all best get going. I'll head back to town and find a place for Miss Hattie to hide until the day after tomorrow. This trail is a bit rough, but you won't find anyone else on it, and it'll get you to Oneonta by the third day. Remember to look for lanterns with ribbons, or the quilts. Godspeed, my prayers are with you."

Miss Hattie said, "When you gits to Canada, plants a peach tree fer me. If'n I git a chance, I'll be up ta makes you dat cobblah. God Bless."

Calvin took the seat in front with Miss Alice joining him. Smitty helped Trent climb in. The others jumped into the back of the buckboard and climbed under the tarp. Smitty looked at Miss Hattie and Quaker Jowett.

CHAPTER XXVII

A Day in Court

The sun beat down hot, but thunder rumbled in the distance. Judge Markette was the first into the courtroom, benefit of his insomnia. He walked around the rectangular space and faced the bench, as sunrise etched its way through the windows behind him. He walked past the table set up for Penn and one of the deputies. Penn had been offered a lawyer but refused. Normally, the sheriff would have represented the state. When the judge told Calderon of that potential task, he was less than happy about it, and was quite relieved when told there wouldn't be a need for him to do so after all.

Judge Markette would have a deputy on either side of him, and one would swear in the witnesses. He looked at the flag in the corner of the room. He thought about liberty, about being free to pursue a man's dream. One man's liberty was gone, and another man's was soon to belong to the state. He reminded himself that justice was blind, meaning impartial to a man's way of life, and simply sought the truth. Many times the truth came easy to the judge, but not this time. He walked up to his bench. He sat down on the elevated chair and looked out on the empty spectator benches. Some of the men who would sit on these benches would gladly free Penn, his friends. Some were the men outside the jailhouse ready to hang him. Markette knew his job was to give each of them an opportunity to think more like the other before this trial ended, so that when the hangman's noose ended a man's life both sides would understand the reason for that man's fate.

Markette saw the glass that would hold his lemonade. Sunlight was streaming through the large windowpanes in front of him now. He struck the gavel once and the sound echoed throughout the large room. He sat for a peaceful moment; he thought, "My last until the trial ends." The judge took a last look around; he exited to the small room behind the bench.

*   *   *

Townspeople chattered amid the benches in the back of the room, as Sheriff Calderon escorted Miss Westcott up to the judge's bench. She placed the pitcher of lemonade on the bench next to the gavel. She touched the smooth head of the gavel and felt its weight. She thought of the gavel's power to stop everyone in the court from talking. Miss Westcott was too shy to satisfy the temptation to bang the gavel to silence the courtroom. She stepped back down to stand next to Calderon. He was searching the crowd for people on the list, the list of witnesses.

He spied Dillancy and Hubbartt off to one side, speaking with one another. Calderon wondered about the others. He worried that most of the people in the crowd weren't there seeking justice, but rather seeking the spectacle of a hanging. He had been present for a number of trials, and thought about the tension that built just before the verdict was read. Many folks held their breath at that moment; Calderon had watched their eyes. He saw the gleam, a life about to change forever. He remembered the Lizzy Borden trial. The sheriff there had said folks came from miles around to see the woman who some thought had chopped up her family with an ax, regular folks with a taste for blood. Sheriff Calderon knew that was how a man like James Penn could murder.

*   *   *

Quaker Jowett wondered if anyone else in town was aware that he could hide a slave in broad daylight in Kingston. He was proud of the fact that Harriet and Marion, the town gossips, were instrumental in hiding the runaway slave. Quaker Jowett knew these women well, as they had maligned the character of many a townsperson. A number of the town's elite had befriended the sisters to avoid being scrutinized. Quaker Jowett refused to take part in their destructive pleasure.

He understood that with gossips, much like a child with a temper-tantrum, if one reacted to the gossip, it was successful. He didn't have an aversion to the sisters until they hurt a young newlywed couple. The couple had come from Albany and intended on farming. A year after the couple had arrived in Kingston, the sisters took to instructing the young bride on how to manage her husband. Seeing as how these two sisters had scarce been with a man, the instructions failed and led to a great deal of discord. When the young couple's first child was born, the sisters expected the child to be named after one of them, and when that did not occur, the child was deemed a bastard, not in the eyes of God, but from the tongues of those harpies. The young couple had fled to Newburgh in poor spirits.

Quaker Jowett wished to spit out his detest, but that was impolite in front of a lady. He reminded himself of his deceit and smiled, as he stepped into the garden behind the great house the sisters had inherited from their parents. Harriet and Marion would usually be in the garden for entertaining, but on Mondays the slaves took to the wash. Quaker Jowett walked ahead of Miss Hattie, but she clung to that strong calloused hand for strength. He spoke to the other slaves, as he had in the past.

"Miss Louisa, I beg a favor of you," he said. "I need your help in hiding something that I will retrieve tomorrow or the next day." Quaker Jowett smiled at her sweetly.

Miss Louisa knew by that round-faced smile what Quaker Jowett was getting to. She smiled at him and said, "Course I'll he'ps you. Slaves cain always comes inta de kitchen, as de mistresses ain't never come in dere." Miss Hattie stepped past Quaker Jowett.

He reminded her, "I'll be back in a day or two, no more. Listen to Miss Louisa, and know I would not put you in harm's way." Quaker Jowett wished he had an alternative as he saw the fear in Miss Hattie's eyes.

She said, "God Bless you," held his calloused hand for a moment longer, and then turned away. Quaker Jowett took coins from his pocket, and as he looked down to count them, Miss Louisa placed her hand over his.

"Ain't no need to spoils a good deed wif dat." Quaker Jowett returned the money to his pouch, promising himself he would bring supplies. Miss Louisa enjoyed books now that he had taught her to read. He looked out at the garden and remembered a warm summer's day when she was reading to the children. The whole world hushed to hear her voice speak the words in the book. At the end of the story, the children beamed, but Miss Louisa had the biggest smile. At that moment, Quaker Jowett understood the parable of teaching a man to fish.

He bid the women good day and stepped back out onto the street through the front gate, having entered the gardens through a trail in the woods. Marion and Harriet were most likely in the parlor discussing the murder of poor Mister Simms, a man they once claimed was having relations with two of their slaves. Quaker Jowett could only think the women were jealous. He smiled, and even found himself letting out a bit of a giggle, as he thought about these women hiding a runaway slave.

Deputy Bielk brought Penn into the court through the doorway that led to the jailhouse. Penn clanked his way into the room and settled into the chair nearest the sheriff. Penn was embarrassed as the gathered spectators whispered to one another, getting all the more louder for a moment. He looked down at the table before him. He was thirsty and the water looked refreshing, but as he started to move his hand, there came a clanking sound. He stopped himself from moving and hoped he wouldn't be asked questions any time soon.

Calderon raised his hand to quiet the crowd. Even the whispers among the masses created a bit of a din. After a few moments, the crowd was quiet enough for him to speak.

"All rise," he said loudly. A few of the folks stood and the remainder followed along as if in church. He continued, "The Honorable Paxton Markette is presenting." Judge Markette came out of the back room wearing a long black robe, making his stern face appear all the more menacing. The judge wanted to correct the sheriff, "presiding not presenting," but that could wait for a recess.

Markette sat in his chair above the crowd and banged the gavel hard. His deep voice resonated around the high ceiling as he said, "Court is now in session." He looked out at the people chattering in the back, as a schoolmarm waits for disobedient children to hush before beginning a lesson. He decided these people needed an education, and said, "Ladies and gentlemen. This is court, actually this is my court. I can have anyone leave by telling one of these bailiffs to remove the offending party. That means if you make me angry, I kick you out. For those who don't know, talking while I'm talking makes me angry." The room became very quiet. Judge Markette smiled, his only reward for the obedient farmers and dockhands.

The judge sipped his lemonade; he could hear the ice chips clanking together. He mouthed a thank you to Miss Westcott, and she blushed. Markette continued his instruction, as he said, "I want to hear the evidence against Mister James Penn before I hear his defense. I would like to hear from Barnaby Bathers."

Bathers stood up and stepped past Luke and Pieter to get out of the bench and up toward the judge. He looked at the judge, who pointed to an empty chair beside his chair. Hank Stratton came over and held up a bible. Bathers looked at the bible and then at the deputy; he was confused.

Hank whispered, "Put your right hand on top of the bible." Bathers looked at Stratton as if he had asked him to swallow a frog.

"I ain't putting my hand on that book," he said. A few of the people in the back laughed, until Bathers turned and glared at them.

Judge Markette said, "Mister Bathers, I need you to swear to God that what you are about to tell me is the truth. I want you to put your right hand on the book and say 'I do' when the bailiff finishes." Bathers opened his mouth to say something, and the judge looked down at him. "Just listen to what the bailiff says."

Hank felt that being a bailiff was a demotion, but he didn't want to tangle with the judge. He said to Bathers, "Do you swear to tell the truth, the whole truth, and nothing but the truth, so help you God?" Bathers looked at the judge and then back at Hank.

"I do." He quickly removed his hand from the bible as if he had just touched a hot stove.

From the back of the courthouse came, "You can kiss the bride," from a man named Petersen. Laughter erupted in the courthouse. Bathers glared at Petersen, the judge glared at Petersen, and Joseph went over and escorted Petersen out of the courthouse without a fuss. Laughter erupted again when Petersen made kissing sounds. Penn had his head down on the table before him. Judge Markette banged his gavel twice, but there was still some chuckling. He banged the gavel again; tittering. He continued the testimony of Bathers.

"Tell me what happened the night Jeffrey Simms was killed." the judge commanded.

Bathers took a deep breath. He said, "Well, I was heading over to see Simms to get him to sign about water rights. We had words earlier that night, but then we settled everything, so I figured to get the water rights while we was still on good terms. So, I seen a lantern on in the barn and I headed in. I didn't see anybody, so I took a step further into the barn and almost tripped over Simms. He was lying there in the barn all bloody. I knelt down to help him onto my horse, get him to Doc Hamilton, but he was hurt bad. When I asked him what happened, who done this, he said James Penn."

Whispers filled the courthouse at the sound of Penn's name. Penn lifted his head off the table; he looked at Bathers with confusion, as if he was hearing this for the first time. The judge banged his gavel, while Bathers smiled on the inside.

Markette asked, "Anything else?"

Bathers said, "I don't know if Penn was working alone, could have been others involved?" Loud whispering brought another swift bangs of the gavel.

"What proof do you have of this?" He always challenged hearsay.

"Dillancy and his friend Hubbartt over there." Bathers pointed at them. The crowd grumbled.

"They've been spreading some mean-spirited rumors about me," Bathers said defensively. "Making some good folks question what happened. Makes me think they have something to hide." Dillancy and Hubbartt both stood up in the back of the courtroom.

Dillancy yelled, "Anybody suspicious of you came to that on their own!"

"We told the truth and we're going to keep telling the truth!" added Hubbartt. Joseph weaved his way through the benches toward the two men. Judge Markette banged his gavel and motioned for the two to sit back down; they complied.

"I will not allow outbursts in my courtroom," said the judge harshly. "Gentlemen, please remain seated. I will hear from you later." Bathers appeared a bit upset at the judge's words.

"Mr. Bathers, do you have any proof of others being involved in the crime?" the judge asked. He slowly loosened his grip on the gavel.

Bathers conceded, "Not that I can put my hands on. I guess not, your honor."

"Good, then you will serve as my example for the court. To all of you who will be testifying, if you tell me something, be sure to have proof to support your statement, otherwise, I may not consider it. Mr. Bathers makes me question his motives, when he makes a statement he can't support with facts. I hope I have made myself clear." He turned to Bathers, and said, "You may step down. You can leave the chair." Bathers left the witness stand and glared at Dillancy and Hubbartt. Hank noticed the eye contact. A clanking at the front of the courthouse distracted the deputy; Penn drank from his glass of water.

Markette looked at his notes and said, "I would like to hear from Doctor Hamilton." He looked up to the courtroom. Calderon stepped forward.

"Doctor Hamilton is still on his way to the court," he said. Markette acknowledged the information.

"Then let's hear from you, Sheriff," he said. Calderon took the witness chair. He placed his hand on the bible. Hank smiled at him.

"Do you swear to tell the truth, the whole truth, and nothing but the truth, so help you God?"

"I do." The volume of his voice even surprised Calderon a bit. Hank nodded his head to say, "Well, all right."

Judge Markette asked, "Sheriff Calderon, what do you know about the murder of Jeffrey Simms?"

"Mr. Bathers came to me to tell me what happened. He said it in his testimony." The sheriff looked at the judge.

"I heard from Mister Bathers, and now I want to hear from you," said the judge. "Tell me what you know."

Calderon said, "Well, he said Mr. Simms had been murdered and that Simms mentioned Penn's name before he died. He said Simms gave him a button, a button I later matched to Penn's vest. Bathers found Penn's knife next to the body. When I saw the body of Simms, I knew he was dead. Penn wasn't at his farm when we arrived, so my deputy waited for him. James Penn has been in jail since and denies he had anything to do with the murder of Jeffrey Simms." Penn watched the sheriff throughout the sheriff's testimony. He remembered the button, one he had lost weeks ago. Then he thought about the knife, a knife he left in his barn for cutting cord on bails of hay. Calderon looked at the judge; he was done.

Markette asked, "Did Mr. Penn put up a struggle when he was found at his farm?" The judge sipped at his lemonade.

"No sir, he seemed surprised that we were there."

"What do you make of it? A man killed a friend and apparently left the city in his buckboard, only to return to his farm and be surprised to see the law waiting for him." Calderon thought for a long moment.

"It doesn't make sense, but a lot of things about this case don't make sense." The sheriff began thinking and almost missed the judge's next question.

"Did Mr. Bathers go with you to arrest Mister Penn?"

"Yes, he went with me, but Penn wasn't there."

"Did you ask him, or did he volunteer?"

"He volunteered."

"You saw Simms's body before burial; did you see any knife wounds?"

Calderon thought for a moment and said, "His body was a bit bloody, but I didn't see any knife wounds."

"Thank you, Sheriff, you can take your seat," said Judge Markette politely. "May I hear from the doctor, um, Doctor Hamilton, now.

Calderon blurted out, "I do believe Mister Bathers is telling the truth." Markette looked a bit annoyed. The sheriff realized he had impulsively supported an old friend, wondering if he was telling the truth.

"That's quite all right, Sheriff," he said sharply. "Mr. Bathers is not on trial here. Please take your seat."

Calderon felt he had done more harm than good for Barnaby Bathers. He stepped down and walked past Penn. The sheriff stood back by the door to the jailhouse. Doc Hamilton had come into the courthouse just before the end of the sheriff's testimony. He was escorted up toward the judge. Markette was more annoyed than he had thought.

He saw the doctor coming toward him and asked in an irritated tone, "Who are you?" Doc Hamilton was taken aback and raised his black leather bag.

"I'm Doctor Hamilton," he said, just as irritably, "and I was busy with a call to Mrs. Kaijal." He turned to the crowd in the benches and said loudly, "And no the baby hasn't come, yet." Utterances of regret floated through the courthouse.

The doctor was sworn in, and he took the chair next to the judge. He gazed at James Penn, who looked weak. Penn had always been a rather quiet man, but had never appeared so vulnerable to Doc Hamilton.

The judge asked, "Doctor Hamilton, you saw the body of Jeffrey Simms the day he died?"

"Yes, your Honor. I went to his farm that night with Jacob Knufield. Unfortunately, Jeffrey Simms had died. His body lay in the barn. He had been struck in the head with a blunt object."

Judge Markette was a little surprised and asked, "Was that the blow that killed him?"

"Yes, it was the blow to the head that killed him. Although there was a knife next to the body, I did not find any stab wounds on examination." Doc Hamilton had been talking to the crowd in general, but noticed that a cluster of three young women, including Miss Westcott, were consoling one another and weeping. He felt a bit self-conscious about his testimony.

Judge Markette was not as sensitive, and asked, "Was there any other evidence found at the body?" He was very curious about the answer to this question.

Doc Hamilton said, "A button was apparently found in the hand of Simms, but it made no imprint on the hand."

"How is that important?" asked the judge.

The doctor explained, "Well, when a body dies, muscles have a tendency to contract. I'd expect some kind of mark on the hand, but there wasn't any." The judge looked lost in thought for a moment, as Doc Hamilton waited for further questions.

The judge finally said, "You may step down." He looked out over the spectators and saw the young women crying. He said, "We'll recess for lunch at this point." He checked his gold pocket watch, the one with the inscription from his children that read "Justice for All." "I expect we'll all be back at one this afternoon."

Markette whispered to Doc Hamilton, who was standing next to the bench, "May I see you in chambers?" Calderon was a little surprised. He felt as sheriff, he should be made aware of any new evidence. He wanted to follow the two men into the judge's chambers, but knew it was by invitation only, and he watched as they disappeared behind the door.

CHAPTER XXVIII

Sigh of Relief

Judge Markette spoke with Doc Hamilton for fifteen minutes. Then the judge came out of chambers and told Joseph that court would resume the next morning at nine. He gave instructions to the deputy that he would be returning to his room at the boarding house and did not want to be disturbed. Shortly after that, Doc Hamilton came out of the chambers and rode off in his surrey. Joseph passed the word on to Calderon, who was most anxious to see the judge. He reviewed Doc Hamilton's testimony over and over in his head, but didn't hear anything new. He thought the judge must have heard something that caused him to get the doctor to investigate further.

*   *   *

Quaker Jowett stepped through the jailhouse door with a basket of food for Penn. Inside the basket was a peach cobbler, a signal that the passengers were back on the train. Jowett didn't feel Penn was in the right frame of mind to hear about Miss Hattie's determination to right a wrong. He passed the basket to Hank Stratton, who examined the contents and noticed the peach cobbler.

"Looks like he has enough cobbler there to feed three people," Hank commented. Penn smiled for the first time in what seemed to be a month. Quaker Jowett said, "Peach cobbler is his favorite, but I'm sure he'll share." Hank handed the basket back to Quaker Jowett and opened the cell for him.

Quaker Jowett asked Penn, "How much time do we have?"

"Depends on if I win or lose," Penn said smiling through the joke. "I've been told I have to go back at one. I'd rather just stay down here. There was a button and knife of mine found at the . . ." He choked up, and started to shed the tears he knew should have come days ago. Quaker Jowett stood by feeling a bit helpless. When a woman cries, he thought, she wants someone to hold her. When a man cries, he wants to be alone. He couldn't leave Penn alone, and so just let him cry. Penn finally wiped away the tears and took a bite of chicken. He said nothing of his tears, and Quaker Jowett wasn't about to mention it.

Instead he said, "It's still hot out there, even though thunderstorms keep passing through. Of course, it's pretty hot in here."

"Not so bad." Penn didn't look at Quaker Jowett, just took small bites of cornbread with honey butter. He asked, "Is everything safe at the farmhouse?"

"Hank said everything was fine; no more shooting."

"I wish I could sleep, maybe tonight. I really don't know what is going to happen in that courtroom. People say there is God's purpose in everything. I have prayed that the purpose in this be revealed to me." Penn stopped eating and placed the yellow bread in the basket. Quaker Jowett wanted to provide words of comfort, but James needed more than words.

A silence hung between them. Quaker Jowett heard the sheriff telling his deputies something about court not being held that afternoon, but starting again in the morning. Penn was lost and confused in thought. Penn opened his mouth twice; each time Quaker Jowett leaned a little closer, but heard no voice.

Penn looked at the floor and said, "I've lost hope, Quaker Jowett. I've lost the meaning in everything that I knew. I never understood how important hope was to me, but in that courtroom, hearing what was said, I felt my heart lower to the floor and I had no strength in my arms to pick it up. It was as if everything I lived for was gone. Without hope, each breath is drawn to draw another." Penn kept staring at the floor, while Quaker Jowett tried to grasp the meaning of what he had just said.

"Then we should pray that hope returns to your life," he said. Penn turned to face Quaker Jowett. With a lifeless expression on his face, he said, "I don't even have the strength to pray." Quaker Jowett touched his arm.

"Then I shall pray for us both."

*   *   *

The Clemmons twins sat on the porch of the boarding house watching children play in a nearby park. Jones absently gazed at the two grown men just itching to run off and play. He wished he could live life as simply. Kingman sat watching young girls pass and thinking about how to get in to see Penn.

Kingman reviewed aloud, "We need to see Penn, challenge him to reveal the whereabouts of the slaves."

Jones added, "Can't get in the cell with him, so it has to sound good."

"Threatening the life of a slave, that's it."

"But lawmen are constantly around him. One of us will need time alone with him." He watched a couple strolling along holding hands; won't last, he thought.

"Need a distraction." The woman Kingman had slept with strolled by and ignored the tipping of his hat. He thought about calling her a whore; he didn't need the attention.

"Heard tell at the trial, Bathers's testimony was all about Penn doing the killing."

"We might be able to use him."

*   *   *

Joseph and Hank stood in Simms's barn. Hay lay strewn about the floor, and there were fewer tools than one might expect. The animals had been fed, by a neighbor most likely, probably taking care of them in the early morning to avoid looters. Hank wished they had the men to protect the property, but they only had two volunteers at Simms's farm, and one of them had fallen asleep the night before last.

Hank put his hand up to halt Joseph. Joseph listened intently, but heard only the sounds of chickens in the yard and a horse chewing on oats in a stall. Hank looked down and saw the blood stain just ahead of his left boot. Hank and Joseph stepped around the spot where Simms had taken his last breath. These men weren't particularly superstitious, but if one can avoid standing on the spot of a tragic death, so much the better.

Hank had had to listen to Mr. Merriwether, a neighbor, talk about seeing the ghost of Simms in his yard. He had tried to reassure the older man that spirits didn't exist, but the old codger wouldn't let it go.

Finally Hank had just said, "If the ghost shows up again, tell him to come to the jailhouse and he can speak to Penn directly." Mr. Merriwether liked the plan; he really liked that plan. Hank patted him on the shoulder before returning to the jailhouse.

Now Hank and Joseph searched the barn for a blunt object. Hank felt the task was hopeless and wouldn't necessarily prove anything. Calderon said the judge wanted the murder weapon. Because the knife didn't kill Simms, the supposed blunt object might be able to tell them something.

The heat of the day was at its peak and began to seep into the shady barn. As luck would have it, the horse relieved himself as they searched near the stall. Joseph and Hank began coughing, which led to laughter between the men. They stepped out of the barn to catch a breath of fresh air, eyes tearing.

Joseph said, "That is the nastiest horse I ever smelled."

Hank joked, "You go around smelling horses, that's good for me to know." Joseph playfully smacked Hank on the shoulder. As Hank turned away from Joseph he caught a glimpse of a cluster of tools outside the barn.

Hank stepped over to the tools and Joseph followed. Amid the hoe and rake was a shovel. Hank slowly removed the shovel and saw a bit of dried brown crust on the backside.

Joseph said with amazement, "Son of a . . . ; you found it!"

Hank looked at the shovel and said, "Where do you hide something you really don't want found? In plain sight." The men placed the flat-head shovel in the back of their wagon and headed back to town.

*   *   *

Miss Alice pulled the buckboard to the side of the road. She was tired and in need of rest. Calvin wondered about the stop, when at least five more hours of daylight was in the sky and there wasn't anybody on the rocky road.

Miss Alice confessed, "I's done drained, cain't we stop?"

"No, we has to keeps going. Soon as Miss Hattie tells de truf, dey'll be comin ta find us ta stops dat truf. We's got ta keeps goin." Calvin took the reins from Miss Alice. He said, "Ain't nobody on dis here road, so's you cain sleeps in back, but when you's wakes up, treats me like a slave, don't be kinds to me, lest we have company." Calvin kept the buckboard slow as Miss Alice stepped into the back.

Miss Alice lay with her head over Trent and Miss Dorothy. She said through the floorboards, "We's high up on a mountainside."

Miss Dorothy said excitedly, "What does you see? Does you sees Canada?" She reached out and found Trent's hand, giving it a squeeze. They turned heads to smile at one another in the dim light in the buckboard. They gazed into each other's eyes.

Miss Alice said, "I see green hills as far as my eyes can see. Off to one side is a beautiful lake." She yawned. "I see a small village off in the distance, by the road . . . ." She was fast asleep when Trent kissed Miss Dorothy.

CHAPTER XXIX

Getting One's Bearings

The next morning found the slaves waking to the first light of the day. A mist hung in the air; Miss Alice knew the day would be hot, as her clothes were already sticking to her skin. She wished for a bath, but knew a luxury like that would wait. Miss Dorothy put together a quick breakfast of brown bread, dried beef, and apples. Water was running low, so ale would do for this meal.

Trent limped around putting up the tarp and bedrolls. Calvin studied the map and the vista. He knew they were on the right road, but was unsure of what lay ahead. He prayed it would lead them to Oneonta. Miss Alice put up the supplies for Miss Dorothy and Trent for the journey. She stepped over to Calvin.

"You best be getting that buckboard on the road. I don't want to wait to get to Oneonta." Calvin looked at her.

"Now dat's de way ta talks to me," he smiled.

Miss Alice said, "De mistress wants all o' us houseslaves ta talks like dat." She smiled at her achievement.

"You think Misser James' gonna be all right?" Miss Dorothy asked.

"Dat's up ta de white folks," said Calvin.

Miss Alice dropped her head and held her hands together in front of her. The others did the same.

From the mountaintop, Miss Alice prayed, "Dear God, please take care of those who have been separated from us."

*   *   *

"Do you swear to tell the truth, the whole truth, and nothing but the truth, so help you God," said Joseph with a smile. Hank thought it odd that his fellow lawman was swearing him in. "I do," he said.

Judge Markette asked, "Deputy Stratton, you recently searched the Simms farm, please tell us what you found."

Hank cleared his throat and said, "I was asked by the sheriff to go with Deputy Joseph Bielk and search the Simms farm for any blunt object. While Deputy Bielk and I were there, we found a flat-head shovel in with a bunch of other tools. I took the shovel out and found dried blood on the back of it, the rain had only cleaned the front. I brought the shovel back."

Joseph brought forth the shovel to a buzz of excitement in the crowd. The judge waved him up to the bench and examined the shovel, looking closely at dried patch of blood. He then handed it back to the waiting deputy, who took it over to the sheriff.

The judge said to Hank, "Did you find anything else related to the death of Mister Simms?" He glanced peripherally at the women who had been weeping yesterday. He wished he could ask them to leave.

"Well, it's a pretty heavy shovel and would take a great deal of strength to strike someone that hard with it." Hank had nothing more to add.

"You may take your seat. I'd like to hear from Doctor Hamilton again." The judge looked about the courtroom, but Doc Hamilton wasn't present. He looked at the sheriff in an annoyed manner. He said, "Sheriff, do you know where the doctor is?"

Calderon said, "He had to see one of his patients. He'll be back this afternoon." The judge looked as if the doctor had just eaten his lunch.

Markette saw the sun shining through the large windows in back of the crowd. He wondered how those poor people could stand the heat even with the windows open.

"Well, I might as well hear from Mr. Dillancy," he said. "If he could come forward and be sworn in?" Judge Markette recognized the face when Dillancy rose up from the bench on the left. Dillancy stepped forward and sat in the witness chair. He was sworn in.

Markette asked, "What do you know about the night Mister Simms was murdered?"

"Well I was at the tavern with Simms on the night he was murdered," Dillancy replied. "Bathers was angry with Mister Simms, and let him know it. I was worried for Jeffrey, um Mister Simms, and warned him to watch himself."

"And what does this have to do with the murder of Simms?"

Dillancy said awkwardly, "I just think it's odd that Bathers was so angry with him and then is the only one to find him and hear Simms blame Penn."

The judge asked, "Did you see Mr. Bathers again that night?"

"Yes, he was sleeping outside the tavern when I left with Simms." He hoped he didn't ask any questions about what they did to Bathers.

"Did you see Mister Simms or Mister Bathers later on that night?"

Dillancy simply said, "No."

"Thank you, you may sit down again." Dillancy took his seat next to Hubbartt, while the judge sipped at his lemonade. Calderon found it difficult to determine if the judge was thinking over the testimony or bored.

Judge Markette set the glass down and said, "Since Doctor Hamilton is out saving lives, I would like to hear from Mister Hubbartt." Hubbartt came forth and took the seat next to the judge. He was sworn in.

"Tell me what happened that night," the judge asked. Hubbartt shifted in the chair to be more comfortable.

Hubbartt said, "Well, Mister Bathers and Mister Simms had an argument in the tavern. I thought there would be a fight, but the tavern owner, Nate, got between the men and settled them down. The two were fighting over water rights. Simms told Bathers he couldn't give him water rights, because he would lose too many crops. Bathers wanted nothing of it, said he'd lose sheep, especially if there was a drought. I left with Simms and Dillancy. Bathers was outside sleeping it off."

Judge Markette asked, "Did you see either Mister Simms or Mister Bathers later on that night?"

Hubbartt said evenly, "No, I did not."

"Thank you, you may take your seat."

Hubbartt sat back down next to Dillancy. He turned to speak with his friend and saw the face of Bathers sitting just behind them. Bathers leaned forward.

Bathers whispered, "Town just ain't as safe as it used to be, especially for farmers." Dillancy looked forward while Hubbartt turned back toward the judge. Judge Markette took notice of the interchange between the three men and made a mental note to ask them during the recess. He quickly surveyed the crowd, and still saw no Doctor Hamilton.

"Seeing as how the good doctor is still out, we'll take a recess until one this afternoon." He looked at the sheriff and said sternly, "I hope all of the people on my list will be here promptly at one."

*   *   *

Miss Marion and Miss Harriet visited the kitchen in the lower level of their home. Three slaves worked diligently preparing the evening's feast. The sisters were checking on the meal before returning to the courtroom. Miss Harriet thought Miss Marion favored the judge, in part because she denied it vehemently. Miss Marion looked forward to discussing the trial at their dinner party.

Miss Louisa was directing Miss Hattie in turning the spit just so to roast the pig slowly. Miss Hattie had done so a hundred times before, but let Miss Louisa direct her, as it was Miss Louisa's kitchen. The giant pig turned slowly on the spit, as Miss Marion and Miss Harriet rounded the corner into the kitchen. Beads of sweat dripped from Miss Hattie's cheeks; she was ever so careful not to let her sweat fall on the meat.

Miss Marion asked, "Will that pig be roasted by tonight?" Miss Hattie looked at Miss Louisa, who would answer that question.

Miss Louisa said, "Yes, Ma'am." Miss Harriet pulled the top off a pot of sweet potatoes that weren't yet cooking. She swung the metal arm to position the kettle over the flames of the fire.

"Need to have the sweet potatoes done as well," said Miss Harriet. "Miss Louisa, they will be served with butter and brown sugar."

"Yes, Ma'am." The sisters left the kitchen as their skin was beginning to 'glow'. Miss Hattie smiled at Miss Louisa, as she moved the metal bar holding the kettle to take the potatoes off the flame.

Miss Hattie said, "Good to knows somethin's ain't so different." She used the back of her hand to wipe the sweat from her cheek.

"Sisters would shrivels up and die without us," said Miss Louisa. Miss Hattie's right arm was tiring from turning the spit's handle, and she switched to her left. Miss Louisa polished the fruit.

Miss Hattie asked, "How comes you doesn't runs ta Canada?"

"Ain't so bad here," Miss Louisa replied. "Them sisters don't ever hits us, or treats us bad. Don't know anything else."

"I don't knows if I'd stay still, if'n I has a choice."

"You witnessin' on Mister Penn, how's that?" Miss Louisa stopped polishing for a moment.

Miss Hattie said, "Misser James done puts his life on de line fer us. Cain't let him lose his life if'n I cain stop it, taint right by God." Miss Louisa looked into Miss Hattie's dark eyes in a kind, sorrowful way.

She said solemnly, "They'll send you back south; I done seen it before." Miss Hattie looked down at the stone floor, her arm continuing to crank the spit.

"God doesn't gives a person more'n de person cain take," she said softly.

* * *

Doc Hamilton was sworn in, and Judge Markette slowly poured himself a tall glass of lemonade. Townspeople shuffled into place on the benches in the courtroom, even more than had been there that morning. Rumors flew around the room like buzzing flies, as spectators created reasons for the judge's request to speak with the doctor again.

When all was settled, the judge asked, "Doctor Hamilton, you examined the body of the late Mister Simms. Did you observe any knife wounds?"

Doc Hamilton replied, "No, I did not." A few spectators in the court chattered, until the judge banged his gavel. Markette waved at Joseph to approach the bench. Joseph carried the shovel in his hand.

The judge asked the doctor, "You said he was struck with a blunt object, causing his death. Could the shovel in Deputy Bielk's hand be that blunt object?" Doc Hamilton put his hand out for the shovel. He took the shovel in hand, examined the area of dried blood, and turned to the judge.

"This could very well be the object." He took the shovel in both hands and took a short swing from left to right. The judge stared for a moment. He motioned for the sheriff to come forward again. Calderon stepped forward. The judge whispered a question to him and he responded by showing his right hand.

Markette turned back to the doctor and asked, "Why did you swing the shovel in the manner you did?" Doc Hamilton initially looked puzzled, but realized his actions.

"That would be the striking blow that felled Jeffrey Simms," he said. A muffled shriek came from the cluster of grieving young women. Tears followed; Judge Markette would have cleared them from the courthouse, except that would have given them even more attention.

He observed aloud, "Am I to assume the killer was left-handed?"

Doc Hamilton said, "I don't know that as a fact. Most people would strike the blow using the strength of their dominant hand. I do know the person would have to be rather strong to strike such a blow."

"Thank you, Doctor Hamilton," said the judge. "You may go back to your patients." Doc Hamilton walked out of the courthouse. Markette looked about the courthouse. He said, "I would like to hear from Jenny Jenkins." He looked about the courthouse, but did not recognize her face in the crowd. As he looked, Markette missed Bathers' wicked smile. Barnaby Bathers had told Jenny he would cut out her tongue before she got a chance to tell anyone what he had done. He knew she'd keep her mouth shut.

CHAPTER XXX

Throwing the Hounds Off the Scent

Bathers left the courthouse with a queasiness he hadn't felt since hitting Simms with the shovel. He heard that doubt was beginning to grow among the townspeople. He wanted to feel better; he wanted the comfort of relations with a woman.

He walked swiftly toward the white two-story rooming house where Jenny shared a room with her children. Those children would be working the fields this time of day, he thought as he opened the crooked gate to get to the house. He pulled the metal hook next to the door that shifted a string, causing the bell to ring above Mrs. Thatcher's room. Mrs. Thatcher was a bespectacled, dowdy woman whom Bathers controlled with lavish compliments. He let her think he was respectful of elders to the point of giving her the ability to make him leave.

Mrs. Thatcher answered the door in an apron dusted with flour. She looked twice at Bathers. He smiled at her, but her expression remained one of disdain, or she had had too much cheese. Bathers had trouble distinguishing between the two at times.

Mrs. Thatcher was succinct: "Go away." Bathers knew it wasn't the cheese. He placed a booted foot in the doorway.

"Mrs. Thatcher, I just want to see Jenny to apologize. I was rather angry with her the other day, and she was angry with me." He tried to give her the look of a broken-hearted boy.

"She will not see you and if you force the issue, I will dispatch for the sheriff." The old woman stood firm. Bathers used a bit of force to get past the doorway. Mrs. Thatcher struggled in vain to keep him out.

"I told you to leave," she said with great conviction. "Don't make me cut a switch." Bathers hadn't been struck with a switch since he was fourteen years old; he fought back a laugh.

"I don't want to be disrespectful to my elders, Mrs. Thatcher, but I do need to see Jenny." Bathers thought, "a few soft words and I'll have what I want." Jenny appeared at the top of the stairs. Bathers and Jenny stared at one another, while Mrs. Thatcher straightened her apron and looked between the two.

Jenny said, "I won't be seein' you no more, Barnaby Bathers." At that point, Bathers knew he'd have to take what he wanted. He raced up the stairs two at a time. Jenny ran back to her room, screaming. She closed the door behind her, turned the lock, and screamed again. Bathers tried the door handle, and pounded on the door. Jenny just kept screaming for dear life. Three other roomers opened doors to get a peek at the man causing the disturbance, but when they saw Bathers, each one closed his door quickly, hoping it wouldn't be next.

Jenny's voice eventually became hoarse, and she slid down the door and cried. She didn't know when Bathers left, and she didn't care. She cried out her frustration at being with a man such as that, but she couldn't cry out her self-loathing for only being able to attract men like that. Jenny realized she had to leave Kingston.

Bathers was steaming on the inside for a fight. He'd tear the head off the next man who crossed him. He headed toward the saloon, crossing through a small alley between buildings. The alley was cooler than the streets, as shadows were just beginning to noticeably lengthen. His mind filled with rage at the entire damn town.

That may have been why he didn't notice Kingman in front of him, until he heard the click of a gun behind his right ear. Bathers lifted his hands slowly to express his desire to live another day. He turned slightly and peripherally saw the sneer on Jones's face behind him. He swore one day that Jones would hear that same click, just before he blew Jones's head off.

Bathers said irritably, "What the hell do you want?" Kingman took a few steps closer. Jones thought if he had to kill Bathers, Kingman would be splattered with blood. Kingman looked about the alley; no one else was in sight. He momentarily studied the anger in Bathers' eyes.

"We can help each other or hurt each other," he said finally, and awaited a response, but none was in the giving. He continued, "Barnaby, your friend Penn has something we need to get back. I'm going to tell you what it is, but if you cross me, I'll let Jones here take care of you. Most likely, he'll stake you in a swamp, rub deer's blood over your privates, and wait for the gators. Do you understand?" Bathers glared at Kingman. Kingman turned to walk away.

"I understand," Bathers said quickly. "What's he got of yours?" Bathers knew that once he had this information he'd be on better footing with these men.

Kingman looked straight at him. "He's hiding runaway slaves on his farm. We need to get those slaves back before the town hangs him." Kingman watched Bathers's eyes to see how this information registered.

"What do you want me to do?"

"You and the sheriff are good friends," Kingman explained. "I want you to use that friendship to get a message to Penn." Bathers looked a bit disappointed. He gazed at the bricks lining the alley. He looked back at Kingman. Kingman's dark, thick eyebrows shifted on his forehead.

Bathers said, "Sheriff and I had a bit of a falling out. I ain't allowed in the jailhouse." He wondered what would happen next. He thought hard about anything he could give them, so they'd know he was on their side. Jones looked at Kingman as if a shared secret could be a secret once again.

"Penn's good friends with Quaker Jowett," Bathers blurted. "I seen him at the jail once." Kingman's eyebrows relaxed, a good sign.

Kingman asked, "What's he look like?" Bathers described the portly man and the house he shared with his cousin. Jones and Kingman left the alley; Bathers was no longer looking for a fight.

*   *   *

Quaker Jowett spent a few moments with Miss Hattie to discuss how they'd get her into the courthouse the next day. He knew Deputy Joseph Bielk was sympathetic to Penn's plight; he was on duty in the jailhouse in the morning. Quaker Jowett could tell Miss Hattie was frightened, and comfort came in holding onto strong hands. After a few more moments, he swore he'd be back in the morning.

Quaker Jowett took the trail behind Marion and Harriet's house to Crown Street. He was heading toward the jailhouse as fireflies had just come out in the evening sky. Cool breezes blew through the streets of Kingston bringing much needed relief from the sweltering day.

He walked down Crown toward the alley to the jailhouse. As he passed a lone willow tree, he was suddenly approached by a stranger, the man he had seen coming out of the jailhouse. Kingman stood blocking his path;

Quaker Jowett placed him as the man who had met up with Penn on the trail. His knees knocked a bit out of fear of the bounty hunter. Jones sensed the fear, a sense that eluded Kingman for the moment.

Kingman said, "You are the one called Quaker Jowett. I am Kingman, and I have a proposition for you." Kingman wanted Quaker Jowett to ask about the proposition; he wasn't disappointed.

"My name is Kingman," he repeated. "I know about the slaves, I know Penn hid them in the barn, because we caught them, not all of them. We have one who is pretty sickly and she'll tell us about the rest, but I fear by the time she does, she won't have long to live."

Quaker Jowett said absently, "Miss Alice." He didn't realize his mistake and never would know that he had given a name to Jones and Kingman. They could use the name to get Penn to cooperate. Quaker Jowett was lost in thought.

Kingman continued, "I need to take this property back to the South, but I want them all. Don't get as much if they die on the way."

"But they don't complain as much, neither," Jones pointed out. Kingman tried to look as if he had little concern.

"Why don't you go into the jailhouse and tell Penn he can have Miss Alice back alive if he cooperates. I can guarantee you the slaves will all reach the South alive." Quaker Jowett thought to himself, "What kind of a guarantee is that?" He had to go along, though, to get away from them.

"I'll speak with Mister Penn," he said quietly. "I'm sure he'll want to help you, if he can." Jones looked into the man's eyes to see if he was lying, but it was too hard to tell. Quaker Jowett walked past the men and into the jailhouse.

*   *   *

Penn could see that Quaker Jowett was deeply troubled, and he wanted to turn away from what was probably more bad news. He wanted his old life back. He wanted to go back to his farm and make cider for all of his neighbors. Hank let Jowett into the jail cell. The clank of the door sounded hollow and permanent to Penn.

Quaker Jowett said, "I have news both good and bad." He could tell by Penn's lifeless expression that Penn would be of little help in resolving the matter of Kingman. Penn wanted to tell him to leave the good news and take the bad news with him.

Quaker Jowett continued, "Two men approached me a moment ago. One of them was Kingman. I don't believe him for a minute, but he said he captured one of the slaves, a sickly one. I don't know if he used the name or I did, but Miss Alice's name was mentioned. He would have mentioned the others if he had them." Penn tried to think, but thinking was so difficult, there were too many thoughts. He took a deep breath and let it out slowly.

"I believe he is bluffing," he said. "So, why are we taking this seriously?" Penn was worn too thin to think this through.

Quaker Jowett explained, "I need to send these men out of the city." He desperately wanted to tell Penn about Miss Hattie, but knew the strain would be unbearable. Penn would protest, and he would be in the middle even more so than now. Penn sipped water while collecting his thoughts.

"We have a chance of throwing these men off the trail of the slaves," he said.

Quaker Jowett thought to himself, "I need to get Miss Hattie here in the morning. If they follow me, I'm sure to lead them to her, and she won't get to testify."

"Yes, yes, I see," he said. "What can we tell them?"

Penn thought some more about the situation.

"Okay, tell them the group went west to Oneonta," he finally replied.

"Won't that lead them to the slaves?" Quaker Jowett was truly puzzled. He thought the fatigue had gotten to Penn.

"He won't believe you," Penn said. "Trust me, he won't believe you'd send him after the others. He'll go in the direction you don't send him." Penn impressed himself with the way he had thought this through. He allowed a fraction of a smile upon his lips. Jowett had no sound reason to argue the point.

"I'll tell them the rest of the slaves headed west to Oneonta," he agreed. "I'll bet they're close to Oneonta, by now, anyway."

"I pray you are right, Brother Benjamin." Penn took a slow deep breath, as if all of his energy was left just for breathing. He asked, "The good news?"

Quaker Jowett replied, "Good news is the townspeople no longer believe you killed Simms. I'm praying the judge has the same thoughts about the situation." He noticed Penn's pale skin, the sunken cheeks, and his darkened eyes. He said, "I still feel guilty about getting you into this mess."

"I've told you before, I made the choice," Penn said weakly. "I'm sorry Quaker Jowett, but I am so tired; I need to rest, please forgive me." Penn laid down on the straw bed in his clothing. Quaker Jowett stood up and called for Hank to release him.

Quaker Jowett stepped onto the wooden porch of the jailhouse. He stood for a moment; over near an old oak tree across the street stood the two men from the alley. He approached them.

Quaker Jowett said, "Mister Penn feels you have given him no choice. He doesn't want the slaves to come to harm." Jones stared at Quaker Jowett, while Kingman nodded in agreement.

Kingman said, "Your friend is making a wise choice. Tell me where they have gone and we'll reunite them."

"I need your word that the slaves will come to no harm," the Quaker said nervously. He prayed Penn was right.

Kingman said, "You have my word." Kingman gave his word easily, as easily as it would be broken if need be.

"Penn told me they headed west to Oneonta. Doesn't make much sense to me, but that is what he told me."

"Fine, you have given us what we needed to know." Kingman turned to leave. Jones stared at the Quaker, as he wasn't so sure.

Quaker Jowett said, "You will keep them safe." Kingman turned with a big smile on his face.

"You have my word as a gentleman." Jones and Kingman left Quaker Jowett standing by the oak tree.

Jones said to Kingman, "Gentleman?" Quaker Jowett walked back toward Crown street.

Kingman laughed and said, "I never said I was a gentleman. Let's go get them slaves." In his exuberance, Kingman slapped Jones on the back. Jones was thinking.

He stopped and said, "He's lying. He knows more than he's telling you." Kingman looked at Jones as if he should have brought this up five minutes ago.

"You want to go back and beat the crap out of him?" Kingman said irritatedly. "Of course he's lying. We'll head north."

Jones said, "I'm not so sure that is what he's lying about. I think we should follow him." Kingman looked at Jones with exasperation.

"I'm not following him," he snarled. "He isn't going to hide those slaves in Kingston. Penn took a big risk hiding them out on his farm. You haven't been yourself this hunt. Focus on the quarry; let's get them." Jones stared at Kingman as if he was looking through him.

"Then we head north," said Jones reluctantly. The men continued down the alley, unaware of Joseph Bielk in the nearby shadows.

CHAPTER XXXI
To Tell the Truth

Early morning light brought a cool comfort to the day, as Jones walked about the near empty streets of Kingston, frustrated with waiting for Kingman to wake and the Clemmons twins to stop eating. He thought about the trail north and catching up with the slaves. Jones was weary of the trail, even though he could expect a good bounty.

He walked down the street behind some rather fancy houses with tea gardens, as Quaker Jowett made his way along the trail to the house of Marion and Harriet. In the woods just before the street, he spied the man who had stood with Kingman. The men had not left then. Quaker Jowett continued along the trail to a corner lot beyond his destination. He realized he couldn't tend to getting Miss Hattie to the courthouse. He wished he could speak with her, but knew that he couldn't.

He walked toward the bakery one block over. He nibbled on a cinnamon roll and glanced at the street through the window far too often. As he watched, the stranger who had been with Kingman continued past the bakery. Quaker Jowett needed to speak with Joseph Bielk. The deputy had agreed to help him.

Quaker Jowett rushed down the road toward the jailhouse. He'd need to reach Penn before court began, to let him know what had happened.

*   *   *

The gavel came down with a loud bang, startling some of the spectators. Judge Markette was in no mood to trifle with those that would keep him from doing his job. His head was pounding, and sight in one eye blurred. He felt as if an ice pick was sliding into his eye and being twisted. The sparkles he saw that morning foretold of his misfortune, but he had to finish the trial.

He gazed out at the spectators and wished there were fewer people in his courthouse. Calderon brought in Penn in shackles. Penn's wrists and ankles held the bruises from previous days. The judge looked at Penn; Penn seemed a bit older, a bit greyer.

Markette said, "The court wants to hear from Jenny Jenkins." He looked out over the crowd with his good eye, but there wasn't anyone standing. He noticed Bathers smiling; that's what he wanted, to see that man's face. The judge motioned to Hank Stratton.

Hank disappeared into the jailhouse, then promptly returned followed by Jenny Jenkins. Jenny peered about the room, visibly nervous. The judge didn't see her fear; he was busy watching Bathers's rage build, as the smile was replaced with tight, pursed lips. Jenny was sworn in; Bathers steamed.

Judge Markette asked, "Miss Jenkins, can you tell us what you know about the murder of Mister Simms?'

Jenny said cautiously, "Well, my gentleman friend . . ." Bathers stood up and pointed directly at Jenny.

"Don't you dare!" he shouted. Jenny was ready to run; her heart raced. Markette scowled at Bathers.

"Sheriff, if that man speaks again in my courtroom, I want him thrown in jail." Markette looked over at the sheriff and said, "Do you understand my order?" Calderon nodded his head in agreement. He thought the judge was trying to show him how it was done, but Markette wanted the deputies ready to arrest Bathers if need be. He was reassured when his right hand felt the derringer in his vest pocket.

"Yes sir," said Calderon. He saw the fear in Jenny's eyes. Judge Markette stared at Bathers, as Bathers glared at Jenny.

The judge said to Bathers authoritatively, "This is my courtroom, do not forget it." He turned to Jenny and said, "Now, please tell me what you know." Jenny looked at the judge for a long moment, then turned to the spectators, but then turned back to the judge.

Jenny said, "My gentleman friend, Mr. Bathers . . ." Hushed whispers rippled throughout the courtroom; Markette banged his gavel in annoyance. His migraine flared at the sound, the ice pick drove deeper, and he wished he were in a dark, quiet room. He turned back to Jenny.

Jenny said quietly, "My friend, Mister Bathers, was drunk and tol' me he had killed Mr. Simms by accident. He said he had gone to see Simms and Simms tol' him he wasn't gonna get water rights. He got angry and threatened Simms with the shovel, but struck him by accident. Simms fell down dead." The courthouse was silent. Jenny started to cry, while Bathers used every ounce of self-restraint to keep himself from jumping up at the witness stand and strangling the crap out of her.

Markette asked, "Is this the truth, or are you spiteful, because he chose to stay with his wife instead of leaving her for you?" Jenny was shocked, speechless. She had come forward after her life was threatened. She told the truth and wasn't believed.

Jenny could think of nothing more. "That's the truth, sir," she said.

"Are you a good Christian woman?" asked the judge. Jenny was confused. She felt she was the one on trial.

"Excuse me?" she uttered. Judge Markette looked at the young woman who was about to cry for the second time in his courtroom.

"Are you a good Christian woman?" the judge asked pointedly. "You have been laying down with a married man. I want to know if you have been with men for money?" Jenny was nervous, on the verge of tears.

"Pardon me?" she asked again. Judge Markette appeared annoyed.

"Have you been with other men for money, prostitution?" Jenny could feel the warmth of a flush as her face reddened.

"Three years ago, I was left with two children and no money," she explained. "I have found good work since then, but when my husband left, I had to feed my children." She paused to fight back tears. Her voice cracked as she said quietly, "I did take money from men."

Judge Markette said in an even tone, "I appreciate your honesty, but you have been involved in criminal behavior, and that makes me suspicious of your testimony. You may take your seat." Jenny sat for a moment feeling desperately sad, with only a hint of the anger that would grow over the coming hours.

"What was I supposed to do?" she protested. "I had to feed my children." Judge Markette was again annoyed.

"You made the wrong choice. That is all this court is concerned about. Please take your seat." Jenny left the court in tears, while Bathers smiled.

The judge paused, and then said, "I do believe there is only one person left to hear from by this court. Mister James Penn, please come forward." Penn had appeared to be watching the testimony of the others, but he was merely staring in their direction. After a moment, he looked at the judge and realized what had been said. He stood quickly, sitting right back down, as if unaware of the weight of the chains that clanked abruptly.

Penn shuffled to the witness chair, his chains clanking as he walked. He shifted his body in quarter circles to turn around so he could sit down. Penn was sworn in, his chains resting on the bible, a book that represented the freedom of his soul. He rubbed his wrists as he sat waiting for the questions from the judge. Judge Markette looked at him.

He asked, "Mister Penn, tell us about what happened the night Jeffrey Simms was killed?"

Penn answered honestly, "I didn't know what happened to Jeffrey, um, Jeffrey Simms, until I was brought to the jail by the sheriff. Then I found out he had been killed. I was not at the tavern that night and I hadn't seen him for three days. I don't know who killed him." Penn looked at the judge.

"Why would Simms say your name before he died?" asked the judge.

Penn thought for a moment, and then said, "I don't know why he would have said my name." Penn wanted to provide a reason, but there wasn't one, at least none he knew. Bathers sat quietly in the crowd, wishing he was a foot shorter.

"And the knife and button, how do you explain these things?" Judge Markette sipped at the glass of lemonade on his bench.

Penn answered politely, "The knife found at his farm is mine, and the button is from my vest. Both were not there by my accord. The knife had been in my barn to cut cord for bailing hay, and the button came off my vest a week ago." Penn breathed a bit easier, although his left ankle was sore. Markette hadn't heard anything yet from Penn that would exonerate him.

He said, "You deny killing Jeffrey Simms."

Penn agreed honestly, "Yes, I did not kill Jeffrey. Why would I kill him? We didn't have any bad blood between us."

"Is there anyone who was with you on the night of the murder?" the judge asked.

Penn was tired and unaware of his pending error in judgment, as he said, "No, not really." Judge Markette appeared puzzled to Penn.

"What do you mean?" he probed. "Is it yes or no?" Penn realized the error. His heart began to race. He took a few deep breaths.

"No, nobody was with me." He tried to swallow, but his mouth was dry. He explained, "I am confused by this whole trial. My friend is dead and all I know is I didn't kill him, but I don't know who did."

Judge Markette had heard enough. "Mister Penn is there anyone you'd like this court to hear from in your defense?"

Penn was quick to say, "No, your honor. I don't believe so." He wondered how far the slaves had traveled; had they arrived in Oneonta? Judge Markette looked out over the courthouse.

"Court is recessed until this afternoon. We will return at one-thirty."

Spectators began moving out into the noonday sun, squinting and shading their eyes, like the coal miners in Pennsylvania.

Joseph Bielk stood with a hand on the doorknob to the courthouse. He slid the door open and heard the final words of Judge Markette's message to the court. Panic set in. He rushed Miss Hattie and her escort back toward the jailhouse. He had to think quickly, to hide them.

*   *   *

Carl Johnson, the manager of the First Bank of New York, was attending Penn's trial, while his clerk dutifully awaited confirmation of the funds before dispensing them to the tall ungentlemanly fellow from the South. Winslow Stacks was quite relieved when the wire was returned and he was cleared to count out the ten and twenty dollar notes to Mr. Kingman. Kingman's attitude reminded him of his childhood days of being called "sticks" for his slight stature. Johnson stepped through the heavy door to the bank as Kingman scooped up his money, with another silent curse to the robber. He knew Jones would be angered by the delay.

"Penn may be sentenced this afternoon," reported Johnson. Stacks bid Mr. Kingman good day, hoping the Southerner would leave quickly.

Stacks asked, "Did he defend himself, tell the judge where he was the night of the murder?" This was a question speculated about in almost every corner of Kingston.

"Just stuck to his story of being home, alone." Kingman heard the bankers review the numerous reasons why people weren't believing Penn's story, including being spotted on the road south of town. He stepped out of the bank and saw Jones stewing outside, while the Clemmons brothers whacked at one another with sticks.

"Jones, you're gonna thank me for sticking around here so long in the day," Kingman said. Jones wasn't losing any of his irritable edge without an explanation. Kingman continued, "Penn is sticking to his story; slaves must be closer than we thought."

CHAPTER XXXII

A Witness to Character

Penn came clanking down the hallway toward the jailhouse; Calderon held the door open. Miss Hattie and Smitty froze and their muscles tensed, as they recognized the sound of chains on a man. Miss Hattie took a deep breath and set back to dusting. Smitty stepped back over to grab a broom and began sweeping. The sheriff walked Penn through the jailhouse; Penn's gaze was on the floor as he shuffled his feet.

Miss Hattie wanted to go to him and hug him; his spirit seemed so withered. Smitty just watched him walk lifelessly into the cell. He swept closer to the cell. Calderon eyed the colored people in his jailhouse.

Joseph said, "They were sent over from Marion and Harriet to do the cleaning. They wouldn't take no for an answer, you know how the sisters can be." Calderon didn't like the town gossips, but appreciated that someone else would do the cleaning for them. He went into his office and closed the door behind him. Joseph knew the sheriff was concerned about something, but the closed door meant he didn't want to talk.

Smitty swept over to the bars of the cell. He looked about the room twice; only the four of them were there.

Smitty whispered to Penn, "Misser James, don't gets too excited, but it's us." Penn looked up at Smitty and for the first time truly wished the bars weren't in his way. Then a frown fell from his smile.

Penn asked, "What are you doing here?" He sat on his straw bed and looked around the room. He noticed Joseph, and nodded in appreciation of the deputy's help.

"God tells Miss Hattie we gots ta comes here an' tells de truf," Smitty replied.

Penn was dejected. "You were supposed to be going to Canada," he said in a worn voice. "You were supposed to be free." Miss Hattie stepped close to the bars and stared James Penn in the eyes.

She said, "You been 'cused a sumpthin' you ain't done. I prays ta God and He tells me to comes here and tell de judge you was wif me, wif us. If'n I goes ta Canada, I's never be free, cause I would has yer soul on me." Miss Hattie gave him a smile that let him know she'd be all right. Penn didn't believe she'd be all right, but the smile was comforting.

Smitty added, "I's here ta sees what dey been feedin' you." Penn can't help but chuckle, causing the others to laugh.

"They'll send you back South," Penn said somberly. Smitty continued to absently sweep the floor.

Smitty replied, "We knows, but dey ain't gonna kill us, cause we has skills."

"I don't know if I'll get a chance to say this . . . ." The door to the sheriff's office opened. Calderon stepped out, turned, and went back in for something forgotten. Penn said quickly, "Thank you." The sheriff came back out of his office to see the two cleaning.

He said to Joseph, "Don't forget to get meals for the help. I'll be right back." He left the jailhouse. Miss Hattie began singing a spiritual that stopped everyone except Miss Hattie and Smitty.

Quaker Jowett saw the sheriff leave the jailhouse. He walked up onto the wooden steps. Jones and Kingman were right behind him. The three men stood just outside the jailhouse.

Kingman said, "Tell Penn if he lied to us, we'll kill the slave we got."

Quaker Jowett, nervous for an entirely different reason, said, "I'll tell him." He chose his words carefully. "I'm sure he didn't lie to you."

Jones took a step forward, just as Joseph's hand was on the handle of the door. Joseph had decided it would be best to keep others from seeing the slaves talking with Penn.

Jones said, "If he's lying, we know where to find him and his friends." He heard the singing and stared at the window behind Quaker Jowett.

"Isn't that church choir up the street beautiful?" Quaker Jowett wanted to step in between Jones and the window, but that would only make Jones more suspicious.

Jones and Kingman hadn't spent much time in church and weren't aware the singing wouldn't travel that far. The men left the porch and took to saddles as they rode off. Quaker Jowett's knees were ready to buckle. He made it inside the door, collapsing on a bench next to the entrance. Miss Hattie stopped singing.

Quaker Jowett gasped, "Bounty hunters were just on the porch." He took a deep breath. "They're gone." The Quaker could see the fear in Miss Hattie's face. He said, "Don't worry, they're gone."

*   *   *

Judge Markette worried that he was wasting his time reconvening the court, but he had his doubts. The spectators in the packed courthouse wanted a verdict. The judge looked straight at James Penn and asked, "Is there anybody you'd like to call forward as a witness for you?"

Joseph Bielk said, "Your Honor, I have a witness that can prove James Penn wasn't anywhere near the Simms farm on the night of the murder." Markette didn't like surprises, but was willing to tolerate this one.

"Bring him forward," he said. Joseph brought forth Miss Hattie and Smitty. Miss Hattie stepped up close to the judge. Her dark eyes met the judge's brown eyes.

Joseph said, "This is Miss Hattie and Smitty." He pointed for Smitty to sit down.

Judge Markette nodded to Miss Hattie. "Please take a seat." She sat down, and Joseph stepped toward her. He showed her how to place her hand on the bible, and she did so.

"Do you swear to tell the truth, the whole truth, and nothing but the truth, so help you, God." Miss Hattie looked at Joseph and then at the judge.

She said in a mildly surprised tone, "I always does." A few spectators chuckled, making Miss Hattie a bit more uneasy. Smitty looked at Miss Hattie and nodded his head, as if to say, "go on."

"Do you know who killed Jeffrey Simms?" asked the judge.

Miss Hattie looked down and spoke softly as she said, "No, I doesn't judge." She knew never to look a white man in the face when speaking to him. Judge Markette could barely hear her, and this was important testimony.

"Speak louder, please," he instructed. Miss Hattie continued to gaze at the floor.

"No, I doesn't judge," she said a little more loudly.

"Then what business do you have with this court?"

Miss Hattie replied confidently, "I knows Misser James Penn ain't de killer o' dat man, 'cause he were he'pin' me an' Smitty dat night." She pointed to Smitty. She continued, "We was out in de woods near a place called Suffern."

"And how was he helping you?"

Miss Hattie looked at Penn. He had a sad look on his face.

"I knows I's supposed ta tell de truf," she said shyly, "but I doesn't really wants ta answer dat questions." She didn't turn to look at the judge.

"I'm telling you to answer the question, so you'd best answer it now," he said curtly. His head felt like it was going to explode as the migraine worsened.

Miss Hattie sat upright and with as much dignity as she could muster said, "He were he'pin' me ta 'scape. I's a runsaway slave from Georgia." The stunned spectators ignored the gavel and chattered away. Markette knew better than to try to silence the crowd after that remark. He waited, to teach the town another lesson in law.

"Is that true?" he asked finally.

Miss Hattie said, "Yes sah, dat's de truf." She knew God had brought her here for something, and this was it. She relied on His strength, as hers was gone. Judge Markette had no other option.

The judge said, "Your testimony is irrelevant. You understand I must place you in custody to be returned to your rightful owner." Miss Hattie nearly fell off the chair. Smitty's face was drained of all life. Miss Hattie held on to her dignity, as she was there to let the judge know about Misser James.

"I un'erstan's," she said firmly, "but de truf has ta be tol'. You mus' believes me." Smitty stepped forward, with Joseph beside him.

Smitty said to the judge, "if'n you doesn't believes her, den I doesn't reckon you'd believes me, 'cause Miss Hattie is da mos' God-fearin' woman I knows. But I'as dere, I'as wid Misser James Penn dat night Misser Simms was killt. We was out in dem woods de whole night."

Judge Markette shook his head back and forth slowly. "Why should I believe either one of you? You are runaway slaves. You are property that belongs back down south."

Smitty piped up, "Dat don't means we ain't tellin' de truf. We knows you all'd be sendin' us back ta de Souf, we knows we could be hanged fer runnin', but we cain't lets Misser James be hanged fer somethin' he ain't done." Smitty's muscles tightened as he waited for the crack of a whip or rod. It didn't come.

"Although I applaud your efforts to get Mr. Penn released," the judge said evenly, "and I don't overlook the fact that he may be innocent, I cannot allow the testimony of property to sway me. You are committing a crime, and this can't be taken lightly." Miss Hattie looked to Smitty.

Smitty said to her, "So's we done come here fer nothin'." Miss Hattie looked at Penn; his hands covered his face. Penn couldn't bear to see them taken from the courtroom. The chains on his wrists were heavy, but he held them up.

"You came here to be returned to your rightful owners. The law is clear. You may step down." Judge Markette felt an increase in the intensity of the ice pick pain in his eye. Joseph assisted Miss Hattie in understanding the judge's order.

Miss Hattie said to Smitty, "We comes here ta fulfills a promise ta God. We wouldn't leaves Misser James ta de white man's law an' lets him be hanged fer a murder he ain't done. We has ta comes here. Dey cain own our'n bodies, but not our'n souls." Miss Hattie left the chair to go with Joseph, as chatter erupted among the spectators.

"Remove these two slaves to the jailhouse," the judge yelled above the din to the sheriff.

Miss Hattie and Smitty left with Joseph without a struggle. Penn rose from his chair.

"You can't do that!" he cried angrily. "These people are in the North; they're free." Calderon eased Penn back into his chair.

Markette responded by saying dispassionately, "According to the Slave Act of 1850, they must be returned to their rightful owner. Mr. Penn you will be . . ."

"Your Honor, please," came a voice from the crowd. In the courtroom stood a tall, slender man in his fifties; a man who couldn't help but be noticed. He walked toward the judge. Penn recognized him; he kept his seat.

Markette demanded, "Who are you?" He dreaded surprises. The man stopped in front of the judge.

"My name is Irvin Keagle," he said clearly, "and I can testify to Mister Penn's innocence."

Markette sighed, shrugged, and pointed to the witness chair. Hank swore the man in.

"All right," asked the judge. "How do you know Mr. Penn is innocent?"

"Because I was with him that night," Keagle replied.

"Now, before you answer this question, think carefully. Were you with him and those slaves?" Keagle didn't have to think.

"Yes, your honor," he answered quickly. "I was the conductor of the last stop before Penn took them. I met Mister Penn across the New York border, and he took the slaves into New York."

Judge Markette clarified, "You were helping those runaway slaves?"

Keagle replied, "Yes, your honor. We met near Suffern, New York. Mr. Penn was to help the slaves toward Canada. We met the night Simms was killed. For the moment, I am a free man, and I make this statement in good conscience. I understand I will be placed under arrest and jailed for what I have told you, so be it." Keagle sat looking at the judge.

The judge pondered the veracity of the statement. He was irritated, and knew the law had to be upheld.

"So be it! Sheriff!" He looked around the courtroom, and the sheriff had just come back through the doorway to the jailhouse. He continued, "Sheriff, take this man into custody." He pointed at Keagle.

Calderon and Hank took hold of Keagle. Hank took him away to the jailhouse; Calderon remained, standing beside Penn.

Judge Markette looked around the room once more and then said, "If there are no more witnesses, I shall make my ruling." The court was silent once again. Judge Markette wanted to maintain the silence for another three or four hours, but he knew his bladder wouldn't hold out. It was clear to him.

Bathers shouted from a bench off to the left-hand side of the court, "You can't believe him!" Bathers got to his feet. He shouted as the judge banged his gavel, "He's lying for Penn." Markette banged the gavel twice more. Joseph and Hank returned to the courthouse and moved up behind Bathers.

Markette said as evenly as he could, considering his anger, "Mister Bathers you are in enough trouble." Waves of pain shot through his eye. He continued, "Your story has come into question. Anything you say today will be discussed at your trial. Sheriff, take Mr. Bathers to the jail."

Bathers was irate and shouted, "I will not go! I didn't kill him." Bathers reached for his gun, but his holster was empty. His arms twisted up behind him as Joseph had his left arm and Hank his right. The judge had his derringer in hand. Bathers struggled with the deputies, and a few bystanders joined the fray to subdue him. Dillancy rested on top of Bathers's torso, while Hubbartt lay across Bathers's legs.

Hubbartt chided Bathers, "Looks like you are getting yours, Barnaby." Bathers struggled even more after the words. Dillancy and Hubbartt took a few jabs at Bather's sides.

Dillancy added, "Don't struggle, we'll only beat you down." Bathers stopped struggling. The men gradually got him to his feet and walked him toward the doorway to the jailhouse. Hank had a rifle at Bathers's back.

As they passed Calderon, the sheriff said to Bathers, "You always did let your temper get the best of you." Bathers grimaced at him and moved on.

Markette had been watching Penn, who actually looked sorrowful when the men struck Bathers.

The judge summed up his verdict by saying, "According to the Slave Act of 1850, I am obliged by the United States government to punish those aiding slaves. In Albany, I sentenced a man to a month in jail, because he did not stop a slave running down the street. The man was minding his own business when bounty hunters yelled to deputize him. He was arrested, and I sentenced him. This is the law." He paused and sipped his lemonade. Chatter erupted among the spectators, but the judge did not bang his gavel. He raised his hand and the room fell silent.

The judge continued, "As for Mister Penn, he will serve one year in jail for aiding runaway slaves. Mr. Keagle will also serve one year in jail for aiding runaway slaves. The slaves will be returned to their rightful owners. Mr. Bathers will return to Albany with me for a fair trial. This court is adjourned." Judge Markette banged the gavel once, and it was over. He sat there for a moment, while conversation grew louder and louder among the spectators.

The judge stood and stepped into the small room that would no longer be his chambers. The small room had no window, but was quiet. He took a cushion from the chair and lay down on the floor in the darkness.

CHAPTER XXXIII

The Price of Freedom

Barnaby Bathers looked like the "Wild Man of Borneo" from the circus that had come through Kingston the previous year. His blood-shot eyes were filled with fire, as his hair appeared to go in every direction at once. He crouched in the wagon behind iron bars. As passersby came close enough, he spit at them regardless of age or sex. Bathers was truly mad in the eyes of the citizens of Kingston. He was headed to Albany for his trial, accused of the murder of Jeffrey Simms. Calderon had wanted Bathers to be charged with assaulting Jenny Jenkins, but the judge declined.

As the wagon rolled out of town that morning, a sense of calm returned to Kingston. Townspeople were saying hello to the sheriff and his deputies as they passed by the jailhouse. Calderon arranged for Deputies Briarton and Sanders to spend two nights at the hotel and have all the food and drink they should care to have during those nights. He made sure the deputies from Newburgh were paid before heading to the hotel.

Sheriff Calderon had one more piece of business that morning. Hank Stratton had gathered the volunteers who had helped during the crisis. Calderon shook the hand of each volunteer and gave him a silver dollar. He knew it wasn't expected, but it was what the county could do for them. The sheriff bid them well and went into the jailhouse; his deputies followed.

Calderon would have thought the four people inside his jail cell were sitting in someone's parlor if it weren't for the bars. Miss Hattie rested on one straw bed, while Keagle and Penn sat upon the other. Smitty sat in the corner weaving five twigs together. Calderon wondered what was to happen to the slaves. He had wired the sheriffs in Atlanta and Charleston in an effort to get them back to their rightful owners.

JONATHAN A. POHL

Penn said, "I don't think I would have been freed without your help." Smitty shook his head back and forth in disagreement.

"Dat judge, he don't believes us."

Keagle explained, "Law says you can't be a witness, because you are owned, you are considered property." He took a bite of an apple.

Miss Hattie asked, "Den de judge ain't intrested in de truf?" She shook her head in disapproval. "Well, God is intrested in de truf."

Smitty continued to weave the twigs as he said, "Don't rightly knows what's gonna happen to us. Miss Hattie said God's been lookin' out fer us, and we's gonna be all right." Miss Hattie smiled.

"God seems ta have taken a likin' ta you, Misser Smitty," she said. "Cain't sees you ta be treated poorly." She let out a little laughter. The laughter was infectious, as the four of them shared in it.

Penn said seriously, "Miss Hattie, I didn't want you to come back, but I can't thank you enough for it." He put down the piece of cornbread he was eating.

"You doesn't has ta thanks me. Thanks de Lord, He was de one guidin' me." Miss Hattie looked up with a quick silent prayer.

Smitty smiled and said, "You cain thanks Miss Hattie, she done convinces me ta returns wid her." Smitty turned to Miss Hattie and said, "Miss Hattie, you's a good woman." Miss Hattie smiled back at him.

She thought for a moment, and said, "Misser James done saved our'n lives an' fer a moment we was free."

Penn said softly, "I am free, in here." He pointed to his chest, and Miss Hattie let out a big smile. The four sat quietly for a moment.

They could hear the voices of townspeople passing by the jail. Bits of conversation floated into the cell.

One woman said, "People shouldn't be owned."

Another man questioned, "I can agree they're property in the South, but in the North?"

A young girl said, "He was brave to help them slaves."

And her friend questioned, "Is he gonna be a slave?"

The young girl replied, "No."

An older man said, "Course they're property, been bred thata way."

But his companion said, "They ain't horses. Come back to free a white man knowing they'd go back to slavery."

Keagle, Penn, Smitty, and Miss Hattie looked at one another and listened to the townspeople talking as they passed by. Miss Hattie said a prayer to herself, thanking God for the witnesses to what they had done. Keagle thought a change was taking place outside that courthouse. Kingston would never be the same. Smitty wondered if any of them would step forward and bear witness to the south. Penn felt sorry for his friend Simms, losing his life over water. Penn said a silent prayer for the soul of his friend.

*　　*　　*

Quaker Jowett stepped into the jailhouse with a large basket giving off sweet smells every dog in the county must have been drooling over. Hank Stratton reached out to take the basket, and the Quaker pulled it closer to himself.

"This basket was made special by Miss Louisa for the four prisoners," he said. He thought he heard Hank moan with disappointment as he stepped over to the cell.

The basket was given to the four. Deputy Stratton didn't check the basket for two reasons. The first reason being the way the four prisoners had accepted their respective fates; the other being how hard it was to pass the basket off to them in the first place.

Miss Hattie reached in and pulled out a smaller basket of fresh cornbread with honeybutter. The four broke off pieces and ate. Smitty took the ceramic jug of fresh cider and sipped. Penn held out his hand for the jug. Smitty moved his sleeve over to wipe off the top of the jug.

Penn laughed and said, "Smitty I'd be honored to drink from the same jug as you."

Smitty smiled at Penn and said quietly, "I hopes them young'uns in Canada gits de same chance one day." Smitty handed Penn the jug. Keagle found the roasted chicken in the basket and devoured a leg, while Miss Hattie ate collard greens.

Quaker Jowett said excitedly, "The whole town is talking about the trial. People are more sympathetic to the plight of slavery than ever before."

Smitty asked politely, "What dey gonna do?"

"I don't rightly know, but Miss Westcott confronted Miss Harriet and Miss Marion about the treatment of the slaves in her kitchen. People are speaking out more." Miss Hattie let out a "whoop," surprising the group.

"Dat's why we's comes here," she said. "De Lord wants us to get folks talkin' 'bout slavery. Get dem thinkin' 'bout right an' wrong." Quaker Jowett sensed the hope in that jail cell.

Jones and Kingman entered the jailhouse, suddenly creating a vacuum that sucked away that hope. Jones was dour, but Kingman had a smile on his face. Kingman walked over to Calderon, who had stepped out of his office. He handed the sheriff two sheets of paper and said, "I think you have property that belongs to the people who hired me."

Calderon let out a deep breath. Exasperated, he said, "I have Smitty and Miss Hattie in my jail. I see you have papers of claim that these two are runaway slaves."

Jones said to the slaves, "Can run, but we always get you back. You belong to the South." Calderon glared at Jones. Kingman shifted his body to focus the sheriff's attention on himself.

"Sheriff," he said, "I have a locked wagon outside and am willing to sign off on these prisoners. I'd like to make Newburgh before nightfall." Jones took a step toward the jail cell, and the clank of the chains was heard. He held two sets of chains that they'd have the smithy lock on. Jones thought for a moment that Smitty could easily do the job for free.

Penn saw the sparkle fade in Miss Hattie's eyes at the sound of the chains. Smitty's posture shifted, as he hunched over. Keagle wanted to provide words of comfort, but none existed for a moment like this.

Calderon studied the paperwork to give the prisoners a bit of time to talk. Hank called Jones over so he could take a look at the shackles. He'd heard of bounty hunters using spiked shackles that cut into the ankles of prisoners. The prisoners had a moment to themselves.

Keagle said, "I hate to see you go back."

Penn added, "I pray they don't hang you." Worry in Penn's blue eyes led to tears from Miss Hattie's dark brown eyes.

"They ain't goin' ta hang us," she said reassuringly.

Smitty, who wasn't as sure, asked, "How cain you be knowin' dat?" Miss Hattie looked at the larger man.

"'Cause you has a trade, blacksmithin'. Dat day cain't do widout." Smitty couldn't argue with her on that. Penn wanted to ask her how she knew about herself, but dared not.

Smitty asked plainly, "An you?" Miss Hattie was not in the least bit put off.

"Mos' o' dose good ol' boys doesn't knows who dere Mammie really is, so dey wouldn't wants ta hurt me." The three men smiled at Miss Hattie.

Penn said, "I wish you a safe journey, Miss Hattie. I won't ever forget you." Penn hugged Miss Hattie, while Keagle shook Smitty's hand.

Miss Hattie said, "It ain't you I doesn't wants ta forgit us. It's dose people in dat courtroom. Dey'a talkin' now, an' I hopes dey keeps on talkin' 'bout us. We done saves each othah's life when it would has been easiah ta lets each othah die." Penn swallowed hard and hugged her again. Smitty shook Penn's hand while Keagle hugged Miss Hattie.

Keagle said to Miss Hattie, "I don't know if they'll remember, but they are talking now. We can hear them in the street." Smitty pulled a long shaven stick with several holes from his pocket. He handed it to Penn, who recognized the flute.

"'Spect yous needin' more music in your life," Smitty said.

"I expect I do," said Penn.

"Thank yous fah treatin' mah likes a man."

"I should be thanking you Smitty, for letting me be a man." The handshake between them turned into a hug.

"Thank you Smitty." Jones grunted his disgust.

Joseph kept Jones from entering the cell. He invited Miss Hattie and Smitty out. Jones and Kingman placed temporary shackles on the slaves, until they could get to the blacksmith.

Jones said to Smitty and Miss Hattie, "I don't want any trouble out of the two of you." He placed cotter pins in the holes to lock the metal shackles in place.

Kingman turned to the sheriff and said, "Thank you for your help." Calderon stared Kingman straight in the eye. "I am releasing these two prisoners into your custody," he said sternly. "These prisoners are to be transported directly to the sheriffs' offices in Atlanta and Charleston. According to the laws of the state of New York, these prisoners are under my jurisdiction until they reach their destinations. If for any reason, they do not get there safely, I get to come after you." Calderon did not look away from Kingman's blue eyes. Kingman understood him—didn't really care, but understood him. Jones had a bit of fire in his eyes, but had no choice in the matter.

Penn heard the clanking he had carried into the courtroom as Miss Hattie and Smitty were led away. Keagle placed his arm on Penn's shoulder.

CHAPTER XXXIV

Train to Points . . .

Judge Markette had slept through most of the previous day, most unlike him, but he was ready to greet this morning. Daylight had broken an hour ago, and he was ready to get back to Albany. Calderon met the judge at his room. The two had shared a long conversation concerning the verdict the night before. Sheriff Calderon understood why the slaves would have to go back South, even if he disagreed with the law.

He said, "I want to thank you for coming down to Kingston."

Markette shook the sheriff's hand. He felt relieved; his head pain was gone. He looked carefully at Calderon. "Sheriff you need to keep the peace around here. That means putting men like Bathers behind bars."

Calderon admitted, "I understand how I went wrong with Bathers, and I won't make that mistake twice.

Markette fastened the leather strap on his bag. He said, "Good for you, sheriff. Who knows what would have been different if Bathers had found himself on the inside of a jail cell more often." Calderon felt a twinge of guilt for allowing Bathers to stay free. He wondered if Simms would be alive. The judge saw the look on Calderon's face.

"Don't blame yourself, it wasn't your fault. Bathers did the killing." Calderon let out a long, low sigh.

"Your job is to keep the peace," Markette continued. "When a man like Bathers starts trouble, you put him behind bars. The townspeople may be frightened of the bully, but they should be even more afraid of you. You put the bullies in jail, and the folks of this town will be behind you." A moment of silence passed between the men.

Sheriff Calderon asked, "You ever think you'll get down here again?"

"Is that an invitation?"

Sheriff Calderon was taken a bit back. "Absolutely," he said, "you are more than welcome to stay at my place. I'll take you fishing." Judge Markette let out a smile.

"I'd like that. Place looks like there would be good fishing. I best be getting home." Judge Markette and Sheriff Calderon shook hands as they walked out to the judge's surrey.

*   *   *

Keagle listened to the birds chirping outside the jailhouse. He wished he was on the road to New Jersey to get back to his own life. The hardware store wasn't much, but it was his. Doors being locked for a year wouldn't bode well for business. He wondered if Mrs. Hanniford would miss him on Thursdays when she cleaned his place, the small three rooms above the hardware store.

Penn was reading his bible. He put it away.

Keagle said, "Somebody will have to take our places."

"I have a few friends looking after my farm," Penn said. Keagle thought for a moment.

"I meant on the railroad," he pointed out.

"There's always somebody out there. I took Quaker Jowett's place."

Keagle asked, "Do you think the South is winning?"

Penn shook his head.

"If the South was winning, I wouldn't be here right now. There will always be someone to help the slaves to freedom, even if it's a hundred and fifty years from now." Keagle sat on the straw mattress across from Penn.

"Will it ever end?" he wondered.

"Only way to stop it is if everyone who disagrees comes forward. There are many more people that don't own slaves than those who do." Hank Stratton came out of the sheriff's office and over to the jail cell.

He said to Keagle, "Write down who you want the telegram sent to and what it should say. I'll be sending it later today." Hank handed Keagle a pencil and piece of paper.

Keagle said, "I want to thank you for this. I own a small hardware store, and I'll surely need someone to run the business for a year." He held the paper on his leg and tried writing out his message.

Penn rested with his eyes closed. He imagined himself on his farm watching thirty families and their children running frantically through the orchards picking up every apple in sight. Hubbartt, Dillancy, Simms,

Bielk, and Penn sorting through the bushels of apples, pressing the ones without worms into cider. Huge bushels of apples pressed down into five or six gallons of cider.

Penn remembered the eyes of the children, wide open as the apples crunched down beneath the wooden plate, their juice spilling out into the bucket. Dillancy would go into the barn and bring out three or four ceramic jugs of cool cider. Each child would wish that he or she could be the first to taste the cider, but the honor was always given to Penn.

He opened his eyes to the sight of a bird in the window just beyond the bars of the cell. Keagle was feeding the bird, but then it took flight. Penn thought of the story Miss Hattie had told him the night before about her dream, about the last bird falling. He wondered if this bird was a sign that Miss Hattie would be well.

*   *   *

Smitty wished he could stand up and move his old bones, but the best he could do was lean over as he stood. Miss Hattie didn't mind sitting so much, as she did a lot of sitting while cooking or sewing. She missed Smitty's pipe of tobacco, but there wasn't any use in complaining. Kingman and Jones were most disagreeable, quick with the whip. Miss Hattie had soiled herself twice so far this trip.

Smitty asked, "Miss Hattie, when I gits ta Heaven, will God tells me why?" He had a sorrowful look on his face. Miss Hattie wasn't sure she understood the question.

Miss Hattie asked, "Tells you why?" Smitty knelt down to look at her.

"Tells me why he done let one man treats anothah dis way." Smitty looked as if tears were gonna bust out of his brown eyes. Miss Hattie wasn't sure how to answer.

"I doesn't know why dis happens," she said, "but God has a plans fer us. We doesn't go through dese trials fer nothin', Smitty. Dere is a bettah place waitin' on us." Smitty looked away from Miss Hattie.

"Sometimes, I don't rightly knows." he said. He felt weak and tired; he wanted an end to the suffering. Smitty felt Miss Hattie's arms around him. The warmth of her skin and the sound of her breathing were comforting. Smitty wanted to sink into those arms and cry like a baby, but he wouldn't allow himself to cry, he was a man.

Miss Hattie held the large man in her arms. He needed strength, the strength of faith. Miss Hattie began to sing softly, Amazing Grace.

Jones and Kingman were inside the tavern eating a warm supper and drinking cool ale. As with their noontime meal, they planned to toss the scraps to the slaves. They acted like animals, anyway, thought Jones, soiling themselves.

Kingman said, "At least we got a couple hundred coming to us, won't find them others."

"I can track them. They went west." Jones wanted to assure Kingman he was still on the scent.

Kingman said, "We best get back home. Clemmons brothers will be wanting their share." He thought it best not to blame leaving on Jones's irritability. Kingman cut another big chunk of steak. Juice dripped from his mouth as he ate the red meat. Jones sipped his ale, a drip wandering down his cheek which met with his sleeve.

Jones said, "Any word on other runaways?" Jones didn't really want to get home. He chugged more ale. He wanted desperately to be there, to walk into his house and feel comfort, but now all he would feel was cold and alone.

Kingman said, "You must be looking forward to seeing your wife." Jones put down his tankard and looked at Kingman.

Jones said honestly, "I can't wait to see her again." He hoped that day would come soon.

Kingman said, "Never understood a man settling for one woman. I'm not one of those rich plantation owners that can have mistresses, so I have to settle for women friends." Jones wanted to leave the tavern. He pushed his plate away from him. Kingman cut another piece of steak. Jones saw the chunk of meat get chewed into smaller bits.

Kingman said, "I'm goin' ta piss outside." He got up and headed out the door. Jones remained seated.

The tavern was quiet, and through an open window, Jones heard, "how sweet the sound, that saved a poor wretch like me . . ." Jones reached for the golden locket in his pants pocket. He popped the latch and gazed at the picture of his wife and himself. She had pulled it from her neck and thrown it on the ground before leaving. Jones closed his eyes, and it was her voice he heard in the choir; her voice singing, "I once was lost . . ." He was torn between sitting, listening to the song, and wanting to leave everything, ride until he was exhausted.

Jones got up and took his plate half full of steak, potato, and corn out to the slaves. He didn't want her to stop singing, but he knew it was right. He handed Smitty a fresh tankard of ale. Jones didn't say a word; he knew this was his last hunt. He turned and went back into the tavern. Smitty and Miss Hattie just looked at each other for a moment. Miss Hattie said grace.

*   *   *

Moonlight shone through the clouds, as Calvin sat in the darkness. The horses drank from a pool of water at the side of the road. Miss Alice had helped Calvin get Trent and Miss Dorothy out of the buckboard and replaced the planks. The four stood outside of a house in the town of Oneonta. The map directed them north toward Canada, but Calvin wasn't aware of the dangers that lay ahead.

Miss Alice pointed out, "On the gate, there is a lantern with a blue ribbon."

Calvin said, "Dats what Misser Quaker Jowett said to looks fer. Do we goes in?"

Miss Dorothy said, "We has ta trust dey'll he'p us."

Trent said, "We doesn't has much o' a choice."

Get Published, Inc!
Thorofare, NJ 08086
09 February, 2010
BA2010040